SI. ⏤L

#1, SILK ⏤L SERIES

ARIANA NASH

Silk & Steel

Ariana Nash

Dark Fantasy Author

Subscribe to Ariana's mailing list & get the exclusive story 'Sealed with a Kiss' free.

Copyright © 2018 Ariana Nash

Cover Design - Covers By Combs

Edited by Michelle Rascon

December 2018. US Edition. All rights reserved.

No part of this book may be reproduced in any form or by any electronic or mechanical means, including information storage and retrieval systems, without written permission from the author, except for the use of brief quotations in a book review.

All characters and events in this publication, other than those clearly in the public domain, are fictions, and any resemblance to real persons, living or dead, is purely coincidental.

Edited in US English.

Version 1.

www.pippadacosta.com

LOST

This land lost its name,
When the dragons came.
In fire and ice and pain,
They spread their reign.
Buried and forgot,
Cities fell to rot.
Now there's nothing left,
For us elves to protect.

— ELVEN
FOLKSONG

CHAPTER 1

*E*roan

The iron door rattled on its hinges and groaned open, spilling silvery light inside. Gloom fled to the corners, leaving behind a figure with broad shoulders. *Male*, Eroan thought. Curious scents of warm leather and citrus tickled his nose. After the wet and rotted smell of the prison, he welcomed any change in the air, even if it meant his visitor had returned.

Eroan kept his head low and his eyes down, hiding any signs of relief on his face. The shackles holding his wrists high bit deeper. He'd been so long in the dark, he'd almost forgotten he was a living thing. The constant, beating pain was a cruel reminder. This visitor was a cruel reminder too.

He knew what happened next. It had been the same for hours now. Days, even.

The male came forward, blocking more light, lessening its stab against Eroan's light-sensitive eyes. He turned his face away, but the male's proud outline still burned in his mind. Other images burned there too. The male's half-smile, the glitter of dragon-sight in his green eyes. Eroan had rarely gotten so close to their kind without killing them.

His mission would have been successful if not for this one.

"You need to eat." The male's gravelly undertone rumbled.

He needed nothing from *him*.

A tray clattered against the stone floor. The sweet smell of fruit turned Eroan's hollow stomach.

Moments passed. The male's rhythmic breathing, slow and steady, accompanied the scent of warm leather rising from his hooded cloak, and with it the lemony bite of all dragonkin. A scent most elves were taught to flee from.

"Were you alone, elf?" the dragonkin asked. The questions were the same every time. "Will there be another attempt on her life? How many of your kind are left in our lands?" More questions.

Always the same. And not once had Eroan answered.

Steely fingers suddenly dug into Eroan's chin, forcing him to look, to *see*. Up close, the dragonkin's green eyes seemed as brittle and sharp as glass, like a glance could cut. His smile was a sharp thing too.

"I could torture you." The dragonkin's smile vanished behind a sneer.

Eroan's straining arms twitched, and the chains slung above his head rattled against stone. *He has me in body, but not in spirit.* He gave him nothing, no sneer, no wince, just

2

peered deep into the dragonkin's eyes. Eyes that had undoubtedly seen the death of a thousand elves, that had witnessed villages burn. If they had souls, this dragon's would be dark. *He could torture me. He should. Why does he wait?*

Eroan recalled that cold look when their swords had clashed. He'd cut through countless tower guards, severing them from their life-strings as easily as snipping at thread, but not this one. This one had refused to fall. This dragonkin had fought with a passion not found in the others, as though their battle were a personal one. Either he truly loved the queen he protected, or he was a creature full of fiery hate that scorched whatever he touched.

The dragonkin's fingers tightened, digging in, hurting, but just as the pain became too sharp, he tore his hand free and stepped back, grunting dismissively.

Eroan collapsed against the wall, letting the chains hold him. Cold stone burned into raw skin. His shoulder muscles strained and twitched. Pain throbbed down his neck too, but he kept his head up, kept it turned away.

"I cannot..." Whatever the dragon had been about to say, he let it trail off and reached for the ornate brooch fixing the cloak around his neck, teasing his fingers over the serpent design.

Eroan wondered idly if he could kill him with that brooch pin. Of course, to do that, he'd need to be free.

The dragon saw him watching and dropped his hand. "You do not have long, elf." His jeweled eyes glowed. Myths told of how the dragonkin were made of glass and forged inside great fire-spewing mountains in a frozen land. Not this one. This one had something else inside. Some other wildfire fueling him.

The dragon turned, sweeping his cloak around him, and headed out the door.

"What is your name?" The question growled over Eroan's tongue and scratched over cracked lips. He almost didn't recognize the rumbling voice as his own.

The dragon hesitated, then partially turned his head to peer over his shoulder. The fire was gone from his eyes, and something else lurked there now, some softer weakness that belied everything Eroan had seen. His cheek fluttered, an inner war raging.

The answer would have a cost, Eroan realized. He shouldn't have asked. He let his head drop, tired of holding it up, of holding himself up. Tiredness ate at his body and bones. The shivers started up again, rattling the chains and weakening his defiance. This dragonkin was right. He did not have long.

"My name is Lysander."

The door slammed, the lock clunked, and Eroan was plunged into darkness.

CHAPTER 2

He gave me a name. But more than that, he'd given Eroan thoughts to cling to in the dark. Lysander. He knew of him. All elvenkind knew of the prince. But this prince was not the pride of the crown. That fell to the queen's other son. It seemed unusual that Lysander would be the one to visit and not someone more familiar with torture. That was assuming princes did not often visit the tower dungeons. Although, for all Eroan knew of dragons and their inner-ways, perhaps torturing elves *was* Lysander's duty.

Over and over, Eroan's thoughts tumbled in the dark. Better to think on the riddle of Lysander instead of the shame his own failure had brought upon the Order. By now, *his* name was a dead thing. His survival unimportant. Only striking a blow to the heart of the crown had mattered, and he'd failed. They had all failed. Should he somehow escape, he would still be dead to his own kind. Until the mission was done.

Pain beat through his jaw from grinding his teeth. Pain had long ago stolen any feeling in his arms, chained high enough that he could not rest without pulling open raw wounds. All he knew was pain, so that even the smallest of movements turned to wrenching agony.

When the door groaned open and the prince came again, Eroan's body had grown heavier, like this stone prison was swallowing him, making him a part of its walls.

He lifted his head, fighting the dull, thumping heat beating down his neck. Muscles shuddered, rattling his chains.

This time, the prince crouched in the middle of the chamber and set the food-tray down beside him. That same citrus and leathery scent had followed him inside. Eroan breathed it in, letting it cool his throat and sink deeper into his lungs. After breathing in the stench of his own making, he welcomed the swirl of fresh air.

The questions would begin now. Questions about his people, their forces, on and on. But the prince held his tongue and a quiet settled.

Dressed in a tan jerkin and similar trousers, all laced at the seams with silvery thread, the prince likely believed he was hiding his lineage behind drab clothing, but his pedigree was in every stitch, in the shine of his well-worn boots, in the neat braid running the length of his dark hair, tied off with a band threaded with an emerald and pearl.

The prince picked something green and hard from the tray's selection of food and offered it to Eroan.

Even if Eroan were to surrender and take his gift, the chains meant he couldn't reach for it. The prince didn't seem inclined to bring it any closer and had no intention of freeing him, so Eroan ignored the food. And him.

The prince drew in a breath, bit down on the morsel with a loud crunch, and swallowed noisily. "It's good."

Hunger gnawed at Eroan's insides, twisting them into knots. In the fog choking his thoughts, he tried to recall the last time he'd eaten. Before his pride of elves had left for the tower. They'd camped on the border with the burned forest and shared stone-roasted rabbit. His mouth watered at the memory. Eroan licked his cracked lips.

"You should keep your strength up. You'll need it."

The words, curiously kind, drew Eroan's gaze. The prince's jeweled gaze wandered downward, roaming over Eroan's chest where it lingered a moment before flicking back to his face. "You're making things much worse."

Worse? How could it be worse? Cycles of planning. Lives lost in the pursuit of the information that had gotten him through the palace walls. There would not be another opportunity. This had been their last hope to stop her. The elves were too few and the queen too strong a force to be stopped. It could not get *worse*.

"I suppose you've heard of how we deal with thieves and assassins?" Finished with his snack, the prince brushed his hands together, leaving the quiet heavy with threat. "How we torture elves, keeping them alive for weeks, months even, toying with them as... *pets*." His smile turned cruel and served as a reminder of how his current human appearance was one half of his being—the half that tricked and deceived.

Eroan had heard tales, seen the shredded remains of his Order brothers and sisters discarded along the border-lines, smelled dragon on them and heard the beasts' shattering roars. He knew what fate awaited him. He had known it since the day the Order had taken him in.

The prince rose to his feet and brushed dust off his fine clothes. "I should have killed you, it would have been kinder."

The sheathed dagger at the prince's hip glinted. He hadn't been without it during their meetings. When they'd clashed the night of Eroan's capture, blades sparking, the prince had been armed with two great curved swords the likes of which Eroan had never seen before. Those weapons had sung in the prince's hands. But now, reduced to a jailor, the prince carried only that small dagger. Why did he carry any weapons at all in his home? Decoration, probably.

I should have killed you... The prince's words sailed back to him, finally breaking through the fog. "Then do it," Eroan growled. "Take that dagger in your belt and cut my throat. End it now." It was a coward's way out, a moment of weakness, and Eroan winced, turning his head away, disgusted at his own begging tone. He should not want for this to end, not while the mission had yet to be done.

The prince settled his hand on the dagger and tapped his fingers on the handle, thinking it over. "A braver man might."

"Brave?" Eroan chuckled darkly. "How brave do you have to be to kill a chained elf?"

The prince's lips lifted, tucking the corner of a smile into his cheek. "Know so much, do you?"

"Enough."

"Of course, you elves know everything there is to know. Butchers, you call us. Beasts." He flicked his wrist, adding a flourish. "You're right, but you are not so innocent." He kicked the tray toward Eroan, spilling fruit and bread across the floor. "Eat or don't. It's of little concern to me."

The prince left and slammed the door behind him with enough force to shake free a cloud of dust. Where slits of light crept between the seals, the prince's shadow lingered.

He hadn't asked his questions, Eroan realized. He'd come with food and nothing else. What game was this? "Why do you come here?" Eroan whispered, eyeing that closed door, examining every rusted bolt, every gnarled hinge in the foolish hope that the closed door wouldn't be the last thing he saw.

The shadows beneath moved and vanished, and Eroan was alone once more.

A FITFUL SLEEP wrapped him in jagged thorns and squeezed, jolting him awake to the agony of needles scattering across sore muscles. He blinked into the gloom and tried to remember what it felt like to feel the sun on his face. Just a little light... He ached to see it again, to feel some warmth.

"You've had enough time—" Unfamiliar male voices traveled beneath the closed door.

"You will get nothing from him." The prince. Eroan recognized that voice at least.

"He'll talk. They always do." A third, and the door lock *thunked*.

Three entered. The prince hung back while the other two approached, boots clunking. The one to the right smelled of wet metal and grinned like Eroan was a prize he'd been waiting for. "A fine specimen," he said, ragged voice slanted by a harsh guttural accent. His mop of dark hair half-covered his face, partially shielding one ruby red eye. The other shone an icy blue.

The third carried a flickering lantern and stood tall and still, keeping his distance. His clothes, like the prince's, appeared informal but had an unmistakably refined edge. Eroan studied that tall one, read the fine stitching, the familiar but bitter scent. His hair, currently tied back loosely with a leather band, was so black it looked like ink spilled over his shoulder. Lysander's brother, Prince Akiem. He had to be.

Eroan's heart spluttered, trying to dump adrenaline into his veins for all the good it would do him. The shivering started up again, rattling his teeth together. He hated this, hated that he appeared weak, hated that they had reduced him to a thing in chains. That hate stirred his blood and drove rods through his legs, lending him the strength to stand. The room tipped, Eroan's vision blurred, but he saw Akiem raise a single dark eyebrow and that small thing felt like a victory. *See me, notice me, understand who I am and that you cannot break me!*

The older prince nodded, and Red-Eye lunged.

A rough hand burned over Eroan's ribs, another scorched his hip. The chains jerked, hauling him higher, onto his toes. Fiery agony lashed down his back, forcing seized muscles to contract. All of it at once sent the room spinning. Every touch burned like a brand. He locked his teeth together to keep from crying out, but a groan slipped through.

Red-Eye's hand closed around his throat and squeezed.

The dragonkin's wicked, snarling face filled Eroan's vision. Skin rough. Teeth sharp. His metallic smell laced Eroan's throat. "Let's start with a name, elf."

Eroan bared his teeth in a snarl, but all it bought him was a punch in the gut, throwing him forward into Red-Eye's rough-handed embrace. Red-Eye muscled him back against the wall. Eroan's gut heaved, ejecting nothing. He coughed, wheezed, fighting for air to fill him again.

"There's a pretty elf," Red-Eye caught his jaw and hissed his next words against Eroan's lips. "You and I are going to get real close..."

This one was the kind he'd been expecting from the beginning. The only surprise was how long it had taken the dragonkin to reveal their claws.

Eroan tried to tear free from Red-Eye's grip, but his fingers dug into Eroan's cheeks, cutting the inside against his teeth. Eroan tasted blood. Heat and fire and pain beat through him like a drum, over and over, but he would not give this beast the satisfaction of hearing him whimper or beg or cry out.

The tip of a blade trailed down Eroan's neck, over his collarbone, sinking deeper as it reached his left pectoral muscle. Their gazes locked, even as Eroan trembled. His body was a tool, the physical pain, temporary. This would end. Red-Eye could cut him, it changed nothing. They could never take his spirit.

"A name," Red-Eye purred, his breath dank with stale mead. "There's no harm in giving us your name, now is there."

The blade-tip burned its way through Eroan's skin, sinking in. Blood trickled, cooling as it dripped. He felt it all, but his stare continued to drill into Red-Eye's. Wicked glee sparkled in the dragon's mismatched eyes. This was the beginning, the beast's gaze promised, and the journey would be a long one.

Eroan bared his teeth in a spiteful grin.

"You won't get it." Prince Lysander's voice broke through the madness. The prince watched from his position near the wall, by the door, behind Red-Eye, his gaze shallow and bored. "He'd rather die. Just for a name." Lysander picked at a nail.

Red-Eye chuckled. The sound of that laugh crawled beneath Eroan's skin and lit a flutter of fear. "He'll die when I allow it. Leave, prince, if you do not have the stomach for it."

Lysander sighed and pushed off the wall. "Do what you will, this foolishness is a waste of my time." He waved a hand, dismissing them all, and left through the open door.

Eroan skipped his gaze to Akiem. The older brother regarded Lysander's departure carefully, until he was out of sight, then turned his attention once more to Red-Eye. The older prince had an iron-coldness about him as though he wore unseen armor. Like nothing could touch him. *Nothing* had in all the decades he'd been alive. And nothing likely would...

Strength bled from Eroan, a drip at a time.

"Inform me when you've made progress," Akiem said.

"And Lysander?" Red-Eye asked, pulling back to admire the rivulets of blood running down Eroan's chest.

"He won't be coming here again." Akiem set his lamp down, left the chamber, and closed the door. The lock clunked like the fall of an executioner's axe.

Orange lantern light danced over Red-Eye, making

shadows crawl across his face. His smile was a hungry, lurid thing, like the beast it belonged to. "You'll tell me your name, elf, if I have to cut it from your lips."

He ran his tongue across his teeth and slowly, carefully, pushed his blade between Eroan's ribs.

CHAPTER 3

*L*ysander

"HE KNOWS NOTHING," Lysander said. "Their assassins never do. He's a tool."

"*It*," his mother corrected. "They are objects. Nothing more."

Lysander gave her a blank look, one he'd mastered long ago. She returned with a glare, which must have taken effort while the males of her harem licked and suckled their way along her body.

She lay propped on her side among a bed of silks and satin while the males writhed around her, tending to her in almost every way. Had Lysander not been present, they'd be fucking her in every crevice and hole they could find. If the prince stayed too long, his presence wouldn't be enough to deter them. That was his dear mother's spell, one that didn't work on him. Not that it mattered. She had many ways to fuck him over without using her body.

"*It* knows nothing," she added. "The elf will be dead soon enough. Let us talk of more pressing matters. Our alliance with the Bronze needs addressing. His promises are all air and whispers. I need commitment if I am to have his armies under me." Lysander's mother trailed off as she noticed his gaze had wandered. "You like that one?" she asked, nodding at the male pressed against her back, sucking at her neck. Warning embers flashed in her dark eyes.

Silently cursing his own foolishness, Lysander looked up, anywhere but at her, at them. "No, Mother, I—"

"No?" she sat up, peeling her harem off her one by one. Doe-eyed and amiable, they fell away, sexed-up and drunk on her scent.

She rose gracefully from the bed, stunning in her nakedness, draped in a dark lace gown. Smooth black hair poured over her shoulders and tumbled over her milk-white breasts. On the bed, her puddle of males fell upon one another, tongues licking, hands stroking.

He knew his mother's games well enough by now to know she had summoned him here precisely because this display would get under his skin.

Lysander's heart galloped. The situation was rapidly unraveling, and she had hold of his strings.

She strode toward him like a storm poured into female form. As *dragon*, she was a monstrous force. As queen, she was worshipped, admired, loved by all. All but those who truly knew her. Those like Lysander.

She paused beside him, her heady scent working to soothe his runaway thoughts. Even as her blood-brood, he couldn't escape all her spells. She studied him, her lips lifting in a curious smile. She lowered her hand, found his hardening arousal through his trousers, and pushed her palm in, dancing his desires toward the edge of pain. "Hmmm," she purred in his ear. The sound was meant to be a comforting one from his time as a kit in the brood. These days it chilled his blood.

Fighting it did nothing. Fighting *her* did nothing. A heady mix of fear and lust swirled through his thoughts, turning them inside out. The more he feared the result of his own desires, the more those desires strummed through him. He wanted to back away, to flee this room, flee her, but a larger part of him wanted to stay, wanted this to happen, wanted her to fuck him, for her harem to fuck him and him them. If he even hinted at how dark his desires went, her punishment would be swift and severe.

She turned and crooked her finger at the blond, pulling him from the harem's affections. He came forward, as naked as the day he first learned how to tuck his wings away and take human form. Long, golden hair stroked his broad shoulders. His clear strength of body declared him prime breeding stock. Of course, Mother would have nothing less than perfection in her bed. These males were bred to breed, over and over, and the blond looked as though he liked nothing better.

Lysander imagined how his tongue might swirl in that sensitive spot between his shoulder and collarbone, how he might make the male arch beneath him.

The tip of the blond's tongue found the corner of his mouth at the same time as his hand cupped his own erect shaft. His thumb lightly brushed over the tip. Unbidden, Lysander sucked in a breath.

Mother leaned closer. "You disgust me." Her purrs turned sharp and her words to venom. "How am I supposed to breed from you?" Her hand found Lysander's arousal again, discovering how he'd further hardened. She squeezed, sending a painful, pleasurable shudder through Lysander. "You will couple with a bronze. One of my choosing."

Her hand massaged, but it wasn't her hand he was thinking of. The male stood before him now, cock gripped, hand slowly working himself from the base to the glistening tip, his eyes on Lysander's, pulling the prince down and down, further into desire.

A twitch betrayed him. That and the very obvious erection his mother massaged through his trousers. She knew exactly how to arouse, how to bring him to the edge, but keep him from falling over.

"I'll make it so you will couple with the bronze heir," she said, "and you will fuck her until she drowns in your seed. Those brutes will be mine." Her hand shifted, stealing another small sound from Lysander. "If you can't do this, what use are you?"

The blond's eyes softened, pupils widening. Lysander imagined tasting his wet mouth, imagined diving his tongue in, gripping him hard and making him groan for him, even as part of him screamed to stop this madness. "Mother." His voice cracked. He gripped her hand, intent on pushing her off but stalling before the thought turned into action. "Mother, I cannot—"

Her hand snapped shut. Lysander's knees buckled, pain lancing through his balls. He'd have dropped to his knees if she hadn't caught his shoulder and held him up. "I'll rip your cock off, you sniveling broken kit. Do as I command it or I'll have you tortured and killed alongside that worthless elf you're so fixated upon."

The elf. The stubborn, stupid elf. There was something about him, something important, something at the back of Lysander's mind that wouldn't shake free since they'd fought outside the queen's chambers. He wasn't sure yet why he had returned to the elf time and time again, but there was a reason. Perhaps it was more to do with Lysander than the elf, and why the prince had stopped the elf from killing the queen, a decision he was coming to regret. "Give me the elf," he gasped, blinking through tears. "And I'll couple with a bronze."

"What?" She blissfully released his cock and him.

He staggered but quickly caught himself.

"The elf? Why would you..." She smiled, interrupting her own thoughts. Something had occurred to her, some dark thought she liked the sound of. "I see." Turning toward the blond, she clasped him by the cock, prompting a pathetic mew, and steered him back toward the males on her bed.

Lysander looked away, toward the windows, and tried to fight the heat spreading through him. Need throbbed hot and heavy and wasn't fading. The desire was worse now she had her hands off him and on *the blond*. Vicious jealousy. The need to own, to hoard, to have. The dragons' curse. He ground his teeth, disgusted at himself, at her, at this fucking wreck they called a brood. She would not share them with him, not because she couldn't but because he was a broken, tainted thing and ever since she'd sensed that about him, she'd punished him at every turn.

She gently lay the male on the bed, pushing him back. The others had withdrawn to watch. Was Lysander the same as them, he wondered, something to be fucked and tossed aside by Queen Elisandra?

"I have not dismissed you."

He'd made it two steps toward the door before she'd noticed. Turning himself into rigid, unfeeling steel, he faced her and swallowed hard. She straddled the male, allowed him a moment to angle his cock so she could take all of him in, then she rocked, riding her male specimen, looking every part the queen determined to claw her way to the top by any means, and if she had to do it by fucking half the male dragons in the realm and swelling the ranks with her twisted amethyst brood, then so be it.

Wrong.

So wrong.

"Watch how it's done, Lysander." She threw a smile over her shoulder, body rocking.

Lysander lowered his gaze from her joyous grin and settled it on the male lost to her. He gripped her legs, fingers denting her thighs, his face slack, eyes ablaze, succumbing to the pleasure she gave. He wanted the blond under him like that. His fingers digging into *his* thighs. He wanted to rip him from her clutches and fuck him as she watched just to make her rage and scream. Make her see. She'd probably kill him afterward, but it might just be worth it.

Lysander's engorged cock twitched. She noticed him adjust his trousers, trying to lessen the pressure, and snarled a deep growl, sounding more dragon than woman. "Dare touch yourself, and your precious elf dies." Her words struck like whip lashes.

Lysander's upper lip rippled but his snarl was silent, and for the first time in a long time, the mental grip on his form shivered, threatening to collapse around him. She saw it all, saw his eyes blaze brighter, saw his skin shimmer, scales shifting, rattling, and she laughed her bitch-queen laugh.

She fucked the blond with Lysander watching because she could and because she knew he had no choice. His own twisted desires throbbed and needed and ached and all he could think was how he wanted his mother, the Dragon Queen, to suffer as he had his entire life.

roan

As RED-EYE'S blade took its bites, Eroan buried his thoughts deeper, losing himself inside warm memories of home, where the air smelled of wet grass and the sun beat down, where Janna's laugh could lift any mood and Curan's scowl was an ever-present threat.

Red-Eye had stripped Eroan's clothes hours ago and set to work carving into his thighs. Cold, slick sweat chilled his skin, turning him into a shivering, weak thing. He hated it, hated the slippery feel of shame and disgrace roll over inside, but he held onto his words through every cut, through every one of the dragon's snarls, and that made him strong, made him powerful.

Red-Eye carved his marks on one thigh and now brought the knife in, close enough to Eroan's personal parts for the chill on his skin to become ice in his veins.

Red-Eye's lascivious smile said it all. Eroan closed his eyes and tried to hide deeper inside himself, somewhere far, far away where the forest was green and the air clean.

Cold metal brushed his scrotum.

Door bolts rattled. Eroan snapped his eyes open as the door swung inward, revealing a slim, feminine figure wrapped in a purple, velvet cloak and cowl.

Red-Eye's knife was gone. Eroan fell forward, panting. A moment's relief. He'd take it.

Her sweet scent found him, a potent mix of floral and honey that tried to cloud his intent. His orders flew in, sharp and precise. *Kill her.* He'd know the scent anywhere, having found it so many times on the elven carcasses strung up along the borders. *Kill the queen.* His one reason for being here stood in front of him.

"Leave," she barked.

Her cowl hid her face, but there was no mistaking the authority in her words. No mistaking her.

Red-Eye whimpered. "It won't be long now—"

A deep, throaty growl rumbled from the woman. Red-Eye mumbled his apologies and scurried from the room, taking his bloodied knives with him.

He had left the door open.

Torches flickered in their hallway brackets, illuminating an empty corridor that snaked away. Eroan searched that space for others, for her guards or princes. Had she truly come alone? What trick was this?

Twisting his wrists, he tested the clamps, disguising the movement behind angling toward her. Pain snapped down his arms, but soon dulled to nothing behind the thoughts of how or why she was here.

The raw wounds at his wrists wept blood and had done

for days. Blood that slickened and oiled his skin, blood he could use...

"My, my... You are quite the catch." She lifted her pale hands and lowered her cowl, revealing a breathtaking beauty difficult to define.

Elven artists had sketched her through the ages, tried to capture the testimony of any who had seen her and survived. Those artists had failed. No pencil could capture something as exquisite as her. Hair blackish-purple, the color of a furious storm, and eyes sparkling with intelligence. Power lurked behind that beauty. A power born of the old gods. A power none could deny.

"I hear you almost made it to my chamber. The closest of all attempts to kill me." Her words flowed like oil, smooth and slow and all-consuming.

Closer, she came. Her intoxicating scent sailed through his senses, trying to distract and disarm. He let his eyelids droop, let her see his fight drain away. Hours, days, weeks, cycles, he'd exposed himself to her intoxicating scent, building resistance so that when the time came, he could drive his dagger home with his eyes wide open. The time spent with those she had killed served a second purpose too. As their bodies bloated and they rotted back into the earth, his hatred became a sword, his disgust became his armor.

"My son was the one who stopped you, did you know?" she asked.

He had known because her son had told him his name. She didn't appear to know her son had been talking, however. Interesting. Another riddle. But one he couldn't waste time thinking on. There was an opportunity here. *Until it is done.*

25

"Ah, yes. Your silence. The famous elven stubborn streak. You'll take your silence with you to your death just like all the others. There cannot be many of you left, and still, you waste lives by sending your best to slay me?"

She moved close and dragged a fingernail down his chest, snagging on Red-Eye's fresh cuts, watching Eroan's face for a reaction. Her dark lashes fluttered delicately, belying the beast inside her.

Already, panting and shivering, he knew he looked like a wretched thing, and let her see how weak they'd made him. Let her think him beaten.

"It saves me having to wipe your kind out at least."

His clamped wrist twitched. He hissed in, making sure to keep her eyes on his face and not allow her to see how the clamp was halfway over his thumb and knuckles —*almost free*. This was his chance. Likely, his last and only chance to end it.

"I see why he asked to keep you. There's something to be said for elven males. Your goddess, Alumn? She has an eye for beauty..." Her touched deepened, roaming over his abdominal muscles, smearing blood and filth across his stomach. Her hand stroked lower, and her fingers found his limp member. An urge to buck and twist twitched through him. He held it back, even as her fingers squeezed, he stared into her multi-faceted eyes. In hundreds of years, no elf had ever been so close to her and lived.

"I've had lesser males than you in my bed." She peered up through her long lashes. "Would you like that?"

He would have preferred death and the risk of condemning his spirit to Ifreann than serving in her bed or in any part of the dragon realms.

She saw the fire in his eyes and laughed, sweet, ringing laughter while turning away. "I've fucked elves before. You're all rather... fragile but full of prideful fire. I suppose you found those I've discarded. I do try to give them back after I'm done." She drifted toward the door, chuckling at her words.

He'd found them, buried them, prayed to Alumn for them. And to have the source of all that horror and heart-break so close... His silence wasn't winning any ground. If she left, he might lose his only chance to strike. He needed a new tactic, a way to reel her in, to lure her close.

He whispered a string of words, keeping them soft, making them tantalizing.

"What was that?"

He spoke again, keeping the words too quiet for her to hear. All dragonkin were curious creatures unable to leave anything unexplored or whispers unheard. She couldn't resist.

Her eyebrows pinched in frustration. Returning to her spot in front of him, she regarded his prone, weakened state, wary, but a chained and broken elf couldn't be a threat to the mightiest of all dragons.

She leaned in, tucked her hair behind her ear, and listened.

"My name is Eroan Ilanea," he breathed, setting his name free. "I was forged in the fires of Ifreann, quenched in Alumn's maelstrom, for a single purpose... to kill the Dragon Queen."

He tore his hand free of the clamp and grabbed for her throat. Agony poured through his muscles, rendering his reach almost useless. His fingers sailed through her hair —*so close*. She caught his clumsy grasp and slammed his arm back against the wall. Bones shattered like twigs. Brittle, sharp agony blasted up his arm. He barked a cry.

Her knee jerked up between his legs. She wedged her forearm under his chin, trapping him against the wall. Her strength was a monstrous thing—bigger than her, more than this room could contain. A strength he had no hope of countering. The prince had been right. Eroan should have eaten, should have stayed strong for an opportunity such as this one. There would not be another. He would die here, in this moment, and he could think only of how his people would weep for another failure.

The queen's eyes glowed with delight. She grinned. "Oh, I like you, *Eroan Ilanea*. You're much too bright a thing for my son to have. Hm..." She ran the tip of her tongue over her top lip. "An elven assassin in my harem. A lesson for your kin, don't you think? And a fate I imagine you believe to be worse than death. Yes, that will do nicely."

Heated pain burned through him, but it meant little compared to the horror her words incited. He could not, would not, be her plaything. He'd take up the first blade he found and plunge it through his own chest before he allowed her to reduce him in such a way.

Until it is done.

But close to her, free of these chains... No elf had survived her for long. He could—*until it was done*—and the queen was dead by his hand. He would survive by any means. Survive her and kill her.

"I came here to offer you a deal," she said. "I planned to put you in my son's service to help satisfy his pathetic *needs*. You would get a second chance at life. But I

28

see a better use for you now, my fiery elf, and perhaps Lysander will obey me with you at my heel."

The purring sound at the back of her throat set Eroan's teeth on edge. She ran her wet, warm tongue up Eroan's cheek, filling his head with her sweetness and magic. Disgust burned in his belly.

"I will kill you, Elisandra," he whispered. "You and your sons, and every dragonkin who crosses me." He knew she wanted to hear the words, to hear the challenge in them, the challenge in *him*, but not as much as he wanted to make them true. He would wreck her brood from the inside out, carve through them one by one until her tower and might crumbled from within its walls.

Her eyes widened, and the Dragon Queen laughed her silky laugh. "You'll try, elf. And you'll fail. As is the destiny of all elves who dare cross me."

She pushed off, and he dropped to his knees and hung from the one remaining wrist-clamp, his broken wrist useless and throbbing at his side, his body a naked, bloody wreck. Inside, wild rage burned and lashed and spat; a rage he knew how to sharpen into a weapon.

The Dragon Queen looked upon him with a triumphant smile on her lips, not knowing this was the beginning of her end. Not knowing *Eroan Ilanea* was the beginning of the end of all dragons.

CHAPTER 5

*D*ragged from his prison, bound in new wrist and ankle shackles, and shoved into a dark, windowless cave, Eroan could do nothing to stop it happening. For a few numb, silent seconds he stood naked and shivering in the dark.

Something thundered behind glistening, wet stone walls.

He looked up and found a grate above. Similar to the one cutting into the soles of his feet. He had moments to wonder what those grates were for when a torrent of water poured in, slamming him to his knees. Shock stole his breath. Panic tore at his chest. He sunk his fingers into the grate and squeezed his eyes closed.

Just water.

He wasn't dying, but by Alumn, it felt like he was. The hard blast bit into countless cuts and poured over his skin, burning like acid. He gritted his teeth against the onslaught and just *breathed. In and out. In and out. Not dying.*

The water shut off, leaving him gasping and wretched.

Old wounds had reopened, spilling streams of blood down his arms. His broken wrist beat in time with his heart. The water would have cleansed Red-Eye's work, clearing out any early infection. It was a good thing. *Yes, a good thing...* If he was being cleansed that likely meant he would be free of the prison and free of the unending darkness... *only to find a new darkness in her bed.*

The guards collected him and led him down internal corridors. Torches warmed his skin as he passed under them. But he ached to feel real light, sunlight. If he didn't see it soon, feel the living earth beneath his feet, all of this would be for nothing. He'd die as surely as a cut rose. Did they know? Or hadn't they let an elf live long enough in captivity for them to realize how he needed the air, the earth, the light, to keep his heart beating?

The challenge of a spiral staircase almost dropped him to his knees for a second time. The guard's firm tugs on his chains kept him up and moving.

Shameful, weak, wretched. He would live with these feelings and use them, turn them into fuel for the fight. But only if he could feel the sun again soon...

"Get it healed up." The guard handed his chain over to the woman. Eroan blinked at her, wondering if she was real or something his mind had concocted.

She dipped her head and led him wordlessly toward a gaping fireplace. Fire licked and danced in the grate. With every step closer, warmth soaked into his skin, seeping into his bones.

"Not there," the guard grunted. He hadn't left, likely assuming Eroan would try to slip his shackles the first chance he got. He wasn't wrong, though Eroan doubted he'd get far, weak as he was. *Keep your strength up. You'll need it*, the prince had told him. He intended on taking that advice now that he was outside that horrid black hole.

"It'll be easier to work the wounds if it isn't shivering," his new chaperone remarked.

The guard grunted, and the female continued to lead Eroan toward the fire. Wood smoke and the fire's accompanying crackle had his thoughts sailing far away to where sprawling forests beckoned and the earth soothed. He clung to that memory of home, wrapping himself in its mental warmth like the fire wrapped him in its real glow. In his mind, he was free and running, and Janna was there, laughing at something he'd said or done. *Don't think about her.*

"Kneel." The woman pushed down on his shoulder.

Head bowed, he knelt in front of the hearth. Firelight washed over his naked thighs, thawing tight muscles.

"It's to be delivered to Elisandra clean and obliging."

"Clean I can do." Her hands roamed Eroan's shoulder but skipped over his back, avoiding where the wounds throbbed the worst. "Obliging? Well, that's up to it."

She set Eroan's chains down and left his side a moment. He heard water sloshing, bowls clanging, but his gaze stayed fixed on the chain's end. For the first time in days, he was untethered. Adrenaline tried to kick in alongside his training, tried to jolt him off his ass and into motion, but all he managed was hastened trembling.

"It's going into shock."

A bowl clunked against the floor behind him.

He stared at the chain.

"Fix that too."

"I'll fix *you*," the woman grumbled quietly.

"If it goes to the queen like that, I'll see the sharp side

of her smile and believe me, Carline, I'll pass that straight on to you. So do whatever it takes. Get it clean and fixed and ready by the time I return."

The sound of his boots thumped out of the room until Eroan heard only the fire crackling and Carline's clothes rustling. Had this been the first night or the third, he might have taken the chain up and struck her with it. Anything to be free. But being free was no longer his purpose. Soon, he would be delivered to the queen and there, by her side, he would have the best chance of finishing her. His pride of elves had struck knowing it was likely their end. They had all died trying to reach her. Only Eroan had survived the queen's last guardian, Prince Lysander. It had to be for a reason. Perhaps the divine Alumn was watching, keeping Eroan alive for when his time to strike would come. He could not run, and he could not fight. But he could wait.

Fingers or cloth touched his back, he couldn't see which, but his skin prickled as though touched with a hot iron. He hissed and jerked away.

"I'll do my best to minimize the pain. Here." She held out a flask.

He looked at the flask, at her, and yearned to pour water over his tongue. Who was she? Wisdom and sympathy softened hard dragon eyes. She was a monster, they all were, but time had worn her sharp edges away. She didn't smile, just looked blankly back at him. She no more wanted an elf here than he wanted to be on his knees in front of her. He took in the room behind her. Vegetables and breads adorned long counters. This was a kitchen of sorts. She was a housekeeper, not another form of torture.

He took the flask to the sound of chains clinking and

drank before she could change her mind and snatch the flask back. Cool wetness touched his parched lips and slid across his tongue. It hurt, everything hurt. His throat spasmed. Water, or whatever poison she'd given him, came back up. He spat and wheezed. "*What is that?!*"

"Mead." She wiped her hands on her apron and moved to stand behind him. "S'all I've got that'll help with the pain." She set to work, dipping a cloth in the water and dabbing near his right shoulder where the wounds weren't as raw. Her fluttering fingertips brought the shivers to the surface of his skin. When she reached the worst of his back, he grabbed the mead and drank deep.

His gut heaved, his body rejecting it. He slammed the back of his hand over his mouth and kept the sweet wine down long enough so it might stay down.

"Once that mead's kicked in, it won't take long to numb you. I'll get you some food once the worst of this mess is dealt with."

She poked and prodded, dabbed and probed, tutted and mumbled, but after the third helping of mead, the pain lessened and Eroan fell into a dreamy daze. Her drag-onkin hands were smoother than he'd expected. Not as smooth or as deft as elven hands, but she had some healer skill.

He took another swig of the mead and closed his eyes against the spinning. In all of this agony, he'd locked himself away. As they had chained him, cut him, none of it had mattered, he had guarded against it all. But here, naked in front of this fire, the wounds weren't the worst of it. His mind, his spirit, those things were weakening, and without those parts of himself, he wasn't even sure who he was anymore.

Eroan Ilanea.

Assassin of the Order.

His pride of elves had come to kill Elisandra.

Over and over he told himself these things, building them up like bricks in a wall.

He was not this wretched thing quivering on his knees. He was elven, proud, free, and strong.

"Easy there." She plucked the flask from his grip, snapping him out of his reverie. "That's enough of that on an empty gut. We can't have you falling into the queen's chamber, now can we."

Mention of the queen rippled a snarl across his lips. Better a snarl than let the trickle of fear sink any deeper and undermine what little strength he had left. What horror awaited him in the brood bed?

His shattered wrist throbbed, a souvenir of his first meeting with the queen. It likely wouldn't be his last.

Carline chuckled. "You have some fire in you yet, I see." She leaned in and set about washing his chest, wringing out her cloth, and changing the water when necessary. He watched her work, catching her occasional curious glances at his face. It was unlikely she had seen many elves up close. Elisandra was right, elves were few. So rare now Eroan knew of only one other clan in the valley. What did she see, this dragonkin female? A killer too? Or a worthless thing, a pet?

He breathed in her scent, marking her in his mind. She smelled of warm bread, mead and smoke, spiced with that now all-too-familiar dragonkin musk.

Her hand roamed lower, across his hipbone. He awkwardly brushed her aside, rattling the chains and setting his wrist on fire.

"Shy?" Her eyes crinkled with humor. "Don't be. She'll soon fuck that out of you."

He blinked. Carline knew he was to be a pet in the queen's bed? He had assumed it would be a secret, that he'd be kept behind closed doors. He couldn't imagine the queen revealing any intimacies with an elf to her brood, but then he knew little of how things worked inside these walls.

Carline frowned at his muddled expression. "I've been told to get you clean. If I miss a bit, it's both our hides she'll skin. So, let's not make an incident out of this and just get it done, shall we?"

He turned his left hand palm-up, keeping his broken-right from moving too much. "I'll do it."

"Very well." She handed over the cloth and watched him clean around his personal areas. The chains made the work awkward, and his broken wrist added to the struggle. When he tried to hand the cloth back, she clicked her tongue. "It will take more than that, pet." She wrung out the cloth and returned, diving her hand between his legs.

He had his hand around her wrist and her arm caught before considering how any defiance might be dealt with. His stare met hers, but she turned away first, taking her cloth with her. "I see you have pride, elf. You had better keep it hidden if you want to survive. Now let's see to that wrist you're favoring."

Survive? "Do you truly think I'll survive this?" The words came out harsher than he'd meant, but the tone was true.

Carline shook her head, more in dismay than answer, and dumped the bowl on her counter. She collected a bundle of bandages and plucked some canes from where they supported her cooking herbs, and fashioned a small splint, then set about wrapping his wrist. He watched her hands move, sensing a little magic tingling through his skin, stealing away the pain. She *was* a healer. Her kind— a dragonkin who cared for others—were rare. As far as he knew, they didn't fix their weak, they ate them.

With the bandages fixed, she washed her hands, grabbed a bread roll and poured something warm and steaming into a food bowl and set the small feast down in front of him. "Eat before you throw up that perfectly good mead all over my kitchen floor." Straightening, she planted her hands on her ample hips and frowned like a disappointed mate. Was it wrong to like this female? It seemed his mind was trying to make a friend in this place of horrors. Only a fool would like his captors.

"I'm going to find you some clothes befitting of your build. I suggest you don't run. A naked elf won't get far in a tower full of hungry dragons."

He had considered it since the guard had left, but the chains and wrapped-wrist would slow him. That and how his head continued to spin. The mead had been deliberate, he realized. If he tried to stand, he'd likely fall before making it two steps. The thought of escape was a sweet dream. One he let go.

"No running?" she asked.

"No running."

After she'd gone, he devoured the food, only slowing when his insides cramped. The warm food and fire helped ease the trembling enough that he tried to stand. Stumbling, he staggered to the counter. Fruit, bowls, plates, a knife... He reached out but stopped. There was nowhere to hide it. Not yet. But once dressed, if he could steal it away and get free... If he could find the queen's chamber...

He staggered to the window. If he could place the part of the tower he was in, he could find the queen's chamber. Find her, kill her, and this hell would be over.

A dark landscape of stone parapets and towers glowed by torchlight outside the window. The forests of home were a long way outside the tower's grounds, beyond the crumbling, ancient steel monuments that clawed at the skies, beyond the sprawl or barrenlands. It had taken days to cross the barrenlands and more to reach the brood's tower. He tried the window latch, finding it locked. Just a breeze, that was all he wanted, to feel fresh air on his face and hear night's sweet song.

A shadow darkened the towers spires. One of the enormous beasts swopped in, its wingspan blocking out everything. It let out a shrill bark, announcing its presence. Eroan braced a hand against the wall and leaned closer. Somewhere far off, another of their brood replied. This one's armored scales shimmered like oil in the darkness, making it almost invisible. The wing beats, too, were virtually silent. It alighted, clutching the tower, throwing its enormous wings back for balance and settled there, scanning the distance. Searching for more elves to feast on, perhaps. Shaking its great head, it swung its gaze toward Eroan's little window and fixed him in its glare. Many believed dragons couldn't smile. On seeing Eroan, this one peeled back its upper lip, deliberately revealing rows of long, jagged teeth.

They were impossible to fight in their natural form, too big, too vicious, and too armored for any elven sword to pierce. Only in human form could they be killed. Eroan knew it was possible because he'd killed one before. But that one hadn't been like this one...

He stared back at the beast now. This thing and its kind had reshaped the world beneath their claws, torn up civilizations and buried them.

It turned its head away, and fixed one eye solidly on Eroan, marking him. He was a small thing, that gaze said, easily crushed. With a sweep of its wings, it took to the air, sending shudders through the tower's walls and rattling the window.

"Ah, that'll be Akiem," Carline said, returning. "Patrols every night. Anyone would think he had nothing better to do." She tutted again, clearly unimpressed with the prince, and set a bundle of clothes down on the end of her countertop.

Akiem. The older prince. The one who had unleashed Red-Eye on him. Anger and shame fizzled through his veins. He tried to watch him soar, but his outline had already vanished against the night sky.

"Now then, let's get you covered up and presentable."

She'd brought for him simple cotton clothes and leather jerkin. Common-wear, he assumed. The type found on house workers. He approached and picked up the jerkin—it reeked of dragon—and dropped it again.

Carline huffed. "Don't be expecting no fancy wear, this is the best I can do. She'll have you dressed to her whim anyway."

Dressed to her whim? He didn't want to think about it or what was to come. He held out his shackled wrists. "How do you suggest I dress while in chains? Should I magic the garments on?"

She arched her eyebrow. "I do believe you're feeling

better, elf. But don't go thinking you can fool me into unchaining you."

It was a genuine question, though he had worded it in a way that had sparked something of a smile to her lips. "How do I get my arms through the sleeves? Tell me that."

Her eyes sparkled. "I don't know, guess you'd better figure it out." She turned away and set about rummaging through her kitchen, muttering to herself.

He picked up the shirt and turned it over, trying to decide the best way of getting his arms through the fabric when it slipped from his aching fingers.

Carline scooped the garment off the floor and shoved it into his chest. "You're more capable than you're letting on."

"Isn't it *your* job to make me presentable?" he asked. "Won't you fail if I'm not dressed?"

She snatched the shirt back, dumped it on the counter and grabbed a mallet. "My patience is not infinite." Grabbing his chains, she yanked him forward and smacked the chain with the mallet, narrowly missing his good hand. "Hold still." She tried again, putting enough force behind it to rattle his teeth.

"Wait—!"

On the third try, the chain cracked enough for her to pull the links apart, separating his hands. He still had the clamps weighing down his wrists, but at least he was able to move his arms independently—and dress.

"There, now get dressed and quit your complaining. And stop smiling, I'm not your friend, so don't go thinking it."

"Thank you."

"And don't thank me either. Neither of us is here by choice."

He dressed, gingerly shrugging the shirt and jerkin over his back, setting his wounds on fire again. The clothes pinched in places, but it felt good to be covered up again, like the layers could somehow offer protection. No boots, though. His feet stayed bare against cold stone.

"She has you working here unwillingly?" he asked.

Carline waved a ladle at him. "Don't ask questions. If you're feeling better, go stand by the fire and wait for him to return. Not another word, you hear?"

Despite the fire in her words, that heat didn't reach her eyes. This old dragon wasn't so hard a thing.

He watched her take a bundle of fine-beans and take a chopping blade to them. One, two, three. Her hands were quick.

"Can I help?"

"Help?" She eyed him, cleaver glinting. "What do you think would happen to me if it was known I had an elf *help* in this kitchen? Don't be foolish, and don't be offering to help anyone but yourself around here. You had it right before. Keep your mouth shut and obey the amethyst. Anything else gives them lashes to whip you with."

She returned to her food preparation and Eroan to the fireplace, where he absorbed the heat while he could. She hadn't seen him slip the paring knife up his sleeve and hopefully wouldn't notice it missing until he was gone from her kitchen. It wasn't much of a weapon but wielded precisely, it could kill as surely as any finely forged sword. He'd had a hunting knife just like it, but that had been taken along with all his other weapons when the prince had bested him.

Eroan only needed one weapon and one more chance to kill.

By the time his head ceased spinning and his wounds stopped their throbbing, the guard returned to escort him on. Eroan didn't speak, didn't bid Carline a goodbye, and she ignored his leaving. She'd likely forget about the elf in her kitchen by the end of the night, but he would remember her, the dragonkin who smelled of smoke and mead.

They walked until his feet had grown sore, roaming farther into the tower's heart. One of the monsters roared far below, shaking the walls. He'd heard similar rumblings in the prison. Dragons returning from their patrols or the same dragon roaring out in triumph, pain or anguish. He couldn't tell which. He'd heard the lower in status a dragon was, the deeper inside the tower it slept, all coiled together like snakes. But not the queen, she lived above them, in all ways.

The knifepoint dug into his wrist where it sat snug inside his wrist-bandage. Should he be searched again, they were unlikely to open the wrappings. If he was being taken to the queen, as the guard had earlier suggested, then his chance to kill her might arrive sooner than he could have hoped. This time, he would be ready.

CHAPTER 6

*L*ysander

LYSANDER COULD BARELY HEAR his thoughts over the disorderly gathering of bronze and amethyst dragons in the great chamber. Mother had dumped some eager bronze female in his lap early on in the celebrations and snarled encouraging words in his ear about fucking her the first chance he got. She wasn't *the* bronze, the one he'd agreed to couple with—that unfortunate agreement was currently being discussed at the end of the table, where Elisandra and the formidable bronze chief, Dokul, sat now. A brute of a dragon, all muscle and bulk. He was built the same as a man, too, like he could break the feasting table in two just by glancing in its general direction. His brood and Lysander's fell about and over each other, oblivious as to the real reason for this friendly get-together.

Lysander watched the bronze help themselves to their food and lead the lower-ranked amethyst into the shadows where they'd undoubtedly try to fuck them. Males and females both, the bronze didn't waste time sticking to the opposite sex. The more they could spread their ferocious seed the better. Lysander couldn't decide if he was openly disgusted or secretly aroused, and that only made this night worse.

"Stop scowling," Akiem said, dropping into the vacated chair beside him.

Lysander shifted in his seat. The bronze lower had stuck around, determined to stick her hand anywhere warm and inviting. He couldn't shove her off his lap without offending Elisandra, and if he did that here and now, she'd couple him with some hideous bronze monster out of spite. Like most things, he was stuck here doing as he was told and knew to make the most of it.

The lower slid across his lap and tried to perch on Akiem's thigh. His brother bared his teeth in a harsh smile, only exciting her more. She leaned forward, sticking her ass in Lysander's face and groped at Akiem's thigh, clearly not getting the hint. All the bronze got off on violence. *No* was the wrong thing to say to her.

"Go get us some wine," Lysander snapped.

She sighed and straightened, looking between them. "I'll do you both if you ask nicely." With that, she sauntered off.

Akiem watched her shapely rear sway. Her collection of strange barrenlands trinkets, metal hoops and rusted springs, jangled around her waist and ankle, advertising her wares. The jewelry was human detritus, left over from the old-world. The bronze had a pathological need to collect shiny shit. Their warren was apparently cluttered with mountains of it. If all went well tonight, Lysander figured he'd soon find out if that rumor was true.

"You fuck her," he told his brother, who continued to watch her.

"I would, if my own brood didn't keep me satisfied." He peeled his stare from her ass and fixed it on Lysander. "Is Mother watching?"

He flicked his gaze over his brother's shoulder and smiled. Mother was indeed watching. She had a face like thunder. Lysander mimed drinking and smiled to indicate her delightful female gift was coming back. "Always, brother," he said to Akiem.

"You screw this up, she'll kill you like she did Amalia."

Hearing that name dealt him a punch in the gut and almost tore the smile off his face. Guarded, he pretended to be interested in a small scuffle breaking out across the table. "You think I don't know that?"

"Can you..." Akiem trailed off.

"Can I what?"

"Can you couple with a bronze?"

Lysander laughed, mostly to hide the sharp twist of his lips. "Believe the rumors, do you? That I can't *perform* my duties?"

Akiem wasn't amused. He rarely was. "Do the bronze lower, right here," he hissed. "Nobody will say another word if they see it now. Better here than—"

"Fuck that." He wasn't some performing freak show. Where was the damn wine?

Akiem leaned closer, bringing his considerable power

ARIANA NASH

with him, making him seem larger than the man. Lysander met his brother's gaze, knowing what was coming. "The bronze couple in public," Akiem said, keeping his voice low. "It's a ritual to them. It proves the joining is consolidated. If you can't do it here, then how are you going to there, among them? And if you fail, Mother will not suffer the embarrassment. She'll instruct Dokul to kill you, probably during the act, if you don't *finish*."

Lysander winced. "Sweet nights, Akiem. I know!" He hadn't thought of much else since Elisandra had first made her intentions to breed-him-off clear. It was always going to happen anyway. She was right about one thing: If he couldn't produce amethyst heirs and strengthen her line, then what good was he? Amalia had refused Elisandra, and she'd died for her obstinacy.

"She didn't give you the lower for her skills in conversation," Akiem said. "You can bet the rumors have traveled beyond the tower. Prince Lysander, her broken son. Dokul is watching."

Tired of hanging on to his fake smile, Lysander let it go and eyed his brother. "Did she send you over here?"

Akiem looked away.

Of course she had.

The lower returned, jug in hand, and poured them both fresh drinks. Lysander took his and drank it all down, hoping it could fill the gaping hole inside him. Slamming the cup down, he stood, cupped the lower's ass and hauled her against his hip, making sure all in the hall got a long look. The lower melted close, already purring, and he knew for sure Elisandra was watching as he guided the lower away from the main hall. He had three options: fuck this lower, bribe her, or kill her. A bribe would come back to bite him in the ass. He'd tried that route before. Elisandra always discovered the lie.

The lower pawed at his arm, his back, and groped at his ass. He guided her into one of the outer corridors where the wind from the balcony arches fluttered the flags and flaming torches.

He could kill her, but without an alibi and with the whole hall having just witnessed them leave together, he was fucked anyway.

She was on him suddenly, a writhing, arching thing, warm and alive beneath his hands. Her mouth sought his, roaming across his jaw. He gave it to her, kissed her, feeling something of a spark shiver lust alight. If he didn't fuck her here and make it good, he'd suffer later.

She plucked his shirt free of his belt and pushed her warm hands up his chest, sweeping over his abs. She smelled of wine and metal, of all things bronze. He shoved her against the wall. Her jingling hoop jewelry chimed. Her wicked smile dumped a ton of lust where it was needed, making him hard. Thank the Great One for His gracious favors. Maybe he could get through this.

She yanked on his belt and palmed his cock through the fabric, purring her pleasure. "She said you wouldn't even get this far. She was wrong, huh?" Her thumb pushed in, pushing over his tip, spilling shivers through him, making his cock jump.

He braced an arm against the wall, hemming her in and tried to shake the rage her words had summoned. This bronze would tell his mother everything. Every word, every touch, wrong or right, hard or soft. All of it. This was a fucking interview.

He caught her jaw and held her locked in place. "You're to report back to her?"

She didn't answer but didn't need to. She grinned and ran the tip of her tongue over her blunt human teeth.

He had no choice at all now. And why was he surprised at that? After twenty-five years, he should have figured it out. His mother owned him. Fuck it, and her, he was getting this done and over with.

He kissed the lower's mouth, pushing hard, driving his tongue in. She writhed and purred. The bronze liked it rough. If he couldn't do it his way, he'd fuck her so hard she'd have no choice but to wipe the knowing-grin off his mother's face.

She fought with his belt, trying to unlatch it. He knocked her hand aside, parted her thighs and sank his hand into the V between her legs, finding her warm, wet and inviting. At least she was easy. Her hot little nub was an easy target too, turning her to liquid in his hands. He could pleasure her with his damn eyes closed. The problem wasn't her, it was him. The lust was fizzling away. There hadn't been much to begin with but knowing his performance would be scrutinized was more than a mood killer, it could be a death sentence.

He slid two fingers into her. She clutched at his back and rocked her hips, then suckled his neck, nipped and dug her fingernails into his shoulder. And his mind started to wander. She was lovely to look at but... Fucking hells. Akiem could do this, so why couldn't he?

"What's wrong?"

Fuck.

"Nothing." He yanked his hand out, caught her hips,

and ground his crotch against hers. C'mon already... He needed to find a way out of this, and fast. Needed to think of something, anything, that'd get him up. He imagined the blond from his mother's bed, imagined his narrow hips beneath his hands, his cock erect and straining between them.

Her hand found him again and stroked some hardness back into play. Pleasure sizzled low in his balls. All right, he could do this.

"You like that."

She sounded like his mother.

He threw his head back and swallowed a bitter laugh. He couldn't do this. "Turn the fuck around." He didn't wait for her to obey. He grabbed her around the waist and shoved her toward the balcony rail. She was pliable in his hands and eager, so eager. It would have to be enough. He yanked her skirt and those ridiculous adornments down her legs, exposing her ass and those sweet, welcoming lips of warm flesh. Spreading his hand on her back, he held her pinned down and freed his erection, waking the bastard thing up with a few rough strokes. *Don't think about Elisandra.*

The blond. Think about him. The blonde's cock in my mouth. Mine in his. His tongue...

"Are we doing this?"

He thrust in, as deep as the fucking thing would go, deep enough to make her quit asking questions and gasp. In his head, it wasn't her taking all of him. It was him, the blond bent over, his hands clutched at the rail, and he had him, his ass so fucking tight, the friction like a drumbeat in his head.

The lower writhed and grunted, punctuating each thrust. Sweet pleasure was building, coiling tighter and tighter, winding Lysander up. Gripping her hips in both hands, he lost his mind to the pounding rhythm, to the idea that he was fucking him, not her. But even then, he knew it was over before it had really begun. She wasn't the blond. Her cunt wasn't what he wanted, and he was so fucked there was no way this was going to end well.

He pulled out and tried to hide his softening dick by working her clit from behind, making her come. He could do that, at least. She screamed her pleasure, but he wasn't fooling anyone. He couldn't even fake his own orgasm.

"We could try again..." She twisted and leaned against the balcony railing, thighs parted like an open invitation.

"Get out of here." He didn't even bother to tidy himself up and fell against the rail, gripping it like he could cling onto the pieces of a life about to fall apart around him.

She snickered, reached up, and planted a little kiss on his lips. "Maybe next time, prince."

Lysander knew he'd failed, and there would not be a next time.

He was done.

Mother would kill him.

He turned, propped a boot on the rail and leaped over the edge, into the dark.

Freedom.

Falling.

The wind bit and scraped his face and tore like hands at his clothes.

Down, down, down. Delay a second too long and it would be over.

His heart hammered, too much alive to throw it all away. He roared out all the anger, all the fear, the rage, and let the shift tear through him. His body breathed outward, magic and power suddenly free, filling him up, emptying him out, unleashing everything, remaking him into his true form.

He flung out long wings, spreading them so wide their sail-like membranes ached as they caught the air. The ground rushed in. Gravity clutched at his gut. He swooped over the rocks, closer than ever before, and soared high, breaking over the wide, winding river. Briny estuary air lapped at his scales. Another roar tore from deep inside. He opened his jaws and howled into the rushing wind. He could fly and not stop, could beat his wings until the muscles burned, until he couldn't fly anymore, and then he'd fall and maybe that time, that one last time, he wouldn't save himself.

He was dead anyway.

He didn't see her, not until claws sliced through his right wing. He rolled mid-flight, trying to shy from the pain. Amethyst scales flashed, her roar thundered, and with gut-sick horror, he watched her sparkling jaws open wide. She struck, plunged her teeth into his neck and tore out some vital part of him. He kicked, raked his claws across her belly, at anything. Her wings beat, slowing their descent and her claws sunk in, digging deeper and deeper around his ribs. Crushing. Killing.

Elisandra lifted her head and bellowed a victory cry.

She let him go.

He tumbled, losing height too quickly. Searing pain snapped up his right side. He tried to fling out his wings, tried to find the horizon in the dark, but something was wrong—his right wing flapped uselessly. The night sky rolled, the ocean glinted, around and around they went. He couldn't catch hold of either and tumbled on, trying to claw at the air in a pathetic attempt to keep himself aloft.

He hit the river like it was stone and the bone-biting cold rushed in to swallow him down.

roan

THE GUARDS LEFT Eroan chained to a wall in what was clearly part of the queen's enormous bedchambers. Floor-standing candelabras chased the dark from the corners and made shadows dance across fluttering window drapes. If he hadn't guessed the room's owner from the plush furnishing, her smell confirmed it. No bed that he could see, although this chamber likely led to others. But at least he was being spared that torture for now.

Left alone, he tugged at the fresh leather cuffs on his wrists. They'd switched the chains for these lighter restraints, and while they didn't pinch and chafe like the chains had, the fact they were made of leather likely meant they weren't coming off anytime soon. Convenient, locking clips fixing his wrists and ankles to the wall-straps implied he might at least get moved around. The new leather collar around his neck wasn't attached to anything. Yet.

He had his paring knife, but until he knew what this new scenario was, he couldn't risk revealing his only weapon.

He was still testing his straps when the door opened and the queen breezed in, wrapped in a combination of purple gossamer and silk. Her hair had been bundled in neat curls. She brought with her the smell of dragon and wine and smoke... and another male...

The man who followed was built like a boulder with eyes just as cold as stone. An odd collection of metal rings and bracelets jangled from his neck, ears, biceps, and wrists. Eroan had seen similar items buried in the forest floor and often overlooked them. But not this dragon, he clearly preferred to collect. That would make him a bronze —they were known for their strange hoarding obsession. Perhaps, the bronze *chief*, considering his size.

"Sit, Dokul," the queen said, softening the word so it sounded less of an order and more of an invitation. She took a jug from a shelf and poured something into two glasses, setting the first before the bronze as he made himself comfortable. Bare-chested, he wore one bronze pauldron at his left shoulder—for decoration more than protection—keeping his sword arm free to move. His hairless head was as smooth as his chest and an unusual sight. Eroan had never seen a hairless male before. He hadn't even known such a thing existed.

Dokul lifted his glass, but as he saw Eroan, his golden eyes narrowed.

Eroan had two of the world's fiercest dragons in his sights. A pity he was chained up, he could have struck a devastating blow to the dragonkin. He held the brute's glare, making it clear he was not beaten, despite what the straps suggested.

"Their forces are building to the east," Elisandra spoke, drawing the bronze's attention back to her. "We must prepare."

"I have it in hand," Dokul rumbled.

"Do you?"

The bronze regarded Elisandra with a look laden with warning. "I remember when you were a fledgling fighting among your brood for scraps, Elisandra. I remember when all the jeweled ones were sprats playing the odds to survive in a chaotic world. Gold, Silver, and *Bronze*." His chest swelled. "I am old enough to remember how the humans rallied their forces. Do not presume to know my mind or how to wage war. *I am war*."

The queen's smile sharpened without moving. She cradled her glass in her hands, appearing as though she was a delicate and obliging thing. It was an act. One Eroan doubted the bronze would fall for if he knew her as he'd said. She laughed softly. "And now I am queen. *Your* queen." She let that sink in. Dokul sniffed and eased back into the chair, making it creak under his muscular bulk. As dragon, he had to be twice her size, and yet she held the power here. How was that possible?

"What do you think of our generosity?" Relaxing in the chair opposite his, Elisandra crossed her legs, making her silks slip at just the right angle to distract a male mind.

"Your brood is most accommodating," he said with a

genuine smile. "I would have agreed to come sooner, but preparations are consuming. You mentioned a coupling?"

"It is time Lysander set to creating his own brood."

"Lysander?" Dokul's brow pinched. He sighed and set his glass down.

"I know what you're going to say. It's been dealt with. He will obey. In every way." For some inexplicable reason, the queen's gaze skipped to Eroan but did so quickly enough the bronze didn't notice.

"The rumors—"

"Rumors?" She laughed sharply. "He is amethyst. He'll fuck what I tell him to."

Dokul's brow lifted. "And the lower's report?"

"He deliberately failed to perform to undermine me." She drank some of her wine and swallowed. "His mind is as sharp as his sword."

"Just not the sword that counts?" the bronze laughed darkly.

"He has been disciplined." Elisandra leaned forward. "His talent in combat is renowned. He stopped *this one*—" she swept her hand at Eroan "—single-handedly after all other guards failed."

Eroan straightened under their sudden scrutiny. Their combined gazes drank him in and made his instincts itch.

"Didn't kill him though?" the bronze smirked again.

"I forbade it. Otherwise, he would have. None can match Lysander in battle, dragon or man."

Dokul arched his golden eyebrow.

"Besides me," the queen purred.

"What say you, elf?" the bronze turned his attention to Eroan.

Eroan had a great deal to say, but much of it would

likely get his tongue cut out. Carline's earlier advice reminded him to keep his words to himself unless he had little other choice.

"He refuses to speak..." Elisandra was saying but trailed off as the bronze rose to his feet and crossed the room.

The knife hidden against Eroan's wrist had adrenaline buzzing through his veins again. Two of the world's most feared creatures stood within striking distance. No elf in history had gotten this close, and yet, tied up, he was useless.

Useless, but for one thing. Words.

"Well?" the bronze asked, close enough now that his stench burned Eroan's throat. The queen stopped beside him, her penetrating eyes narrowing.

Eroan lifted a shoulder. "I was tired. I'd already killed eight. Had he been the first I encountered he would have fallen like—"

Elisandra's hand smacked across his cheek. Her nails, or a ring, cut in and zipped open his skin, dribbling blood down his jaw.

Dokul laughed deeply, and Elisandra's lips twitched. "He lies," the queen spat.

"Oh, I know," the bronze grinned, revealing a discolored metal-capped canine tooth, and stroked his hand over his bald head. "I've seen Lysander fight. Tried to kill him once when he was a kit."

Elisandra blinked, failing to hide her alarm. She hadn't known.

He waved her off. "It was a long time ago, and he clearly survived. I've had my eye on him for a long time. He has great potential. With the right motivation."

Elisandra's mouth twitched again as though he had just

insulted her. Did the bronze imply she could not give her son the correct motivation? It seemed Lysander was a weakness of hers. The bronze knew it. And now so did Eroan. If he could get close to the prince, that weakness might be further exposed.

Dokul squared up to Eroan. He smelled like warm metal, like racks of swords soaked in blood and it was all Eroan could do not to gag.

"There is some fire in you, elf," the male dragonkin remarked. "I think you certainly did prove a fine match for the young prince. Had my guards been stationed at the queen's tower, none of your kind would have breached the walls to begin with." He turned away, allowing Eroan to breathe again. "Elisandra, you really must take my gift of a bronze flight."

"It is not required."

"It's a gift. Gifts never are."

The bronze wanted his flight in her tower, and it had nothing to do with protecting her. If Eroan saw that, so did Elisandra. The queen smiled her polite, courtly smile. "Let us return to discussions of coupling."

He grunted. "I can do much with the prince. I do not need a coupling. I'll take him under my wing and remove him from your embarrassment."

"No."

Dokul gripped the back of his chair. Wood groaned. "You want an alliance, and you want control. Let us not pretend anything else is happening here, Elisandra. If he cannot perform, he'll weaken your line. Let us prevent that mistake. He need not die for your ambitions."

"No," she repeated. "There will be a coupling, or you don't get him."

The bronze folded his arms and glared at the queen. Wherever his thoughts were, his eyes darkened. Then, nodding quietly to himself, he jerked his chin toward Eroan. "I want the elf too."

"The elf is my pet."

Eroan sneered at them both, though neither noticed.

"If I am to lose a bronze to your attempt at spreading your amethyst line throughout mine, then I want a sweetener. We haven't seen an elf in decades. My brood would enjoy playing with that one."

Elisandra blinked quickly and smiled her thin, unassuming smile. "You seem to have forgotten your place. As your queen, I can order you do this with no counteroffer required."

She had something over him, something over all of them that kept them at her heel. It wasn't just her beauty. Even the mighty bronze cowered before her when she wanted him to. But why? Eroan watched every expression, heard every word, even the things unsaid, and learned.

"Then loan me the elf. No permanent harm will come to it, and I'll return it when we're done."

Eroan couldn't swallow his silence any longer. "I am not some beast to be traded!" He yanked on the straps, straining away from the wall. "I have a name, a life. I am Eroan Ilanea, Assassin of the Order."

Elisandra waved her hand. "Yes, yes. Born in the fires of some pit... I heard you the first time. But these are just words that mean nothing. Like you mean nothing, little pet."

"I can see why you have it here." The bronze's golden eyes flashed with malice. "It will be a pleasure to break him."

"Yes. And that pleasure is mine. He is not available. Take my son. Arrange the coupling. If he doesn't perform, kill him."

Dokul sighed. "Very well." He scooped up his drink, downed it in one and bowed his head. "My queen."

CHAPTER 8

$\mathscr{L}$ysander

PAIN. Not even the wine chased it away, and Lysander had tried all the wine he could find. Forgotten how many bottles he'd finished, in fact. A few, at least. More bottles than he had fingers, and still the pain thumped through him. It wasn't the broken wing or the ribs that ached. Those wounds he hid behind his human form. Something inside ached and always had since his earliest memory. Like he was missing a part of himself. Sometimes he barely noticed it, other times he wanted to drink himself into a hole or take up a blade and cut open his veins to release the wretched pain.

This time...

This time he wanted to take a blade to *her*. Maybe the pain would go away if *she* went away.

He had his hands wrapped around the twin blades, welcomed their weight, their extension of his will, and found himself at his mother's receiving chamber before he'd realized he'd been climbing her tower.

He shoved open the door, stumbled, but righted himself quickly enough. *Too much drink*. Damn the drink. Damn the tower, its stairs leaving him breathless. Damn it all.

"Mother?" With the way his call echoed, he knew she wasn't here. Her presence filled a space, leaving little room for anything else.

The bronze, Dokul, had been here. He could smell him, smell the wine they'd shared, smell their scheming. Lysander wiped his sleeve across his mouth to try to wipe the taste of shame off his lips.

His gaze snagged on the elf and for a moment all thoughts of Mother scattered at the sight. She still had him bound, this time with thick leather wrist and ankle cuffs. And a collar. Of course, he had seen Lysander the second he'd entered the room but had stayed elf-quiet. Even now, chained to the wall, it seemed Lysander might blink and the elf would melt into the shadows.

He headed back to the door, intent on leaving, but as he sheathed the blades against his back—taking a few swipes at it, due to the fact the room kept spinning with him in it—his thoughts stalled. He closed the door instead.

Turning his head, he met that elf's icy glare. Defiance kept his expression proud. Even tied as he was, that didn't deter the fierceness in his eyes. He looked at Lysander the same now as he had in the dungeon, like the second he got free he'd kill him. He didn't look nearly as weak as he should have. Didn't they need light to live? This one looked like vengeance alone sustained him.

The elf watched Lysander approach. Keen elven eyes designed for hunting and seeing in low light stared, unblinking. His pupils were full and dark, like a new moon. His mouth held a firm sneer, just for Lysander. And those pointed ears pricked through his long, braided, platinum blond hair, ruffled and knotted from his ordeal. Hair so pale it was almost white.

Ganaoah had cut him up just as Akiem had commanded, carving deep lines down the elf's chest—or so Akiem had said. Lysander couldn't see the wounds beneath the elf's jerkin, but he didn't look sickly. In fact, he seemed to be healing extraordinarily fast. They hadn't gotten answers from him. Torture wouldn't make this one talk. Whatever his life had been like, this elf was honed to kill.

Lysander snatched a chair from a nearby table and planted it facing backward a few strides from the elf. He straddled it so he could brace his arms on the back and stop the walls from moving.

"She has you now, huh?" he asked, wondering if he'd slurred as much out loud as he had in his head. "Then we have that in common."

The elf's eyes narrowed.

"She will fuck anyone and anything if she thinks it'll give her an advantage. Even an *elf*." The disgust in Lysander's voice wasn't for the elf, not really, though from the elf's twitch, he seemed to believe it. Good. He could hurt right alongside Lysander.

He should have stopped this elf, should have cut him down the same way he should have cut out Elisandra from the brood like rot from an apple's core. Akiem would have killed the elf without blinking. Akiem could stop Elisandra... He chuckled at his own foolishness. No dragon could stop the bitch-queen.

"Don't say much, do you?" Lysander rested his chin on his folded arms and watched as the elf tried to read him, to read this situation. He couldn't have missed his stumbling and likely knew he was exceedingly and exquisitely drunk. Would the elf try to talk him around, try to persuade the prince to free him?

"Not to you," the elf finally said.

Oh, so he did speak. Although it had taken so long, Lysander had forgotten the question. He had a smooth voice, this elf. One he imagined didn't have to be raised in anger. He spoke, and his people would listen. He had the arrogance, at least. Who was he? Just another assassin, flung at the brood like arrows from a bow, or was this one something else? Something important, perhaps. Lysander looked closer. He had seen him shirtless and knew those arms were muscled enough to swing a sword without tiring, but not too much that he'd be cumbersome. He was swift, light on his feet. Faster than Lysander, though the prince would never admit it. He had only caught the elf because of a mistake. The elf had rushed his attack, knowing he was running out of time to finish the kill and Lysander had cut him down.

Should have let him have the kill, Lysander thought. He couldn't fathom why he'd saved her. *Should have opened the damn door and let the assassin have her.* He turned his face away, feeling the elf's gaze follow, taking the prince's hesitation in. What did it matter? This elf was as trapped as Lysander.

The elf still watched as though waiting for Lysander to admit what they both knew.

"I don't know who I pity more, you or me," Lysander said.

"Do not pity me."

The prince chuckled. "That leaves me, I suppose."

"Pity is for fools."

Well, all right then. "I still don't know your name."

The elf looked away.

With a sigh, the prince stood, keeping a hand on the chair to hold him steady. "It'll be a shame when she breaks you. And she will. First, you will fight because you think you can win. Then, after much pain," he laughed darkly, "you will accept what she gives you. And inside, you'll become a cold thing. A hard, hollow thing."

That elven defiance flared hotter. He breathed in. His lips turned down, fighting with a sneer. So proud a thing, Lysander thought. Elves all over would cry when he died. Perhaps they already did. One in particular maybe. A mate. Did she weep for him now?

Lysander shoved off the chair and ventured closer. The elf's straps and chains had some slack, enough that he could potentially hook a length of it around the prince's neck if Lysander were to get close enough. It would solve a lot of problems.

Closer, and the elf lifted his chin.

If this nameless elf killed Lysander now, the pain would go away. No more Elisandra, no more shame, no more weakness, no more having to publicly fuck a bronze and face his own death right after. If this elf killed him now, Lysander could fall forever and never hit the ground.

Closer. The elf shifted back an inch and tilted his head, narrowing his eyes, assessing, reading, learning.

This elf hadn't seen half of what the dragonkin would do to him. Maybe Lysander could save him that pain. Take a blade to the elf's throat here and now, and end it before he lost that fire in his eyes.

Lysander reached over his shoulder and freed one of his blades.

The elf breathed in, expanding his chest. His eyes darted from the naked blade to Lysander's face. This close, Lysander could smell the cleaning wraps used on his wounded wrist and smell him, a curiously evocative scent of warm wood and pine, one that reminded the prince of soaring above the forest canopies. He smelled like wildness, like freedom, like all the things he ached for and could never have.

Lysander stretched his arm over the elf's shoulder and spread his hand against the wall. The elf could thrust his arm up, hook the strap around the prince's neck and probably end it in a blink. The elf's breaths quickened, and that telltale muscle fluttered in his cheek. A battle raged inside him, Lysander read. He wanted the prince dead. Every instinct had him thirsting for blood, and a creature like him... He knew how to kill with just his hands. They had fought, blades clashing, and now they fought again, but this time was different. Restrained, like he was, the elf could be Lysander's. *He should be mine and she took him.*

Lysander tested the line between them and leaned in, his mouth close enough to steal the elf's racing breaths. He could pull back, turn his head, he had room, but he didn't move. Because he was stubborn. A stubborn, proud, foolish creature that would meet his end beneath Elisandra's claws. Every defiant act, every fierce rebuttal, would see him ruined. Lysander had hoped to avoid that, but now, even he couldn't save this one. Same as he couldn't save himself.

Parting his lips, Lysander brushed a touch over the corner of the elf's mouth, and when he didn't respond, it was all he could do not to twist a hand in his hair and demand a kiss from him.

"Touch me again and I'll kill you," the elf said, his voice hard.

Lysander would kiss him, take him, own him, twist him to his desires even if he didn't want it until the elf spilled his seed, calling Lysander's name. Desire shuddered through the prince, pulling need into a tight, aching want that had him instantly, painfully hard. Like this, with the elf in chains, it would be so easy. But he wasn't Elisandra. He would never be her. And he wouldn't force this elf. That was her way, not his.

He hooked the tip of his blade under the elf's left wrist strap, and with a quick flick, the leather split, freeing his arm.

Lysander pushed away too fast and staggered as the room spun. The table caught him, holding him up as shame burned the lust away. What thing was he, aroused by a creature, an elf of all things! It didn't matter anyway. Maybe he'd get free, maybe Lysander *could* save him. At least, then, one of them would be free.

Two glasses sat on the table. Lysander imaged Dokul laughing at his failed performance and his mother laughing right along with him. The pair of them would maneuver him, use him, as they saw fit. He was done with it. Done with them.

He swept the glasses aside and relished the sound of them shattering against the stone floor. If only it were that easy to shatter everything else.

He was at the door, his mind far away when the elf spoke. "Why?"

Why free him? Why hadn't he taken the elf when he could have, why had he come here? The answers didn't matter. This was all just a drunken mistake.

Lysander glanced back, and the elf looked on with pity in his eyes. And that made fools of them both.

Lysander left him there, halfway to free and sought out another bottle to drown in.

CHAPTER 9

roan

EROAN WAITED until the sound of the prince's staggers faded into silence before lifting his freed hand. He couldn't fathom why Lysander had done it. Some kind of trap to catch him in the act of escaping? Whatever the reason, it was done, and now Eroan had his opportunity. Not to run, but to kill. He reached up, eased his fingers beneath the wrist-wrapping and pulled the paring knife free. Heart pounding, he cut the leather cuff binding his sore wrist and knelt to slice through an ankle strap.

A fresh, warm, wet-metal smell alerted him too late. Five dragonkin poured into the room, barefooted and eerily quiet. Each wore dark clothes and hoods. Eroan knew assassins when he saw them. He hacked at the remaining strap, finally freeing himself, and looked up from his crouch. They had him boxed in. Golden eyes glowed in their eagerness.

Too many.

"Come easy now, elf." One loomed closer, a hood and rope in his hands.

Eroan feigned left, sending the dragonflight one way while he darted the other. A thick-fingered hand made a grab for him, but he slashed back and up, opening a gash in the bronze's palm. The brute swore, clutching his hand. The others darted forward, startlingly fast for their bulk.

Eroan ducked a second grab and with a vicious jab, punched the paring knife into the dragonkin's chest, sinking the tiny blade deep between two fat ribs. The beast grunted and staggered into one of his companions, wide-eyed and oblivious to the fact he was already dead, it would just take a few seconds more for his body to hit the floor. Eroan never missed the heart.

A fist came from the right, cracked across Eroan's cheek, and dumped him facedown before he knew he'd been hit. A bronze kicked the knife from his hand. It skittered across the stones to where the one he'd stabbed lay dead-eyed and motionless.

Rough hands yanked his arms behind him, twisting his wounded wrist, wrenching a gasp from him, and pulled him to his feet.

Eroan felt laughter bubble inside him. He'd come for the queen, and now these bronze had come for him. Well, he'd take all of them down if he could.

A fist slammed into his gut, folding him around breathless pain. Still, the laughter bubbled. Maybe he was losing his mind. Didn't matter.

"Think that's funny, elf? You won't be laughing soon."

The bronze clamped a massive hand around Eroan's skull and jerked him so close Eroan smelled the sweat on his dark clothes.

"What is this?!" Lysander stood in the doorway, eyes narrowed as he flicked his gaze over the intruders. He drew his blades.

"None of your concern, prince," Eroan's captor snarled.

"Dokul... know you're here?" the prince slurred and staggered, setting one of the bronze sniggering. "Damn you..." Lysander plunged in, faster and lighter than the bronze but it wouldn't last. The prince managed to get a few vicious slashes in before the bronze planted their fists in his face and gut, knocking the drunken fight right out of him. He went down hard, grunting when one of the bronze dealt him a swift kick to the side.

"Stay down, *prince*."

Eroan bucked and twisted, then brought his heel down on the bronze's shin, cracking it hard and fast. His captor swore. His grip loosened, but a bag came down over Eroan's head and a slip-knot tightened at his throat, cutting off his air. The rope yanked backward, digging into his neck. His lungs jerked, chest burning. He clawed at the rope, trying to loosen it. Blood whooshed, his heart pounded, then the knot was worked, and air rushed over Eroan's tongue, filling his lungs. He swayed, staggered, but could see nothing through the bag. His hands were captured and yanked behind him again.

"Piss me off and that happens again," his captor snarled. "There's a good elf."

The wet smell of his breath and the stench of the rotten bag watered Eroan's eyes. Panting, he wheezed and spluttered. This was worse... so much worse.

Fingers dug into his arm and pulled him into motion, out the chamber.

Eroan listened as he was led on. The bronze flight moved without talking. He heard their breaths, their pauses, their careful footfalls. Doors opened and clunked shut behind them. Water dripped and the temperature dropped. They were taking him down, farther into the tower. Cool, fresh air wafted in under the bag and Eroan breathed it deeply. The echo of corridors opened into a larger cavernous space. A distant roar sounded, trembling the air, and he was shoved into a pocket of rock with a hand smothering the bag over his nose and mouth. He writhed enough so he could breathe and listened to the bronze pressed in around him. The roaring ceased, and they moved again. Hands tugged and groped and yanked when he fell or stumbled.

The air and sounds changed. A chill touched Eroan's hands, still bound behind his back, and the ground beneath his bare feet became pebbly and dirt-covered. The sounds of water lapping and the clunk of rigging and his heart raced some more. A boat. They were taking him away from the tower, away from the queen. Whatever Elisandra had over their chief, Dokul, it wasn't enough to stop him from stealing what she saw as hers.

As Eroan was shoved and manhandled into the damp, cold hull, his opportunity to kill the queen slipped farther and farther away. Oars sloshed, the boat rocked, and Eroan's weary thoughts drifted to memories of racing through the tree canopies to where he was free.

CHAPTER 10

$\mathscr{L}$ysander

ELISANDRA PACED THE HALL, her heeled boots striking against stone. "How dare he steal my property!"

Lysander's gaze tracked her every step. His head throbbed, and the kick the bronze had dealt to the ribs beat the same kind of dull, aching heat. Sick and wretched, there was nothing he could do but swallow the self-loathing. If he hadn't been off-his-head drunk, he could have cut those bronze down.

Pain twinged up his side. He adjusted his shoulders against the wall. Battered in dragon form and now human too. A part of him wanted to curl up in a corner and lick his wounds.

"We have a flight to the west, scouring the skies, but the morning light is low on the horizon," Akiem said, tall and proud in his obsidian armor. Three lines of guards stood behind him, blocking much of Lysander's view to the front of the room. "They planned their theft perfectly with the sunrise."

"I don't want to hear how perfectly they planned this!" the queen snapped. "They took my pet from my chamber!"

A door clattered, drawing his brother's and the queen's gazes to the rear of the hall. Dokul was back, this time flanked by six of his own personal guard and armored to the chin in battle gear. To enter the queen's council unbidden was an insult. To enter armed to the teeth was potentially an act of war.

Lysander straightened and felt the burn of his blades against his back. His fingers twitched at the prospect of a fight.

"*You!*" Elisandra pointed a finger, nails shining black. "You did this. Don't try to tell me you didn't."

"This is not my doing," he flatly denied. Another insult.

Elisandra's dark outline wobbled, her human form briefly stuttering.

Lysander snorted. None of the bronze acted without their chief's command. To even admit such a thing was to admit weakness. Did Dokul want the elf so badly as to lie to Elisandra? All of this over one elven assassin. It would have been comical if it weren't for the dead bronze the elf had left behind. A death Lysander was likely partly responsible for. He *had* cut the elf's restraints. Not that the elf had needed help. When Lysander had dragged himself off the floor beside the dead bronze, he'd found the bloody paring knife and tucked it into his boot. There was no need to alert everyone as to how the elf might have managed to get himself a knife from the kitchens and use it. He was a smart one, Lysander had to give him that.

"We were invited here in peace," Dokul's mouth twisted. "And now one of our own has been killed. I demand recompense."

Elisandra's nostrils flared. "Recompense?" Her eyes widened. "For this indiscretion, I'll let you live, that's all the recompense you'll be getting from me." She swept a hand. "Get out. I want all your brood gone by the time the sun reaches its zenith. Should any remain, I will kill them myself."

Dokul's cheek twitched. He jerked his head down, in the briefest of bows that wouldn't see his head bitten off, then he stalked back the way he'd come, his guards clunking along behind him.

When they'd left, Lysander felt Elisandra's gaze crawl over him. "And you?"

He dropped his head back against the wall and blinked at the ceiling. Of course, her wrath would fall on him eventually. "Yes, Mother. What of me?"

"So drunk you killed only one!"

He'd take that credit. It was better than admitting he'd gotten his ass handed to him. "They won't take the elf by wing." He pushed off the wall and walked up the line of mute guards. He knew most by name. Some, he'd personally trained. None cared to look at him now, too afraid his mother would rip their balls off.

"Of course they will," she ranted. "It'll take them days on foot."

True. But Lysander figured they'd gone another way. Something quick, something silent, and something unexpected.

"I'll take my flight and track them," Akiem offered.

Elisandra flicked her eyes to her eldest son. Akiem and his flight were one of the finest. Having them away from the tower left her exposed. Lysander watched his mother think, watched her weigh the odds of an attack. It wouldn't have concerned her before. She'd always had Lysander as her last line of defense. He smiled to himself, still feeling the ghost of her claws in his gut and no doubt she felt it too. They weren't on the best of terms.

"Go, then. You have until nightfall. Return before then, with or without this Eroan Ilanea."

Lysander hid the surprise at hearing the elf's name and focused instead on the passing of the guards. His brother was the last to leave. He ignored Lysander, just like all the others had. Moments later, the tower shook with their battle cries and the beat of their wings.

"Is my coupling with the bronze off the table?"

"Oh no," Elisandra glared. "More than ever, I need that bastard's flights under me. I don't trust him. He is of the old ways, and they were always... difficult. If he won't submit to me, then you'll breed my soldiers under him. This is just a distraction. He took the elf. I know he did. I saw the way he looked at it. He wanted it, even tried to bargain for it."

"Mother—"

"Do not test me. I will carve your heart out and have Akiem seed my power for me."

Lysander felt the dregs of his drunkenness loosen his tongue. "Then send him and be done with it. I can't fuck a bronze—"

Her lips rippled, a snarl breaking through. She threw a hand at him, one that might have backhanded him across

78

the face if he hadn't moved at the last second. "Get out of my sight!"

Lysander dipped his head and turned. He wouldn't run. He'd done enough running. But he couldn't fly either, his mother had seen to that. There were other ways. The stables housed horses for the hunting feasts. It had been a few years since he'd ridden one of the beasts, but he'd cover more ground on four legs than his two.

If Dokul wanted Eroan so badly, maybe there was an opportunity there, but only if Lysander found the elf first.

THE HORSE, a piebald mare, shied from Lysander's touch and whinnied, scraping a hoof against the stall floor. He offered his hand. "Shh, you're not to be dinner today."

The mare eyed him down her long nose and snuffled.

"All right. Normally the situation would be different. Dragons don't often ride horses, but I got a little wing problem, and you're faster than running, so what say we put our differences aside and get along?"

She swished her tail but carefully lowered her head and toed forward.

"I know what it feels like to have a dragon on your back," he said, rubbing at her velvety nose. When she didn't shy, he tossed the reins over her neck. "Maybe I'll let you go after, how does that sound? It's a better chance than the one you have in here." He grabbed a tuft of mane and threw a leg over, heaving himself onto her bareback. The horse restlessly trotted on the spot. "There, not so bad. Prey, predator, these roles don't define us—"

The horse reared, kicking at the air. Lysander clenched

his thighs and hung on, feeling the beast's heart gallop. Then she was off, veering, bucking and racing out of the stables like the place was ablaze. Lysander stayed tucked in and clung on, watching the forest roll and the horse plow into the undergrowth like a thing possessed. Her hooves beat the earth, and with every labored breath, every thunderous leap, Lysander's smile grew. Fuck yeah, this beast could *fly*.

Sunlight sent shafts through the canopy, highlighting old-world wreckage and twisted hulks of metal spewing undergrowth. Over and around the horse darted until, eventually, she slowed to a plodding gait, resigned to the fact the dragon on her back wasn't getting off.

"I should give you a name." Lysander pulled on the reins, turning the horse westward. Golden leaves fell like rain and twirled in the air. He'd forgotten how peaceful the forest was from below its canopy. "She got a name out of him..." he said, thinking of how the elf had stubbornly refused him, but not his mother. "I was so sure he'd take it to his death." The idea that the elf had given his mother something weakened him in Lysander's mind. He'd almost admired the elf's stubbornness. Somewhere inside, he'd hoped this Eroan would hold out, but like everything she touched, Elisandra had broken him.

The horse huffed and plodded on.

"I'd call you after him... *Eroan*." He tasted the name on his lips and then remembered tasting *him*. The corner of the elf's lips, twisted into a snarl, had tasted sweet. That had been a drunken mistake. "We don't generally name our food or our pets..." He'd been making a lot of those mistakes. Recapturing the elf would go a long way to getting his mother off his back, or make an excellent bargaining chip with Dokul. He hadn't yet decided how to play it. Of course, he had to find the bronze party first.

The sound of water rushing drew Lysander off the path. He reached the bank and scanned the wide, swollen river with its low, flooded banks. Twisting on the horse's back, he peered up at the tower through the trees. So large, it still loomed behind, huge and overbearing, like the dragonkin who sat atop it.

Facing the flooded waters again, he considered the time of year. A river would make a fine escape route. It meandered and wandered through the dragonlands. They didn't even need to get far, just far enough to be outside the obvious flightpaths. Once out of sight, they could take to the wing and then the elf would be lost, probably forever. The bronze would have their fun and kill him, eventually.

The horse dropped her head to drink, almost unseating Lysander on her back. He shifted his weight and patted her flank. This had to be the right route. All he had to do was follow the river. "Let's find their boat."

CHAPTER 11

 roan

THE BOAT GROANED, jolting Eroan from a fitful sleep. The vessel scraped and thumped and finally stopped its incessant rocking. The stench of the bag and the rolling motion hadn't done Eroan's gut any favors. Sleep had seemed the only way out, but the dreams waiting for him there hadn't been kind.

Boots stomped nearby. Hands dug into his arms, and like before, he was marched, blind, up a set of steps, onto the deck. Rain patted his shoulders and hissed against the deck boards. He'd barely made it down the springing plank before rain had soaked through the bag and trickled down his back.

Murmurings from the bronze crew revealed they'd hauled the boat out before reaching a narrow section of river and its rapids. Eroan was thankful for that, at least.

Hands pushed down on his shoulders, forcing him to sit on what he assumed to be a fallen log. He listened to fat raindrops *drip-dripping* against nearby leaves, muffling most sounds outside the camp. They were still in the forest then, somewhere the vegetation was thick and not burned to cinders like the grounds around the tower. Pine scented the air when he could catch a breath of it. It could almost be home if not for the stench of dragon.

"Let's get a proper look at you."

The bag vanished from his head.

Eroan blinked into warm orangey hues. Four bronze sat around the beginnings of a campfire. *They'll be lucky to get it started with wet wood*, Eroan thought idly and smiled. Ironic. As human, they couldn't warm themselves. One of them had a flint and steel—a firemaking device—and was trying to summon a spark among damp kindling. Eroan looked away before the laughter he swallowed invited their fists. Outside the camp, a dusky gloom had closed in. Nightfall. They might take to the air once the dark settled. He'd never flown, never had his feet higher than the tree canopy and didn't much relish the thought of being any higher.

His captor, the one who'd floored him with a punch, dug his fingers into the collar still fixed around Eroan's neck and pulled. Thick fingers pushed into Eroan's neck, cutting off his air.

The bronze gave him a long, hungry look before letting go and making his way toward the fire. Eroan coughed and swallowed, drawing the bronze's eye back to him. His gaze lingered too long, shifting to where the thin, rain-soaked cotton shirt clung to Eroan's chest.

Anger sizzled in Eroan's gut, and the bronze's hard mouth pulled into a smirk.

"When was the last time you saw one?"

His captor looked across the sparking fire to his companion. This one had a smooth, shaven head too, and a golden beard cropped short. He scratched at it now and nodded toward Eroan. "Elves," he added.

"Nobody seen 'em in the west since we were kits," Eroan's captor grumbled. "Rare now. Maybe rarer than humans."

The fire caught. Flames licked and fought against the rain. Eventually, they took hold, and Eroan lost his thoughts to the flickering dance. Better that than listen to the bronze remark on how they'd successfully wiped most of the elves decades ago. Eroan's people had been softer then. It had almost cost them everything. Things were different now. His people were different now.

The bronze crew settled around their campfire, coming and going, hunting for game, checking the perimeter. This deep in the forest with the low clouds, they wouldn't be spotted from above.

They skinned and spit roasted rabbit over the fire. Eroan's mouth watered. His captor occasionally sent a glance Eroan's way, catching how Eroan tracked the sizzling meat, and returned to his feast, biting and chewing with more gusto.

"Hungry for some rabbit, huh?" his captor asked.

Thunder rumbled in the distance and the rain started again.

"No."

"No?" the bronze tossed his gnawed-on bone into the

fire and wiped his greasy hands on his leather pants. "If it ain't rabbit, then what do you hunger for, elf?"

Eroan looked down at the litter-strewn forest floor.

"Kerrik, leave it. Dokul'll break you if you break it before he gets his chance."

Eroan wasn't sure who'd spoken. He kept his head down. Maybe if he could make himself into a small, weak thing, this Kerrik would lose interest.

"I ain't gonna do shit."

Eroan saw Kerrik's boots plant in front of him. With his hands bound behind, he wasn't going to be fighting his way out of this. *Stay small.* The anger was back, an ever-present ball of hate for these animals, but if the bronze saw it, this situation would only get worse.

Kerrik's fist locked in Eroan's hair. He jerked Eroan's head back and with his other hand, he cupped his own crotch. "Hungry for this, maybe?"

Pain lashed down Eroan's neck, but it was nothing compared to the disgust burning through his veins. He bared his teeth. "Touch me and your chief will kill you."

"My chief?" Kerrik's thick eyebrow arched. "Dokul doesn't give a shit what I do with you. Just so long as you're still breathing when I'm done." His hand clamped around Eroan's throat and squeezed. "You got a lot of fiery words for a pet elf."

Eroan gritted his teeth. The bronze had him half-lifted off the log. The hand scrunched in his hair twisted, forcing Eroan's head to the side, exposing his neck. Rage scorched his veins and trembled through his muscles.

Kerrik pulled him onto his feet and breathed in behind Eroan's ear. "You smell good. I don't know if I should fuck or eat you. As I can't eat you, I guess we both know what happens next. You ever taken a male like me?"

Kerrik shoved Eroan back. The log tripped him. He went down hard on his side. The bronze reached down with one hand while the other made quick work of his belt.

Eroan snarled, gritting his teeth, breathing hard. This had been coming for hours now, but the bastard bronze wouldn't find him easy.

Kerrik's thick lips curved into a grin. He grabbed for Eroan's arm.

Eroan kicked out, hard and fast, cracking his heel deep into the beast's crotch. The brute screeched and reeled back. The log tripped him too, and he collapsed backward into the campfire, scattering embers, flame, and burning meat.

Eroan was up and running but only managed a few strides before a bronze slammed into him from behind, tackling him against a tree. Rough, gnarled bark chewed at Eroan's cheek and jaw.

"A kick to the balls ain't gonna stop me, you fucker. That's foreplay in our brood."

An arm dug into Eroan's neck, ramming him harder into the tree. He twisted and tugged on the bindings, setting his wrist on fire all over again, but the ropes weren't loosening. Kerrik's fingers groped over his ass, kneading hard enough to bring a hiss to Eroan's lips.

"You just done and gone made it ten times worse," Kerrik snarled into Eroan's ear. "I was gonna take it easy on you, make sure I didn't leave a mark. Now I'm gonna fuck you until you're crying for your bitch of an elf mother."

"Kerrik! You hurt him and Dokul will kill you."

"Listen to your friend," Eroan growled out, tasting blood from a split in his cheek.

The hand was gone from Eroan's ass, but the arm stayed pinned against the back of his neck. Kerrik grunted and let out a deep, guttural moan, then the brute pressed in, plastering his hot body against Eroan's back. Eroan squeezed his eyes. No, Alumn, no! "Damn you and your kind, damn you to Ifreann. Do this and I'll hunt you down, cut off your cock, and ram it down your throat."

His hard arousal dug into Eroan's hip and ground upward. The dragon shuddered his pleasure. "Fucking hells, elf. You're only making me harder with all that sweet talk."

"I've never killed a man with his own penis before, but I'd make an exception for you."

Kerrik laughed a deep, belly laughter. He slapped Eroan's ass and sank his fingers into Eroan's belt, but instead of pulling Eroan's trousers down, he paused. Eroan's heart tried to thump its way out of his chest. This was happening. He'd known of their brutality but had never planned on staying alive long enough to become a victim of it. All he could hope for was that the bastard finished quickly. He'd heal. It wouldn't kill him. He'd suffered wounds, terrible wounds. This would pass.

The arm vanished from Eroan's neck but was quickly replaced by the rough hand at his throat. Kerrik twisted Eroan to face him. The bastard's eyes glowed a brilliant tarnished bronze. He switched his grip to Eroan's hair, knotted his fingers and forced him to his knees.

Eroan twisted and tugged, trying to pull from the hold, but the best he could do was keep his head turned away from the man's erect member. "You want me to suck you off, you risk me biting it off, you piece of dragon krak."

The hand was at Eroan's throat again, and this time it clamped tight, choking off his air.

"If you wanna live, you're gonna suck me dry." Kerrik took his cock in his free hand and stroked the swollen tip between his finger and thumb. He squeezed Eroan's throat tighter still. Stars splashed in Eroan's sight. "Get a good look elf, you're gonna take it all in, and then when I'm done, the rest of my brothers here are gonna fuck you until you're drenched in us. But you'll stay breathing. And when it's over, you'll thank us, and you won't say a fucking word to Dokul, else we'll do it all again."

Eroan jerked and twitched, everything in him trying to fight free. He couldn't reach up to claw the man's grip off him, couldn't pull in enough breath to stop the pounding in his head. They might not want him dead, but it wouldn't take much. A squeeze too tight, a second too long. If he died here, like this, his whole life with the Order had been for nothing.

Kerrik's cruel smile opened and the man licked his lips. He squeezed the end of his flushed cock and shifted his hips, arching at just the right angle for Eroan's lips. When he had angled himself an inch away from Eroan's mouth, he eased his grip on Eroan's throat.

Eroan gasped. He wanted to fight, his pride demanded he fight every second, but there was no way to fight this. With a sickening hollowing in his stomach, he realized this was happening, no matter what he said or did.

Kerrik gazed down between them and stroked his cock, milking a bead of pre-cum to the head. Jaw slack and eyes glazed, he brushed his glistening tip against Eroan's chin, smearing the wetness.

Eroan bared his teeth, and Kerrick's grip tightened. "You're gonna be good, now. Open your mo—"

The sword sang as it flew in a silvery arc straight over Eroan's head. When it struck Kerrik's gut, its song stopped, leaving a crisp silence peppered only by the sound of rain on leaves. The bronze blinked, surprised to find a sword in his gut.

Eroan tore himself free of Kerrik's weakening fingers and staggered back. The blade's sweep and curve were one he'd seen before.

Kerrik fell to a knee, still with his cock in one hand while the other gingerly groped at the sword in his chest.

A growl reverberated through the camp. Deep and menacing.

Lysander stormed from the undergrowth, his one remaining blade swirling in his hand and a smile on his face that said he'd found exactly what he'd been looking for.

CHAPTER 12

$\mathcal{L}$ ysander

LYSANDER TASTED blood in the air and wanted more, so much more. The bronze flight scrabbled in the dirt for their weapons, but it was too little too late. He cut the first down with a quick and clean slash across the male's exposed throat. Two left, and one managed to free his twin daggers for all the good they did him. Lysander's sword severed a hand from its wrist. He kicked the same bronze in the chest and sent him sprawling as the remaining bronze roared and tried to tackle the prince. They moved like cattle, slow and lumbering. Lysander darted to the side and brought his sword down across the back of the male's neck. The blade lodged in the vertebra, sticking fast. He tugged, tore it free, and took a second swing, severing the head from the rest of the body.

Lysander turned in the center of the camp, bloodlust galloping through his veins, but there were no more bronze to kill. Besides the one still propped on his knees with the other blade lodged in his intestines. The bronze's only chance now might be to shift, but with a sword in his gut, there was no knowing where the magic would put that sword. He could shift only to find it embedded in his heart.

The elf—Eroan, Lysander corrected, now that he knew the name—stood, wrists bound, in the same spot he'd been in when Lysander had made his entrance. If he was fazed by any of what he saw, his stoic face showed nothing. He could have at least looked impressed. Lysander was damn impressed. Nobody could have slaughtered three, almost four, bronze in a blink like he just had. It was a shame his mother hadn't been here to witness it. Although had she been, she would have likely found fault with it.

He lifted the bloody sword and approached Eroan. He flicked his gaze up, fast and sharp, either ready to bolt or do something foolish like attack, and with his wrists tied too. "Easy." Lysander stretched out a friendly hand and beckoned with his fingers. "Your wrists?"

Something dangerous twitched beneath the elf's guarded expression. He eyed Lysander's approach, then turned and presented his bound wrists at his lower back. Lysander cut the ropes and moved off in search of a fat leaf he could wipe the blade clean on, but also to get clear. "The group didn't get far from the tower," he spoke, hoping to ease a crackling tension. The elf was wound tight, tighter than the night he'd tried to kill the queen.

Thunder rumbled.

Lysander found a leaf, plucked it free, and wiped the

sword. Eroan had taken a few steps to position himself in front of the kneeling bronze. He looked down at the brute, his profile lean and lethal, the bronze clearly submissive in front of him.

Lysander quietly maneuvered to get a clearer view at the bronze's face. Pale and stricken, the haunted look in his eyes made it clear he knew it wouldn't be over for him anytime soon. Gut wounds could take hours to kill. Maybe Eroan would take pity on him and end it sooner?

Eroan gripped the sword sticking from the bronze's chest and yanked it free, spilling a few pink, wet entrails with it. Lysander figured the elf would cut the bronze's throat now, but instead, he knelt, reached between the bronze's legs with his left hand, cupped the bronze's flaccid cock, and brought the blade down in one surgical slice.

Lysander stopped moving.

The bronze groaned and wept. A string of begs tumbled from his lips. Eroan straightened, dropped the sword, swapped the severed cock to his other hand, grabbed the bronze by the hair, and forced his head back. The elf made a proud sight towering over the bronze, shirt and jerkin soaked through and glued to his skin, hair plastered down his back, but the sight of him forcing the cock into the bronze's mouth was either the most terrifying thing Lysander had ever seen or the most erotic.

Eroan gripped the bronze's jaw, fixing it so he couldn't spit. *"Hungry for this, dragon?"*

Sweet fucking diamonds, weren't elves supposed to be all brightness and light or some shit? Lysander knew their assassins were different but this... this was... he didn't have words to describe this.

The bronze, gagging and choking on his severed penis, finally slumped forward, and when Eroan let go, he collapsed facedown with a dull thud.

Eroan stood breathing hard in the rain, peering down at his prey. Time seemed to slow to a grinding halt, and then, with a blink, Eroan picked up the sword and made straight for Lysander.

Lysander readied the sword's twin in his hands, not entirely sure where this was about to go or how it would end. He'd freed Eroan, but they were still enemies. For all the trouble it caused, Lysander would quite like to keep his cock between his legs.

Eroan turned the blade over, holding it by the steel, and handed it out. "This is yours."

Warily, Lysander took it and lowered both weapons to his sides. So, what was this now? The bronze all lay dead and cooling in the rain, and now the elf had handed him back his blades. Were they enemies still? Or was this some kind of truce?

"You should go," Lysander said, surprising himself. He'd planned on recapturing the elf either for Dokul or his mother, but neither idea felt right after *this*, after a lot of things. Eroan could be free, and that had to be the best outcome here.

Eroan looked around the clearing as though seeing the dead dragonkin for the first time. His brow pinched. "You killed your own?" he asked.

"Not for you, if that's what you think. They stole from the amethyst. I already told you, we don't suffer thieves and assassins."

"They stole *me*. You're letting me go?" Eroan's cool and measured gaze found Lysander again, making his dragon heart flutter just a little bit faster. "I don't understand."

Lysander chuckled. He supposed it was a little odd. A dragon prince allowing the assassin to go free. "That makes two of us. Look, this—" He sheathed one of the swords at his back and gestured at the steaming mess of bodies. "I got here too late. You escaped. Give it a few days and Mother will lose interest in you. Life goes on, for you anyway." Tearing off another leaf from a nearby bush, he concentrated on wiping the second blade instead of facing the elf's scrutiny. "Go. Before I change my mind."

Eroan backed up but instead of running, like he should, he scanned the carnage again, his scowl deepening.

"Elf, you're trying my patience. Akiem's looking for this party. If he finds you, I—"

"Take me back."

"What?"

"Take me back to the tower."

Lysander looked for some signs of a head injury but found none, just a whole lot of wet silvery hair and bright, inquisitive eyes.

He returned the blade to its back-sheath and rolled his shoulders, settling the swords into place. "Are you insane?"

"Why do you keep letting me go?"

"Why won't you leave?" Lysander shook his head and started back the way he'd come. This was absurd. "Run. Don't. I don't care."

Of course, the damn elf was following.

Lysander stopped and sighed out. He looked up, through the canopy, but the sky was hidden behind storm clouds. Thunder rumbled and rainwater trickled down the back of his neck. The elf hadn't gone. He was right behind him. Lysander could feel his presence like a hot electrical current running through his veins. "Go home, elf. Go back to whatever family you have and keep them safe. Don't come back to these lands."

A second passed, then another. Lysander struggled to hear Eroan but knew he was still back there.

"I don't have a family," Eroan said.

Lysander looked back at this paradox of a male with his oddly tipped ears and minimal words. "Then go make one. The only thing that's waiting for you at the tower is torture. Nobody in their right mind walks back into her clutches."

His eyes flicked up. "You're going back to her."

Lysander laughed. Maybe this elf *was* insane. "Because nobody has cut my ropes."

The elf's eyes narrowed, sharpening his glare with intent. "You could have killed me when we first fought, but you didn't."

Lysander laughed him off and stomped through the wet brush. He'd left the horse around here somewhere. "Don't go looking for meanings," he grumbled. "I didn't kill you because she ordered you be kept alive."

"After you'd already captured me."

So clever was he, this elf. Observant, clearly. Lysander would have expected nothing less from an assassin.

"You wanted me to survive."

"I wanted no such thing. I'm her son. I don't let assassins live." He growled low in his throat. "Apart from now. And that offer is fast wearing off." Lysander stopped and whirled. "Back off, *elf*." He let a little more of the dragon bleed through his voice. Magic swelled beneath his skin. "Last chance."

Eroan arched an eyebrow and looked like he might be a second away from smiling. "Or you'll what? Take me back to her?"

Lysander reached behind his shoulders and pulled both blades free. When the elf continued to just blink at him, he lunged, crossing the blades, using them to drive the elf back against a tree. He expected some kind of fight, anything. In fact, he wanted it, *ached* for it even. Murdering the bronze hadn't been enough to satiate the anger building in him but maybe this elf's death would. Only Eroan hadn't lifted a finger to fight him off and looked back at him now, swords crossed beneath his chin, without fear. If anything, this stupid elf appeared mildly intrigued.

"You're not going to kill me, prince." His lips ticked at one corner.

Damn it. Lysander huffed a sigh and pulled his swords back. "I don't need to. You're doing that yourself." He had a death wish, that was the only explanation. The elf *wanted* to die. Well, Lysander had done his part. He'd tried to help. He could do no more. Were all elves this stubborn?

Lysander stomped through the brush. His horse had wandered from the place he had left it, and now the skies had opened and had begun to dump sheets of rain over him.

He stood in the clearing and rubbed water from his face, resisting the urge to growl out a curse. Without the horse, the tower was a few days hike. He should return, and quickly, before Elisandra noticed he was gone. She probably already knew, which meant he'd be in for a world of pain when he returned without his prize.

He sighed, turned, and there he was, Eroan Ilanea,

watching him with curious eyes. Soaked through, his long hair plastered to his face and neck, he still seemed almost serene, like neither of them had just slaughtered a bronze flight, like they were just two people in the woods and all of this was perfectly normal. Maybe it was for elves?

Eroan folded his arms over his chest and shivered. He lowered his gaze, and Lysander found himself wondering what Eroan was thinking. He was in no hurry to deliver this elf to his fate; the fool might think differently about following him back to hell in daylight. "Let's get out of this rain."

CHAPTER 13

*L*ysander uncovered a cavern entrance, one of many at the river's edge, and led the elf down into the dark. Rubble gave way underfoot, but the ceiling appeared stable and watertight. When he turned to tell Eroan they'd best find some dry wood, he found he was alone. Lysander chuckled to himself. The elf was unlikely to have abandoned his suicidal plan to return to the tower. He'd be back. Meanwhile, Lysander set to work clearing a patch of ground and building a fire.

Of all the things he'd seen, Eroan mutilating a bronze almost topped the list. He hadn't witnessed much of what went on before his arrival at the bronze camp, but he'd observed long enough to perfectly aim the sword-throw at the bronze's belly. Those few seconds revealed Eroan on his knees, hands bound, and what was likely a bronze cock in his mouth, though the angle was all wrong to know for sure. The entire flight would have fucked Eroan and probably killed him. Had Lysander taken a different turn off the path, had he gone upriver instead of down... Had he chosen not to come at all, the elf would be dead, and the bronze bastards would have been all the more pleased with themselves.

He had been within his rights to kill them, though Dokul likely wouldn't see it that way. But he hadn't expected to enjoy it, to relish the feel of his blades sinking into bronze flesh—a reminder not to fuck with the amethyst, not to fuck with Lysander. He'd failed when he'd been drunk in the chamber. But not now. It was almost a shame none had lived to tattle on him.

Pebbles skipped into the cavern and Eroan reappeared. He jogged down the mound of rubble and tossed something in front of where Lysander crouched.

Lysander picked up the blocks of stone and metal connected with a small chain and examined it. A pocket firestarter. He'd likely gone back to the bronze camp to retrieve it. "You do realize I'm a dragon?" The question echoed around them.

Eroan's elven eyes sparkled in the near-dark. "I had noticed, but I've also noticed you don't seem inclined to take that form, else you would have attacked the camp very differently." He gestured at Lysander's pile of sticks and leaves. "I'm done with being cold and wet, so if you don't mind, *dragon...*"

Well, that was true enough, though Lysander didn't feel like telling the elf why he couldn't shift. He gathered the leaf litter and struck the steel against the stone. Sparks immediately caught the desiccated wood and minutes later Lysander stoked a roaring fire.

The firelight set their shadows dancing on the walls. These underground caverns could be found all over. Strange little things, Lysander quietly mused as he watched Eroan through the firelight. The elf had removed his jerkin, and now crossed his arms and pulled his clinging, wet shirt over his head. Firelight stroked over his rack of abdominal muscles and then, as he turned, that same light lapped up a defined back. He knelt down and stretched the shirt across a flat stone to dry.

Houses, that was the word the humans had used for these holes in the ground. Lysander lowered his gaze and started to untie his boots. Houses. Boxes. He couldn't see the difference. Apparently, almost all humans had one. They lived in them. Lovingly tended them. Some small, some big. It seemed a waste. Why they didn't all just sleep together was a mystery like many of the human ways, and one Lysander was happy to think on instead of thinking on the way the moving firelight licked over Eroan's sculpted arms. The elf's cuts had healed except for a few scars from the torture he'd endured. If Eroan ever found his torturer, Lysander wondered how long the dragon would last faced with the elf's vengeance.

"Do you know why they wanted me?" Eroan asked, sitting on a rock and draping his arms over his knees. Gathering all his hair in one hand, he pulled it over his shoulder and wrung water from the long tail.

"Because the bronze chief couldn't have you." Eroan's eyebrow lifted. "My mother refused him, so he took you anyway. He denies it, but what he has in strength, he lacks in intelligence."

"The bronze flight called him Dokul."

"A recent name. He's so old he doesn't have a name from before. He's one of the first. I don't know a time without him."

"Gold, Silver, and Bronze," Eroan said, watching

Lysander closely. "Gold and Silver are dead." He said it like a statement, but there was a hint of query in there too, as though he wanted it confirmed.

So, the elves did know a little of dragonkin history. It paid to know your enemy. How well did Eroan believe he knew Lysander? Had the elf studied him from afar? What whispers traveled beyond the cast walls to elven ears, he wondered. "Dokul is the only one to survive the rising. The last of the great metal rulers. The jewel-line, my generation, came next. Faster, more cunning, more vicious in every way. Dokul could not contain us, and so he kneels to Elisandra, same as we all do."

Eroan picked up a stick and teased it between his fingers. "May I ask a personal question?"

Lysander shrugged. He tugged off both boots and dumped them by the fire to dry. "Ask away..."

"Which came first, the dragon or the egg?" A smile pulled at his twitching mouth.

"Really? You're the first elf in forever to have a dragon answering questions and you lead with that?" The elf's mouth quirked and Lysander resisted a small laugh.

"It is a matter of hot debate among elves. Without the egg, there can be no dragon. Without the dragon—"

"I get it." Lysander chuckled. Eroan was screwing with him, perhaps to lighten the gloom hanging over them. It worked. "So there's such a thing as an elf with a sense of humor. Who knew? Such a shame this elf is about to walk voluntarily back to his own execution."

Firelight smoothed Eroan's face, catching in his eyes. A neat little bow of a mouth, one that had tasted oh-so-sweet. It was near to laughing now, and Lysander felt a curious warmth thawing him from the inside. There was a great deal more to this elf than the fleeting glimpses he'd revealed so far. Lysander found himself wanting to peel back those layers to discover what secrets lay beneath. "Why do you insist on going back?"

Eroan snapped the twig and tossed both pieces into the fire. Time ticked on, punctured by the sounds of dripping water and the occasional rumble of thunder.

Lysander clearly wasn't going to get his answer. He shook his head, laughing softly at his own foolishness. A dragon chatting with an elf. By the nights! It was unheard of. "The queen would not approve of my talking with you."

"Then why are you?"

He leaned back, stretched his legs out alongside the fire and braced his arms behind him, soaking up the warmth. He didn't answer because he didn't know the answer. He should have kept the elf bound and gagged the second he'd arrived at the camp, not freed him. It was yet another mistake and one he'd pay dearly for if Elisandra discovered it, but what could his mother do that she hadn't already? She had ordered his death the second he was promised to the bronze brood. She knew he couldn't perform for her and knew he would die, bloody, publicly, and a long way from home. The bitch could rot in her tower for all he cared. She was not getting her claws into *his* elf.

Eroan shifted and stretched out too, drawing Lysander's eye and his thoughts back to how the firelight played over Eroan's long, lean legs, roamed his waist and chest, and how it lapped across his mildly curious expression, softening hard lines. He was so proud a thing, strong and defiant in so many ways. His eyes alone held a fierce but raw honesty. And the rest of him... there wasn't a wasted inch on that body, a body honed and shaped to kill. Lysander had once dreamed he'd be the same as this elf. Powerful. Unyielding. Proud. With his swords swinging and the blood of his enemies spilling, during a battle, he could be the jeweled prince everyone expected him to be. Until the bloodletting ended and he was left empty all over again. Like now. He felt alive *now*. But soon, that rush, that power, would be gone and he'd be back under Elisandra.

Lysander's gaze snagged on the elf's, and for a moment, neither spoke. There was just firelight, warmth, and nothing else between them.

"I find myself asking what a dragon prince has on his mind to make his thoughts so dark a place."

"You really don't have a brood—a family?" Lysander asked, eager to steer the subject away from the thoughts in his head.

Eroan picked up another twig. This one went into the fire too. "Assassins of the Order are unencumbered by relationships. Of any kind."

What a waste of perfectly good genes and a reminder that Lysander was stretched out and at ease with an elf who would likely sever his cock from his balls without so much as a wince. That was a sobering thought. And with it came the sobering image of seeing Eroan do exactly that to a bronze dragonkin twice his bulk.

He swallowed hard. "There's no one waiting for you to return?"

"We don't return—" Eroan lowered his gaze to the fire "—until it is done."

So many of the elves must not have returned. Could he do it, this elf? Could he kill Elisandra? Lysander's heart thudded harder. Fear, anticipation, hope. That was why Eroan wanted to go back. He had nothing else to live for. The queen's death was his only purpose. It didn't matter what she did to him. She could fuck him, cut him, shame him, and as long as he was alive, he'd steal every opportunity to kill her. He'd keep on trying until it was done or until she killed him first.

But Lysander lived that life every day.

He lay back and laced his hands behind his head. He almost wished he'd be around to see his mother's face the moment an elf cut out her heart and made her eat it. It would be all she deserved. She'd likely think she'd broken her little pet elf. She wouldn't even see the blow coming. Similarly, neither would Lysander if Eroan decided their little truce beside the campfire was over. "Are you going to kill me while I sleep?"

The words echoed too long for Lysander's liking. He lifted his head. The elf had propped himself against a rock, his head resting to one side as his chest slowly rose and fell. His lashes fluttered. Soft lips slightly parted. Asleep, he didn't look like the type to brutally stab a dragonkin in the chest and slice the cock off another. Asleep, he looked calm, like a dream, one Lysander could happily lose himself in.

"Guess not," Lysander smirked, and while the elf was out cold, he'd go right ahead and admire the forbidden, fire-licked temptation that was Eroan Ilanea.

CHAPTER 14

 roan

EROAN WOKE with a sickening emptiness in his stomach. Dreams had swept him up, dreams of dragons and males, and what might have happened had Lysander not stormed into the camp, swords swinging.

He rubbed at his face, trying to clear the nightmares from his mind.

The fire had burned down to glowing embers, its soft light barely penetrating the gloom.

Lysander wasn't opposite him, through the flames. Nor was he anywhere inside the den.

"Krak," Eroan swore. He hadn't meant to fall asleep, but the fire and Lysander's resonating voice had pulled him down, down where his body no longer ached for daylight, down where his wrist didn't throb and his gut didn't try to gnaw itself into a tight, aching ball of hunger.

He threw on his dry shirt and emerged from the cavern mouth. The rain had stopped, though heavy dampness still hung to the air. A breeze rustled the trees, revealing glimpses of the starlit sky above. From beneath the canopy, he couldn't get a fix on where in the dragonlands he was. Without Lysander, it would take longer to get back inside the tower, and if he encountered any dragon guards, in his weakened state, he could easily find himself in a situation like the one he'd just escaped. The prince had stolen a moment of Eroan's weakness to leave. But he couldn't have gotten far.

Eroan ventured farther from the cavern, deeper into the forest to be free of the river's burble, and crouched, listening to the forest's song. Water *tap-tapped* on leaves. Bats chittered, hunting fat moths after the storm. The breeze lifted and fell away again, filtering through thick undergrowth. And there, he caught it, the smell of dragon, leather, and steel. Lysander.

Eroan was up and moving, carving silently through the brush. Catching a low-slung branch, he swung into the canopy. Pain snapped and snarled up his arm, almost tripping him out of the trees. He slowed, crouched once more, cradled his wrist, and listened. There. The clang of metal, shortened gasps, and a scent Eroan hadn't ever expected to breathe in again. He pushed off, ran along the tree limb and leaped, landing in a sprint. Crashing through the bushes, he saw the elf ahead, her daggers flashing.

"Stop!"

Lysander feigned left, but the elf let loose a flurry of slashes, driving Lysander backward.

"Stop, Nylena!"

Her eyes flicked to him. Her pointed ears twitched,

but Eroan knew that look. He wore the same one often enough. She wouldn't stop. Not for him, not for anything. He ducked and tackled her clean off her feet so the both of them went sprawling in the dirt. Eroan captured her wrists and pinned her, trapping those lethal daggers with her. She screamed at him, sharp teeth bared and snapping.

"Stop," he said again. She bucked beneath him until he clenched his thighs and pulled her close.

Breaths hissed through her teeth and fury lit her dilated pupils. The fight strummed through her. She'd tear out his throat to get to her prey.

"Nylena, it's me..."

She blinked, lashes fluttering. Her brow creased and finally, the fight melted out of her body beneath him. "Eroan?"

Lysander's movement drew Eroan's gaze. The dragon watched curiously, his blades still exposed, chest heaving. He hadn't escaped Nylena's daggers. A few nicks on his cheek wept blood. Another on his shoulder soaked his shirt, but nothing serious. Nylena was fast but sloppy. He'd tried to train that out of her.

"We thought... we thought you died..." Her eyes darted over his face. Hope initially widened them, but that soon faded, realization sinking in at the sight of the collar around his neck. "No..." she breathed. "Not you, Eroan..."

Shame rolled through him like a sickness. He freed her wrists and straightened. "This dragon—you can't kill him. I need him."

Her gaze lingered on Eroan's face. Fear, horror, he felt all the things she threw his way as though each was a precisely thrown knife. Standing, he pulled her to her feet.

"Stow your weapons," he told her, dropping his tone to one she'd know well. "He's mine."

She swallowed and blinked at Lysander. Eroan knew her thoughts. Why wasn't this dragon dead? Why hadn't Eroan killed him?

"I don't understand," she said.

Her blades were still free. She appeared relaxed, shocked even, but the second Lysander moved into striking distance, she would take the opportunity and go in for the kill again.

"Sheathe your daggers, Nylena." This time, Eroan added weight to his words.

She flinched and backed away from them both. "I can't do that."

"Nylena, you should not be here."

Lysander stepped forward, and Nylena brought her daggers up. Eroan held out a hand, urging the dragon back and took a step in, placing himself between the two of them. She could still fling those daggers sharp and true and she would not miss her target.

"What is this?" she asked. "It's been weeks... When you failed—"

Those words struck like her daggers might. "I have not failed."

"The queen still lives and you..." Her glare settled on the collar. "What are you? You are not one of us. Not any longer. They... own you."

He should have expected the words, he'd been telling himself the same for weeks now, but it wasn't what she thought. How could he tell her how he planned to kill more than the queen, how he would make them all fall, with the prince listening?

"Leave," he ordered.

"You shame the Order." She spat in the dirt.

Would that be how he was remembered? Would Janna weep not for his death, but for the ruined memory of him? He could let Nylena kill Lysander. A prince wasn't a queen, but it would be a blow to her reign. Lysander blinked back at him now. He would not be easy to kill. Nylena wasn't strong enough. Besides, this prince was too valuable. Eroan had worked to win his trust. He could not afford for it all to be wasted. With Lysander's help, he *would* get to the queen.

"Nylena, you don't understand what's happening here. Leave these lands and tell the others not to come. They'll die, and we cannot afford—"

At first, when the ground shook and the air blasted over them, Eroan thought the storm had returned. Leaves tore at his face. He jerked an arm up, shielding his face but when he blinked grit from his eyes, a wall of shifting purple scales slammed down like a waterfall. Half-moon black claws spread wide and dragon's eyes shone like two blazing stars. The beast opened its jaws, rows of teeth glinting, each one the size of Lysander's swords. And then it struck, lightning fast, and where Nylena had been standing moments before, there was only dragon.

Eroan couldn't move. Couldn't breathe. The thing was too big, too close, too much of an enormous force to think around.

The beast reared higher and turned its wicked serpentine smile on him. Those eyes, so dark, bottomless pits of power and hunger and thirst that had wrecked worlds. And he knew those eyes. He'd stared into them as her magic had tried to smother him. Elisandra.

And Nylena was gone.

Another elf dead.

Rage. Foolish and all-consuming.

So many had fallen... so many proud warriors. So many he couldn't save because the queen still lived, and had he succeeded, Nylena would still be alive.

He didn't think. Didn't reason. Eroan strode forward.

A foot slammed down, blocking his path. Claws sank like sword blades into the earth and gouged out grooves.

Fear chipped at the sudden silence in his head.

He knelt, picked up one of Nylena's fallen daggers, and when he lifted his gaze, the queen of dragons peered down at him, mirth gleaming in her eyes.

CHAPTER 15

 ysander

She would kill Eroan.

Lysander's heart thumped like it was trapped behind bars. He had the blades in his hands, but they were useless against her bulk. If he attacked as human, he'd be a distraction, nothing more. If he struck as dragon, she'd tear him to pieces. But he couldn't watch this... He tightened his grip on the blades. Perhaps distraction was the key, buy the elf time to see reason and run.

Eroan knelt, and for a moment relief lifted Lysander's heart. *Yes, kneel to her, it's the only way.* When he straightened, a dagger glinted in Eroan's hand, and the relief turned to lead in Lysander's gut. *No, you fool!* A silly little weapon, barely a toothpick. Eroan would die here. No, this wasn't right. The elf was too bright a thing, too strong, too proud, to die here. It couldn't happen. It *wouldn't* happen.

I keep saving him, but he keeps walking into the jaws of death.

Lysander was moving, running, although none of this felt real. His mother's gaze was fixed on the elf. In seconds, she could crush him, consume him. He'd die just as easily as his friend had.

Not this time, Mother.

A roar tore from his chest, voicing the broiling pit of rage burning him inside. He lifted the blades and plunged down into the back of Elisandra's front foot.

Her bellow rocked the air, the skies, rocked Lysander's chest to his withered soul. He'd never heard a sweeter sound. She lifted her foot, and him with it, clinging to his blades. Air rushed, the ground fell away. If he fell, it might be the end of him, but he'd never felt more alive, more focused, as though some deeper instinct had a hold of him and was driving him forward. Magic and power sang through his veins, the shift calling, but he held it tight, held it close, and instead of freeing the truest part of him, he pulled a blade free, clutched to the other still lodged in her foot, and swung free. He might not make it, he realized, as he let go and fell. Didn't matter. His heart sang, falling... so free... He hit scales and scrabbled to grab hold of something. Anything.

The crown of bone about her head. He grabbed one of its forks. She threw her head high. Starlit skies swirled. His stomach dropped, body suddenly light. There was no clinging to her for long. She'd shake him free, but not before he drove the blade in his hand home.

Her scales hissed and rattled, and with a second sundering roar, she tore at her head, at him.

Lysander saw his moment. Clear. Precise. He tightened his grip on the sword. Calm certainty washed through him. She bowed her head, trying to shake him free. He let go— falling, skidding—sliding over scales, down to her brow, and there, he plunged the sword into the only soft part on a dragon's body. Her eye.

roan

It wouldn't kill her, Eroan thought, as the prince plunged his sword home and true, but the prince must have known that. Why then? Why do this?

The Dragon Queen's screams sliced through Eroan's skull. He staggered under the onslaught of noise and stood frozen as the towering mass of dragon reared up, blocking out the sky. Lysander clung on, little more than a child's doll in her clutches.

Then he remembered the drunken moments, the careful words. *Nobody has cut his ropes.* The prince was trapped too. But this wasn't reason, this was madness. And why now, why here, surely not for... Eroan?

Eroan backed up. The queen threw her head back and forth, but when that didn't shake her parasite free, she tore her son from her eye, capturing him inside her fist, and slammed him into the forest floor. Pinned, he lay still, eyes open, staring at nothing. The queen roared over her kill, claiming her son's limp carcass as hers. And he was surely dead. Old fears, childish fears, urged Eroan to flee. He glanced at the dagger in his hand—so small a weapon in the face of her monstrosity. But he could do this, he could beat this creature alone. His whole life had been honed in pursuit of this moment. For the fallen, for those who hadn't returned, and for a broken prince.

Elisandra's head swiveled down, her gaze falling on Eroan once more. Behind her grin, purple fire burbled.

Attacking her head-on would get him killed alongside the prince. No. There was another way...

He dropped the dagger.

Elisandra huffed a rumbling growl. She swept her wounded foot in and closed her digits around Eroan, then closed tight. He let it happen, let her pull him close to her muzzle, let her peer down at him as though he were nothing but an insect in her clutches and let her grin, revealing rows of curved, lethal teeth, so close now he could reach out and touch one.

Teeth, shaped like Lysander's blades. His blades, Eroan realized, were made from dragon teeth. And one of those blades had pierced the scales on her foot and punctured her eye.

Her closed eye wept tears of blood. Tears for her son, perhaps.

Eroan closed his eyes, listened to her huge wings spread and draw in air, then beat, like thunder, as she took flight.

CHAPTER 17

*ℒ*ysander

LYSANDER KNEW ONLY PAIN. Broken as dragon and broken as man, he had nowhere to hide from the agony. Carline's healing hands rubbed at him like glass and blades and needles and all things made to make him howl and writhe. She tried, he knew she tried, but some things can't be healed. A choice, she had whispered to him in the darkest hours: Never walk as a man or never fly again as a dragon. A broken back or a broken wing? Pick one.

He couldn't.

And so he thrashed in pain for hours, days, weeks, into a timeless ocean of agony where there was nothing worth waking for.

Broken.

In so many ways.

In all ways.

Why wouldn't it end?

Someone nudged his leg and snuffled a gentle greeting. *Brother*, his instincts confirmed. Lysander stared at the wall, at every crack, every crumbling stone, chasing the veins in the tower rather than chasing the truth. Akiem— all magnificent black scale—plodded in front of him, lowered his head between his front feet, and looked Lysander in the eyes.

Lysander stared through his brother's golden eyes, through the wall, out into the space beyond where he would likely never fly again. He didn't want to make this choice. Why hadn't Mother killed him? He couldn't keep on fighting when there was nothing left worth fighting for.

Akiem was gone now, and so were the days and nights. Was the elf gone too? Had she killed him like he'd feared? Eroan. Stupid, stubborn Eroan. Lysander's dreams shifted from cold to warm, and the pain faded, just for a little while. He saw Eroan's gaze through firelight, saw the elf gently smile at some silly thing he'd said about eggs and princes. Lysander couldn't remember the words, but he remembered the thawing feeling those words had gifted him. Like there was something else beyond this hell, some other hope.

"Kit. Dear little kit. You must choose. I cannot choose for you," Carline soothed.

Lysander let his lips ripple a warning to stay away, to leave him be, let him rot for all he cared.

"I cannot see you do this to yourself. You're wasting to nothing. What good does your death do, Lysander? Survive and find a way."

Good? What good was there in the world now? Amalia

had been good. Her laughter had once brightened the tower. And Elisandra had ripped her out of the brood as if she were some cancerous thing, but her only crime had been to search for light and love in a world void of those things.

Lysander heard Carline sigh, then she was gone, and the dreams swirled again, but this time Lysander smelled pine and freshly cut wood, and the rain. Eroan. In here, in his dreams, it didn't matter what Lysander thought or who he admired. In here, he had the elf in chains again, but this time the elf wanted it, and Lysander tasted his mouth one careful, testing kiss at a time. Fire wrapped around his heart, pumping hot blood through his veins, filling his limbs with feeling. Not too much, just enough to lift his head above the dreams.

"Is he alive?" Lysander asked, not even sure who he was asking or how many times he had asked it. "The elf..."

"It's alive," Carline said.

It. Right. Because it was such a crime to think of anything other than dragon as worthy of a name.

Lysander fluttered his eyes open. He couldn't recall turning back to human, couldn't recall the room around him, with its white-washed walls and waxy smell rising from a dozen candles.

Carline knelt at his bedside, wringing out a wet cloth. The lines in her face had gotten harder and her lips paler. Much of her bundle of silvery-peppered hair had escaped its band. A sadness clung to her. He reached out a hand and smiled when she placed hers in his. Her fingers closed, but her sadness only thickened when she met his gaze.

"There was nothing I could do." Her hand squeezed his

and let go. She gathered her rag, bowl and skirts, and left with her words ringing around him. *Nothing she could do?*

He threw his hand back and tried to swallow around the knot in his throat. The choice. A broken wing or a broken back. Fear pinned him still. Either choice was one he couldn't live with. But which had he chosen? He looked down himself, at the bedsheet with its dips and valleys and there at the end, the sheet steepled over his toes. He could feel his legs, couldn't he? Breathing in, he held still and stretched his toes. The sheet shifted.

He'd lost his wing then. Or at least the use of it.

His mouth twisted. He pinched his lips closed then bit into his bottom lip to stop it from trembling.

His flight. His freedom.

He knew. That part of him felt dislodged. Broken inside. There would be no more flying, no more soaring over the forests, no more tasting the wind, letting it caress his scales. Without it, he might as well be a chained thing, a trapped thing.

He threw off the sheet and planted his feet on the floor. What was he then, if not dragon?

A hollowness gnawed at his chest. He wanted to tear the wrongness out of himself, wanted to sink his fingers into something and rip it to shreds.

Sinking his hands into his hair, he rocked while his thoughts unraveled. He couldn't stay together, couldn't hold it in, this slippery feeling that his life was falling away from him. The tears fell, like the rest of him, forever falling. He was breaking apart, turning to dust, becoming nothing.

The moan wasn't his, couldn't be his. All feeling leaked away, fleeing with his tears and moans and cries into an empty room. *Let it go, let it all go. It can't hurt anymore if there's nothing left to break.*

LYSANDER STOOD at a window and stared over the scorched lands to the green and plump forests far beyond, turning golden now the days were shortening. He had always liked autumn. Warm air during the day, but bitterly cold at night. Ice had nipped at his wings when he'd lingered too long in the air, giving his flight a sharp edge he'd often chased.

There would be no more flying... ever.

"Lysander..." Elisandra summoned.

He turned away from the vista back into the gloom of the tower chamber. "Yes, Mother."

"Your escorts will arrive in three days. I suggest you ready yourself for the coupling."

He blinked at her, his thoughts taking a moment to return from his memories. It always surprised him how the amethyst replacing her right eye had a depth to it her true eye never had. She wore her hair down these days and often let it curtain half her face, making that jewel-eye seem like a tantalizing secret. It was no secret, of course, though how she had lost her eye was. By the time he had woken from his stupor, half a thing, she had spun a legend of some great old-world beast that had struck at the heart of her lands. Nobody cared enough about Lysander to think it a coincidence how he too was wounded. She lost an eye. He lost half his life.

"Did you hear me?" she snapped.

"Yes, Mother."

"Good." Her poisonous lips curled into a smile. "Now then..." Her gaze turned sly. "I have a little task. Something I think you can help with. Would you like that, my dear?"

"Of course."

Frustration fluttered her cheek. "Would it kill you to smile once in a while?"

He headed for the door, not caring he hadn't been dismissed. "No, Mother."

"Come to the hall this evening. I have a parting gift for you," she called after him.

He let the chamber door clang shut as answer.

roan

EROAN COULDN'T REMEMBER the last time he'd seen the light. Weeks. Months. His skin sizzled, muscles trembling, his body shrinking around the husk he was becoming. His mind too. He'd thought, perhaps foolishly, that the queen would take him back to her chamber, bind him in leather straps and it would be as before. He'd be a part of her harem and closer than ever. But that hadn't happened. Instead, she'd locked him somewhere dark, somewhere cold, somewhere like the dungeon, only this time the prince hadn't come. Nobody had. And with every second trapped away from light and life, Eroan felt his strength wither and curl inward.

When the dragons finally did come, he could barely lift himself from the mire of his mind. Hands shoved and pulled—every touch a brand—and he couldn't find the energy to fight. They could do anything to him, he realized, and he couldn't stop them. Couldn't lift a hand to plead to see the queen, to let him have that one last chance at killing her.

Nylena had been right. He wasn't Eroan of the Order any longer. Now he was a ghost of a thing. He ached for the light, to feel it on his skin, to breathe it in and let it fill him up so he knew he still lived and this wasn't some wretched afterlife.

Dragonkin tore his soiled clothes off and led him into a deep walk-in bath. Warm water lapped up his thighs. Steam twirled, and he wondered if the males were steam too, or were they real? They moved like smoke. Hands were on him, caressing him, sweeping the dirt off his skin, roaming intimately so that nothing was missed. He briefly thought of the old dragon, Carline, and how he had once thought to stop her from touching him. It was different then. *He* was different then. He'd had a fire inside. But the prison had snuffed out that light.

"They have pretty eyes." The dragonkin male's face was all he could see suddenly. His eyes were slitted, like a snake's, and wide with want.

Eroan lay his head back against the pool's edge and fluttered his eyes closed. Let them have him. Water sloshed. Hands roamed his chest, kneading over his hips and boldly massaging between his legs. His thoughts fluttered too, thoughts of another's touch, so long ago, of Janna and how they'd laughed, tangled together. He'd plucked leaves from her hair, and she'd kissed him on the lips... No, that wasn't him. That was someone else's life, someone who had a purpose, a proud and strong male. The memory of Eroan Ilanea.

Kill the queen.

Until it is done.

He'd lived for the Order. Now he was a husk, a ghost without purpose.

The dragonkin's hand stroked, stoking heat awake low in his stomach, way down low, and he couldn't find it in him to think around the pleasure of feeling something, anything. The dragonkin nursed the spark in him, using his thumb to run up his thick swelling shaft. Eroan could wallow in this warmth. It had been so long since anyone had touched him. So long, he'd feared he'd been forgotten forever.

His thoughts drifted while something important plucked at their edges. The dragonkin's hand tightened, pleasure throbbed, and Eroan arched into his grip. This was wrong. He wasn't here for this, for them. There was another reason for him being here... one he'd almost lost in the dark. It was important. It was everything. If he could just think...

The dragonkin straddled his thighs, gripped his arousal and lowered himself over him.

Wait.

Eroan gasped and gripped the male's shoulders. The dragonkin's eyes flashed.

What had they done to him? The water, was it that? The steam? He couldn't think through the fog, the heat, the want, but he knew, inside, this was wrong.

"Stop," he mumbled and pushed at the male's slippery chest.

The dragonkin seated himself over him, and took him in, inch by careful inch. "Oh no, elf," the dragon purred. "We do not stop for you."

Tight pleasure coiled in Eroan's belly, a pleasure that sickened and sweetened all at once. He tried to push, to twist away, but his head spun, and the fog swelled. A hand captured Eroan's jaw, holding him pinned. And the dragonkin rocked his hips, taking him inside in aching tightness, riding him out.

The second male moved closer, easing into Eroan's vision. A slippery vision of muscles and masculine lines. He stroked his nipples and then lowered his hand toward the waterline to massage his arousal.

What was this madness?

Pleasure spun tighter, building, hardening. Eroan couldn't do this, not with them. There would be nothing left of him if they took this too.

"You like that," the dragon riding him said. "I feel that you do. Don't resist us."

The strength came at him out of the dark, a sudden surge of anger and hatred. He punched the balls of his palms into the male's chest, flinging him backward into the water and out of sight beneath the choppy surface. But the second was on him suddenly, his mouth hot and sharp as it claimed Eroan's. It burned. Stole more of him. Pleasure trilled. He didn't want this, but he couldn't seem to make the thoughts get through to his skin, to his body. Still hard, the second male plunged his head under water and took him in his wet, hot mouth.

"No... no..." Eroan had his hands in the male's hair and meant to pull him off, but the dragon's tongue licked and flicked, tearing a groan from Eroan.

And then, *she* was there.

Dressed in black lace. Lips blood red. One eye amethyst, like her scales, like her fire. He hadn't heard her enter, hadn't seen her walk around the bath to stand opposite. But she was there now, as real as the dragonkin taking Eroan's arousal in so damn deep it brushed the back of the male's throat.

"Out," the queen snapped at the dragonkin lurking nearby. The male jogged from the pool, his head bowed. He padded naked, out of sight.

Eroan dared not take his eyes from the queen.

The second male, the one with Eroan's cock in his mouth, twitched beneath Eroan's hand, still holding him down.

Eroan stared at the queen. He imagined it was her head he held underwater, her lips around his hard need. The fire in her one remaining eye and the smile on her lips told him she knew his thoughts. Maddening ecstasy spooled tighter. Eroan pushed the male's head deeper and arched his arousal deeper, choking the beast.

The dragonkin's teeth sank in. Pain burst behind Eroan's eyes.

Eroan kicked out and jolted from the pool on flimsy, weak legs. His footing slipped. He staggered, almost fell, and then she had him by the back of his collar, yanking him up and back like a pet on a leash.

"That rat almost killed me!" the male in the pool spluttered and wheezed.

Elisandra slammed Eroan face-first into a wall. "What did you expect?" the queen laughed. "Foolish thing." She leaned in, molding herself against him. Her breasts pushed against his back, her hip against his ass. "A little test," she hissed into this ear, "to see if there was any fight left in Eroan Ilanea."

The queen let go, but Eroan stayed pressed against the chilling wall, needing it to hold him up.

"Get him dressed," the queen barked. "A loose shirt. Let Lysander see how his pet quivers."

Lysander.

The prince was alive. Feeling thawed Eroan's heart into something warm and bright again. When the prince hadn't come during those long hours in darkness, he'd assumed she'd killed him in the forest. To hear he was alive...

Eroan turned and let the queen see all of him, see the pride in his eyes even as shivers wrecked him. Naked and wet but for the collar at his neck, he stood exposed and raw, but she saw the fire.

Her good eye twitched wider. The queen drank him in, inch by careful inch, as though committing every hard curve of his muscular design to memory. "Make no mistake. I'm not doing this for you, elf, or him. He will perform, and his childish actions have consequences. You're going to help me with that." She tilted her head and eyed him side-on. "Bring him to me after the celebration," she told her males. Males he hadn't even noticed had been here all along.

She clicked her fingers and the dragonkin scurried off, returning moments later with towels and clothing. In those moments, Eroan hadn't taken his eyes from the queen. This was progress. To see her again, to be this close. She would soon have him closer, and in those moments, opportunity would come. He panted in anticipation, his body buzzing with life like the hit he usually got from basking in daylight, until the room tipped, and the queen's laughter set his thought spinning. He went down onto his knees. No, no... He could not appear so weak!

"Feed him," she chuckled. "Do what's necessary. I can't have him passing out... yet."

She left, and more dragonkin came in. Three attended him. He let them dry him, let them dress him and braid his hair while inside, vengeance fueled a fire of his making. None tried to touch him again. He smiled, garnering odd looks from the dragons. Among all of this madness, he'd won a small victory, and the queen hadn't realized.

Feed him.

Him.

Not it.

DRESSED, fed and dry, the guards led Eroan down corridors, toward distant mumblings that reminded him of ocean waves. With every step, warmth spilled back into his veins, filling him and chasing away the lethargy. Perhaps it was the firelight from the torches or being around company, or more likely it was having a purpose again that drove him forward. But all those thoughts chilled at the sight of the crowd and the wooden stocks.

The stench hit him then. Dragonkin and hot, sizzling meat. The hall was full of the beasts. Some looked his way as he was marched in. So many. Countless. Males. Females. Even a few younger kits. They lay about the room or were seated at the long table, suitable for a hundred at least. There had to be hundreds here, gathered around, watching from archways, balconies, from every window looking inward.

Instincts had Eroan baring his teeth for all the good it did him. The stocks came down, clamping his wrists and neck tight. Trapped, panic tried to rattle through his bones. But he would not let them see him weak. Whatever was about to happen, it would end, and he would be with the queen afterward. Close to her. He'd do anything if it meant he could crush her neck in his hands. All he had to endure was this and the never-ending night of monsters would be over soon.

His gaze snagged on furious green eyes.

Prince Lysander. He stood as still as stone while his kind flowed around him, like water around rock.

Eroan lifted his chin. He still clung to his pride like a shield and showed it to Lysander now, but the prince barely blinked.

A hush came over the room and a chill with it. And still, Lysander stared, his face a deliberate mask, nothing like the animated, relaxed prince from before. Something had happened to him, something to lend him that steel he'd spoken off all those weeks or months ago.

"My dragons, my brood..." Elisandra glided in from Eroan's right, the hem of her lace dress trailing behind her. "We are here to celebrate the joining of two great lines, to celebrate my son's venture on behalf of the amethyst."

She held a coiled whip at her side. He could hardly miss it as she crossed the floor in front of him. She had a destination in mind, and as she reached the table where Lysander had risen, she held the whip out to her son.

"For your new joining," the queen explained, and then louder for them all to hear. "A gift to the bronze for the regrettable deaths of their kin. Deaths wrought by this elf."

Lysander looked down, blinked once, his brow creasing, then carefully took the whip from his mother's hands.

"Fifty lashes," the queen declared. "Ten for each bronze killed."

"Yes, Mother," the prince said. When he looked up, there was nothing in his eyes but cold, hard steel.

CHAPTER 19

*L*ysander

THE WHIP FELT soft and supple in Lysander's hands, but he knew all too well how it liked to bite. He gathered its coils in his left hand and rubbed at his chin with his right, using the motion to wipe off a sneer and replace it with a smile his mother would find more appealing.

The dragonkin watched their prince approach the elf locked in the stocks. His mother watched too, her one-eyed gaze burning into his back. They all fucking watched. Even the elf. The elf who should have fled when he had the chance. The elf who was a damned fool. He had brought this on himself.

Excited, breathless murmurs rippled through his kin. Lysander hated them all, but most of all, he hated himself.

He swallowed, let the whip's coils drop with a wet

sounding slap to the floor, and gripped the handle tighter. He had felt nothing for so long, nothing since he'd roared out his hurt alone in that room, and now this. He could not feel here either. They would sense weakness. His mother would sense weakness.

He drifted around the stocks, dragging the whip's tails with him.

Fifty lashes.

Fifty lashes for five dead bronze. Three, he'd killed. Two, Eroan had dispatched. Although the bronze found with his shriveled cock in his mouth had been more of a dual effort.

While Lysander had been holed up licking his wounds, Dokul had demanded justice. Well, here it was. To deny the bronze their bloodlust would start a war. It didn't matter they shouldn't have taken the elf in the first place. In the name of peace, Lysander had to cleave the elf's back to shreds.

Akiem drifted toward Elisandra. He kept his voice low, but Lysander heard. "Let me," his brother whispered. Something dark twisted inside Lysander.

Elisandra ignored him, and Lysander's smile cut deeper. The last thing he needed was Akiem driving the lashes into Eroan. Like this, he could at least control the damage. And there would be damage. There was no escaping it. Just like there was no escaping every-*fucking*-thing in this tower.

Akiem joined his mother, and both of them watched him now, waiting for him to fail. Lysander jerked the whip back and snapped it down. With a vicious crack, it tore into Eroan's back. The elf jolted, rattling the stocks. Thick silence followed.

Blood crept down Eroan's back, soaking through his shirt.

Lysander tightened his hand on the whip to keep the tremors from showing. His chest heaved from the voice in his head screaming at him to stop, that this was wrong, but to his kin, it looked like rage.

He'd wanted to see Eroan again, but not like this. He'd wanted to sit with him by the fire like they had when they were alone. He had wanted to know more about the elves, about why the elf Nylena had looked at Eroan with such pride in her eyes before she'd thought... what? That he'd become Lysander's pet?

Why didn't you run?!

Another lash. Another jerk. Fabric and skin split apart.

The elf should have run. Lysander would have—he should have taken the skies when he had the chance, and now that chance was taken from him. Because of this elf's stubborn mission. A doomed mission. All the elves died and this one would too.

Another lash. The whip cracked. Eroan grunted, panted. His shoulders heaved and trembled. As Lysander drew the whip back, blood rained across the floor.

Be cold. Be hard. Be steel.

He lashed again.

Be steel.

And again.

And again.

THE REVELRY CONTINUED, all in Lysander's name. He faked his smiles, his laughs, like he wore steel on the outside too. Time stretched long and thin, and with every second, the elf's blood dripped, pooling beneath the stocks. He'd fallen unconscious after the first twenty lashes. After thirty, there was little left of the elf's back. Lysander had almost thrown up his dinner by the fiftieth lash but had somehow kept it down, hidden it all inside.

He wasn't even sure if the elf still breathed. He couldn't look. None of this was supposed to matter. The elf was a tool. A plaything.

His kin wandered around Eroan in stocks and laughed, and Lysander curled his fingers into fists. He hated them. Hated them all. But his hate for Elisandra was a blinding, powerful force. His kind tried to speak with him. He blanked them all, and with every heartbeat, the hateful knot tightened, choking off all feeling. If he stayed too long, he'd do something foolish.

Sometime in the evening, his mother's assistants unlocked Eroan from the stocks and carried the elf's limp body out of the hall. Maybe they'd throw him away. Maybe his mother would finish him off. If Lysander were more like Akiem, or any other dragon, he wouldn't have cared.

But Lysander wasn't like them, any of them... He couldn't allow it. In a few more days, he'd be gone from this wretched place to somewhere Elisandra couldn't reach him. Before he left, he'd do something worthwhile, something to make up for every terrible lash of that whip.

"Lysander... Is everything all right?"

He turned away from his kin's question, set his tankard down on the table and left the hall, careful not to break into a run. Panic gripped his heart.

What if it was too late? His pace quickened, boots thumping on stone.

Akiem stepped out of a side-door, blocking him. "Stop."

Lysander shoved his brother aside and ran faster, heart racing. And there, he made it to the stairs below his mother's tower where the assistants were hauling Eroan's unconscious body between them. "New orders! You're to bring him—it with me."

Narrowed eyes regarded him. "Queen Elisandra said—"

Lysander planted his feet and allowed some of the magic to burn through his gaze, knowing it made his glare sharper, his eyes harder. The twin blades at his back warmed, eager to be freed.

They still wavered because whatever he said, whatever he threatened them with, he wasn't Elisandra.

"Do it." Akiem breezed behind Lysander. "And hurry about it. The queen hates delays."

One brother they could argue with, but not two. Lysander briefly met his brother's gaze and saw a similar anger reflected there. Akiem had likely only helped him to keep him momentarily safe from Elisandra's claws, or maybe he was curious. Whatever the reason, he certainly wasn't stepping in for the elf's benefit. Akiem would make him pay for this, but whatever cost, it would be worth it.

The assistants followed, descending deeper into the tower's heart. Lysander hammered on a closed chamber door and heard familiar grumbles from inside. Good, she was in, and she wouldn't turn him away.

Carline opened the door, squinted at the princes and the bloody elf and let out a deep wearisome sigh. "You amethyst kits, always bringing trouble to my door." She stepped aside.

Lysander ripped the sheet off the bed. "Here." The

assistants dumped Eroan's body on the bed like the elf was trash. He barely reined in the rage. "Get out!" They scurried out, probably already thinking of the cleanest way to tell Elisandra all about Lysander's latest indiscretion.

"Light a fire, prince," Carline said, rolling up her sleeves. She approached the bed and Eroan's prone body.

Akiem glanced at Lysander.

Carline waved a hand. "Either of you. Doesn't matter, just do it."

Lysander assembled the kindling, tossing it into the fireplace grate, anything to keep his mind off what he was doing here. Bringing Eroan here couldn't be another mistake. It felt right. And nothing had felt right in weeks.

"It's not yours..." Akiem propped himself against the wall beside the fireplace and looked down his nose. "She'll punish you."

Laughter tickled Lysander's throat. He snapped a bundle of twigs in two and tossed those into the grate. "What else can she do, brother?" He took the firestarter from his back pocket and paused with it between his fingers. He'd kept it all this time, through the pain, through the long darkness. A darkness he had yet to climb out of.

"Why?" Akiem asked.

Lysander struck the flint, sending sparks flying, and nursed the resulting tiny flames, feeding them fuel, making the flames higher, brighter, hotter, until the fire had a hold of the wood and filled the gate.

"Just let it die," Akiem whispered. "It's kinder if that's what you're worried about."

"No." Lysander straightened and gripped the mantle. He breathed in wood smoke, the same kinda of smoke that had filled their camp. Memories fluttered about him like ghosts.

"Then why?!" Akiem snarled.

He turned his head to meet his brother's gaze. Akiem thought him weak, always had. Siblings killed the weakest one, but when Akiem had tried, he'd learned Lysander bit back. Even now, Lysander saw the hatred in his brother's eyes. It had never left.

He looked over his shoulder at Carline carefully peeling off strips of the elf's shirt. Eroan lay on his chest, an arm hanging off the bed, blood dripping from his limp fingers, his white hair fanned out and matted with blood. If he died... it would break him open.

"If he dies, so does the last of my hope." Lysander watched confusion twist Akiem's expression and felt his hate knot into something ugly inside. "I don't expect you to understand, you never have."

"It's not even dragon." Akiem's eyes flashed. "It's an elf. You do realize that?" Disgust had him recoiling. "You want to fuck him, is that it? Find a horse to fuck out your sick lust if you must. This is... this is twisted—"

The hate blazed, suddenly breaking free. Lysander threw a punch. It cracked satisfyingly against Akiem's jaw, but his brother never had gone down easy and was on him in a next blink, his cold hand at Lysander's throat. They grappled, but Akiem's strength always won out.

Lysander's back hit the wall. Akiem pinned him still, like a kit caught by the scruff of the neck. "You're going to get yourself killed! Is that what you want?!" Akiem breathed in and finally loosened his grip, allowing Lysander to breathe again.

"She's not going to kill me," he spluttered. "She needs

me to spread my seed through the bronze. Afterward..."
He rubbed at his neck. "Maybe."

"There's a limit, Lysander."

"I took her fucking eye, brother. I reached that limit weeks ago."

Akiem suddenly stepped back. "*You* did that? You mutilated her?"

Had his brother really not seen the obvious, and hadn't he cared enough to see? He straightened his shirt with a shrug. "Oh, don't look so shocked."

"Why?"

"Why?" Lysander laughed. "I killed the bronze. The ones Eroan hadn't gotten to yet. I suppose you want to know why I did that too. You don't understand. You can't understand because you've always had control of your life. You don't feel like you're falling every day, you're Prince Akiem! Elisandra's beloved, the crown's favorite!" Lysander laughed and didn't care that it twisted and turned ugly. "You have a brood, you have power. I have nothing and no one, and now she sells me to the fucking bronze like I'm no better than breeding stock. I thought I could be her prince. I thought I could live a lie. I can't!"

"That's ridiculous. None can match you in battle. Our flights admire you for that..."

If nothing else. The way he trailed off, they both knew there was more to that sentence.

"I'm not like you. I'm broken, Akiem. Some days I don't know who I am, but it sure isn't amethyst."

"Will you both stop!" Carline snapped, rising to her feet. Her hands glistened with blood. "I used to throw you both over my knee and whip those little asses of yours until they were pink as peaches. Akiem, shut up and listen to your brother or you'll lose him. And Lysander, quit your complaining. This elf is dying. Help me save it or leave."

Akiem's brow pinched at the old dragon's disrespectful words. When it was clear she had no intention of apologizing, he swung his heated glare back to Lysander. "That elf will be the death of you and I'll have no hand in it." He left, slamming the door so hard it almost bounced off its hinges.

"Good, that's him gone," Carline drew in a breath and planted her hands on her hips. "Now, help me save him like I know you can."

CHAPTER 20

 roan

BLOOD-SOAKED DREAMS PUNCTURED by whip cracks. They boiled and simmered around him, never seeming to end.

Eroan wasn't ready to give up, not yet. He dreamed of a time when he knew nothing but pain, when the Order had found him, starved and wretched, crying in the rain. He hadn't given up then. He dreamed of sending proud, fierce warriors to their deaths and how he'd ached to bring them back, to stop them. But there was no end then, and there couldn't be one now.

"You don't get to end it now. It's not yet done," a voice told him, a voice that somehow found him in the blood-soaked nightmares.

He dreamed of hands on his skin, of lashes slicing through muscle, of a mouth teasing his, of desires and hungers and things yet to be known but he had yearned for

145

all the same. He dreamed of a prince with green eyes full of wonder but also regret. And when he woke, the prince was sitting on the floor, propped against the wall beside a roaring fireplace, his chin on his rising and falling chest, arms folded, eyes closed.

Eroan blinked, wondering if he had conjured this room and the prince. That thought floated, anchorless and free.

"You'll feel a little out of sorts, elf. It's the valerian root. But you'll live."

He shifted his head and recognized the older woman seated at the foot of the bed. She smelled of mead and wood smoke and had the cracks and lines of a hard life mapping her face. The ghost of her healing tingled down his back. Her little smile touched that wrecked, lonely part of him. Just a tiny smile, but it tied him up in knots to see it.

She jerked her chin toward Lysander. "He's exhausted. I wouldn't have been able to save you without him."

He rolled his tongue around his parched mouth. "He did... this... to me." He heard the whip cracks. Felt his back burn.

"Foolish elf," Carline muttered. "He suffered, just like you have. Perhaps more so. Do you think he's never felt that whip lashing his back? Do you think, in that healing haze you're in, that Lysander is free to say no to the queen?"

He hadn't considered it, and when the first lashes had struck, he'd hated them all, Lysander included. He scowled at the old dragon as she rose and brought him a cup. Cradling his head, she helped him drink. Just a few sweet sips, but even that small motion was almost too much for his spinning thoughts. Mead? What was wrong with these dragons? Did they never drink water? "Trying to... get me drunk, old woman?" His voice scratched his tongue and throat.

She rolled her eyes. "Trying to ease your pain, elf."

"I have... a name." He fell onto his back, or tried to until his shoulders blazed as though someone was running knife blades down his spine. Wincing, he coughed out, "Eroan Ilanea."

She set the cup on a bedside table and pulled her chair closer. "Truth be told, I thought you were sure to die, *Eroan*."

He blinked at her face, not so different from the elders of his home village, and waited for the pain to ebb. "You healed me?"

"No. Well, yes. Some." She leaned back, and something in the way she smiled down at him had Eroan wondering what else she wanted to say but clearly couldn't. "We don't breed healers," she added. "Not anymore."

He knew, but let her speak, enjoying the softness of her voice, the warmth of the sheet and the comforting firelight.

"Weakness is cut out of a brood before it can fester," she continued, placing her healers' hands in her lap. "Lysander was destined for death the second he tore from the egg. The older, Akiem, tried it. He survived. I watched him then too. Others have tried to kill him, he's always survived. He has a passion for life but lately..." A shadow passed over her face. "Passion can only get a dragon so far."

"Why are you telling me this?" he whispered, trying to ease the soreness in his throat. He didn't remember crying out but must have.

147

Carline pursed her lips. "You stole my knife."

Eroan let his lips lift into a smile and Carline's mirrored his. She likely knew what he'd done with that knife too.

"You're a slippery thing, Eroan. I was sure you'd die like all the others and yet here you are, months later, your heart still beatin'. I see why he fights for you, even if it's foolish. Like you are foolish."

He laughed then choked on the sound as something inside twisted.

Carline leaned forward. Her smile cooled. "Lysander is a diamond in the rough. Even broken, he is worth a thousand amethyst." The dregs of laughter hardened in her fierce eyes. "I have tried to protect him, tried to steer him right, but like all dragons, he is stubborn. You have that in common."

Eroan let her words sink in and felt as though there was something else inside of them, some greater meaning he didn't understand. He missed the clearness of his thoughts, missed Alumn's light guiding him. He tried to recall the smell of rain and couldn't. All he could smell was dragon and mead.

"Queen Elisandra is a curse upon this land," Carline said, catching Eroan's wandering thoughts. "It was never meant to be this way."

He turned his head and looked closer at this old beast wearing a human face. Something else was happening here, a moment in time that would ring into the future, but he couldn't clear his head enough to grasp a hold of it. "What do you want from me?"

"Protect him. He won't ask for it and will fight you at every step, but you must protect him. He is the future."

Eroan lifted his gaze to the ceiling, feeling the world tip. "Alumn did not bring me here to protect dragons." *She brought me here to kill them.*

Carline chuckled. "Alumn, or fate, whatever you call her, often gives us the things we need exactly when we need them, but we must have our eyes wide open to recognize her gifts. You need him now, same as he needs you, elf. You must simply... open your eyes."

Eroan blinked, and she was gone, her words still fluttering about him like moths in the night. His thoughts cleared, the fire crackled in its grate, the sound sharp in the quiet of the room. Lysander still slept, but there was no sign of the old healer.

He lifted his head. The empty chair was back at the end of the bed. His cup sat on the bedside table. He tasted mead on his tongue. At least, he thought he did. Had he dreamed her?

You need him now...

Her words haunted him as he watched the sleeping prince. Words of protection, words hinting at more. Lysander had been the one to strike each crack of the whip... and now he was here, had been here all along...

Even if he wanted to protect this prince, how could he in a tower full of dragons? Carline's words made no sense. They must have been dreams, he dismissed. Nothing more, and when he closed his eyes, he fell into those dreams again, only this time, they wrapped comfortingly around him.

SUNLIGHT.

Eroan almost wept as light stroked over his face. Clouds sailed across clear blue skies. He closed his eyes and let his lips part, let the warmth feed into his skin. The prince was behind him, standing guard, his presence the only thing anchoring Eroan to the earth, to the now. Life and strength swelled inside him. So long in darkness, so long alone...

He dropped to his knees in the dew-soaked grass and spread his fingers through the vibrant green blades. So little a thing, to feel, but he hadn't been sure he'd feel much of anything again, until now. He bowed forward and breathed in, inflating withered lungs.

Shudders spilled through him, lifting the fine hairs on his arms. He'd been a ghost for so long he'd almost forgotten what it felt like to be whole again.

I am Eroan Ilanea. Assassin of the Order. And I still live. Until it is done.

A shadow fell over him. He lifted a hand to shield his eyes from the glare and absorbed the sight of Lysander's dark outline. The sunlight blinked behind his head, but between shimmers, Eroan caught the strangest smile on the prince's lips.

"We can't stay here," the prince said.

"Moments more..." He wouldn't beg, though he ached to. "Just... a few moments more."

Lysander offered his hand. "She'll come."

The way he said it, he made it sound like it was inevitable, and Eroan supposed it was. He took the prince's hand and accepted the help onto his feet.

"Are you all right?"

Eroan smiled through the shivers. Good shivers. Life sang through his veins, setting him ablaze once more inside. Was he all right? He wanted to laugh, to throw his arms wide and bask in daylight, but Lysander still had hold of his hand, and he found he didn't want to let it go. If Carline's words had been real, he owed this prince his life. "Thank you."

Lysander's throat bobbed as he swallowed. Color touched his face and a shine brightened his eyes, or perhaps that was the touch of sunlight on his skin too. "Don't thank me." He jerked his head. "I..." He held his tongue and swallowed whatever he'd been about to say. "We should get back."

Eroan let his hand slip from Lysander's grip. A strange residual tingle lingered on his fingertips. He curled his hand against his palm, savoring the tantalizing sensation. It reminded Eroan of when he'd woken, his skin alive with a similar hypersensitivity. He'd assumed it was Carline's healing touch, but Lysander's touch, just then, had felt the same.

The prince's eyes darkened. A frown upset his easy smile. "Come, before we're seen."

Eroan's steps felt heavy. He was in no hurry to return to the darkness behind those stone walls. He lingered, breathing in the light, and hadn't realized he'd stopped again until he opened his eyes and found Lysander so close, he saw how delicate the dragon's lashes were, dark accents over jewel eyes.

"Elf," the prince growled, "you're going to be the death of me."

The anger in Lysander's eyes shifted from light to dark in a blink, and that darkness flowed deep, so deep, where something dangerous lurked. The dragon hid deep inside that cave, so well buried that Eroan had briefly forgotten the man standing in front of him was a monster, one he'd dedicated his life to killing.

Lysander's gaze flicked down. Eroan touched the thick leather collar around his own neck and an odd, absent look passed over the prince's face.

"Who were you?" Lysander asked. "Before you came here to die."

"Someone like you. Someone full of pride and honor who thought he could save others."

Lysander laughed softly, and a startling burst of light sparked in Eroan's chest at the deep, chuckling sound. Out here, alone but together, Eroan could almost believe this prince with his half-smile and haunted silences was something other than the monster. But he'd seen the coldness in him, felt it at the crack of a whip too. "You think that's funny?"

"You know what I think is funny," the prince grinned, "that the two most foolish creatures on this earth somehow found one another."

Eroan let his own careful smile play on his lips. "You sound like that Carline."

"She spoke to you, huh?" Lysander asked. They fell into an easy stride back toward the tower walls.

"She did. It was her knife I used to kill the first bronze when they stole me from the queen's chamber."

A sly look came over the prince, and a delightful mischief brightened his face. "Don't be fooled. Carline's the oldest thing in this tower. If she likes you, it's probably because she's measuring you for roasting."

He believed it. "I don't think she cares for the taste of elf."

Lysander laughed again, and Eroan caught himself

wanting to touch that smile, to feel its corner beneath his thumb. He pulled himself away, confusion muddying his thoughts, and gazed over the courtyard garden. The tower walls loomed behind him. Impossibly high. He breathed in, taking the fresh air in deep. It might be the last free breath he took.

In the corner of his eye, he noticed Lysander watching him and how the prince's smile had fallen away, replaced by a long, intense look that had Eroan's breaths shortening. This was... He stopped that thought and shoved it away. He shouldn't be feeling this kernel of need toward a dragon. The prince was one of *them*. And he could be cruel, like them. He'd seen it. Felt the lash of his cruelty still. No, whatever wants Eroan was feeling had more to do with the sun on his face than twisted desire. If anything, he should be thinking of Janna.

He closed his eyes and remembered Janna's light laugh, felt her fluttering kiss brush his lips and heard his last words to her: *I'm sorry*.

CHAPTER 21

*L*ysander

FEAR HELD Lysander rooted to the spot and kept his hands locked at his sides. Fear that if he took a single step closer, if he lifted his hand and tucked that stray curl of white hair back behind Eroan's tipped-ear, it wouldn't stop there. He'd turn the elf's face toward him, and if Eroan didn't stop him, he'd taste those soft lips like he'd ached to since he'd first seen the elf in chains. And if he still wasn't stopped, he'd explore that mouth, and when he was done there, he'd sweep the elf's hair back and taste the curve of his neck.

Eroan lifted his head like he had minutes earlier and fluttered his eyes closed, and all Lysander could think of was how he wanted to run his tongue down the defined jaw, nip at its edges, and make the elf whisper his name.

When Eroan had stood in the sunlight, suddenly aglow with life and light like some divine creature, Lysander had felt the world tip for a different reason, for a new feeling. He wasn't sure when it had happened... Maybe since Eroan's blades had clashed with his swords and they'd fought outside the queen's chamber, maybe later, when he'd tasted Eroan's mouth and heard the elf threaten to kill him. Maybe when he'd freed him, maybe when he'd saved him from the bronze, and he'd watched Eroan exact his revenge, or when he'd spent hour after hour cleaning the terrible gashes—gashes Lysander was responsible for. Maybe it was the sum of all those parts, or maybe it had begun long before that. Before they'd met, and Lysander had just been waiting for someone to try to kill him so he knew what it felt like to truly be alive. Whenever it had clicked into place, he knew it now. A dangerous need, a willingness to protect no matter the cost. He admired Eroan, the foolish elf and his persistence, but it was more... so much more than admiration.

His brother's words stung as he heard them again now. His mother's too. A useless thing. Broken. Damaged. This feeling inside of him when he admired Eroan, it was so wrong, like a creature alive inside of him, eating him up, but gods, he wanted it. He was falling hard into madness and had no idea if he could stop it, or if he should. Tomorrow, he would be leaving for the coast, for the bronze brood, and he'd have to leave Eroan behind, in Elisandra's clutches. The thought made him want to tear his heart out to stop the hurt. If tomorrow was the end, then what was a kiss today? A risk.

His heart raced. Fear. What if Eroan was disgusted too?

But it was just a kiss.

Lysander lifted his hand.

A shadow sailed over them, instantly stealing the sunlight and blasting the courtyard in a frigid wind.

"Quickly!" Lysander grabbed Eroan's hand and pulled him through the doorway behind him.

A roar funneled down the corridor like a rushing torrent of noise. Lysander caught Eroan's glance and nodded. The queen had found them.

roan

"WE'RE GOING to play a game. Our last time, dear son, as you'll be gone from my life tomorrow." The queen laughed but quickly cut herself off by adding, "But not out of reach."

Eroan swallowed, finding he couldn't clear the knot in his throat. His back ached where it pressed down on the soft, quilted bed but that was likely to be the least of the hurt about to be rained down on him. His wrists were bound at either corner of the bed, and right now, a naked blond dragonkin was spending a great deal of time and focus removing Eroan's belt. There were others here. Others from the queen's harem, Eroan assumed. The same ones who had been present at the bathing pool. They lay sprawled at the edges of the bed, watching with heavy sexed-up eyes. And Lysander was as far away as he could get, standing with his back to a window. He hadn't moved from there since the guards had shoved them both inside these chambers.

Eroan hadn't looked to know if the prince was furious or if he'd surrendered himself to whatever was to happen next.

"He likes males, did you know, dear son?" the queen crooned.

Eroan closed his eyes. Then this was to be the induction into her harem. *I'm sorry,* he had told Janna when she had tried to kiss him. She had loved him. But he hadn't loved her, not like she'd wanted.

"Answer me!"

Eroan twitched and opened his eyes to see the blond dragonkin raise an eyebrow.

"No," Lysander said from across the room. Eroan dared not look.

"No what?"

"No, Mother, I did not know."

Lysander's words were clipped, running the razor's edge of rage. Eroan swallowed again.

"I discovered the revelation while he was being cleansed," she went on, sounding giddy with delight. "He's broken. Like you."

"Don't do this," Lysander whispered, so softly Eroan wondered if anyone else had heard.

"What was that, my broken mess of a son? Did you just try to deny me the pleasure of my pet?"

"Stop it, Elisandra," Lysander growled.

"Oh, come now. What did you think was going to happen? Tomorrow you are gone. Let us enjoy a moment together, mother and son. Let us wallow in pleasure. I might even let you have your elf..." Eroan heard her voice trail off and still dared not look over. "What an interesting thought. You've never seen the bronze couple... It's quite the sight. The main attraction—you—must perform with the entire brood watching. Do it well, and you'll find yourself the center of a sexual madness brought about by your entertainment. It would be remiss of me to let you go into that without some practice." She clapped her hands, and her harem melted off the bed. All but the sultry blond. He untied Eroan's trouser laces and jerked them down, over Eroan's hips.

There was little point in resisting. The queen already knew his weakness. And so the blond leaned forward. His mop of hair tickled Eroan's lower belly. His tongue swirled, dipping below his waist, following the defined V downward. The blond lifted his gaze and locked his glare with Eroan's. It shouldn't feel this good, shouldn't bring his body alive, but it did. Unbidden desire stirred low, slowly swelling Eroan's member.

Another clap of her hands and the blond reared up, revealing his own proud, taut erection. Another pulse of desire thumped through Eroan. He bared his teeth, belying his body's betrayal.

Lysander's growl rumbled like distant thunder. "Stop this now, or I'll kill the bronze bitch you've arranged for me and start a war you do not want."

Eroan turned his head to witness Lysander squaring up to his mother. They looked so alike, the same proud lines, the same shapely eyes. Different colored eyes though. Was that normal?

"You think I won't do it?" the prince sneered. "Don't think I don't know how Dokul wants me. Years ago, he tried to take me by force. I almost choked him for it, and he's never forgotten. If I kill his bronze bitch, it just gives him an excuse to have me in his bed and for him to war with you, so don't try to tell me he'll kill me first. He won't. If you want me to fuck you an army of bronze-crossed amethyst, you'll stop this right now!"

Elisandra grinned. Then her laughter sparkled when she couldn't contain her delight any longer. "There's my son. I knew you had some fight left in you."

She might have said something else but the blond lowered his mouth around Eroan's hardening erection and a sudden electric pleasure stole the thoughts from his head. All but one. He didn't want this. He pulled on the ropes at his wrists and tried to twist his hips away. The dragonkin's cold hands claimed his hips and held firm. "Stop," Eroan snarled out.

"You want this to end?" Elisandra asked Lysander. "Or do you want something else, dear son?"

"Don't, Mother."

She clicked her fingers and the blond lifted his mouth off Eroan with a wet sucking pop, leaving Eroan panting, teeth bared.

"Do not threaten me, whelp," the queen snapped, drawing Eroan's gaze again. "You have just begun to understand the world in which we live, in which I must govern. You think you know savagery. You have no idea. This elf, he is a gift, from me to you. Take him and use that memory when you couple and maybe you'll survive the bronze." She gripped her son's face and forced him to look at Eroan.

Heat flushed through him at the thought of Lysander's mouth on him, chilling but at the same time tightening that ball of pleasure, making his member achingly hard. He pulled again at the straps.

Lysander tore his head free of his mother's grip and shoved her hand away. "I'm not fucking him for you."

"Then I will." She beamed. "Maybe he'll survive me. You and I both know most elves don't."

CHAPTER 23

*L*ysander

LYSANDER TRIED to temper the thudding in his chest, the one that matched the hot beat straining his cock against his pants, but really, what was the point in hiding it? He wanted this. He'd started wanting it as soon as the blond had tied Eroan to the bed and stripped him naked, and wanted it a whole lot more when the male had taken Eroan's cock between his lips. There were two ways this could end. He could let his mother fuck Eroan and probably kill him when he didn't play along because, without Lysander, she had no reason to keep Eroan alive. The other option, the one that left him breathless, was for Lysander to give in to his wants, to give in to his mother, and even if Eroan didn't want this, Lysander knew how to make it pleasurable. A few whispers, the right touches.

He'd had male lowers, made them want him, made them beg him to fuck them. Of course, it would be easier if Eroan wanted him too—although nothing about this whole fucked-up scenario likely aroused the elf.

He likes males...

Dare he believe her? And if he did, what did that mean? Here and now, it just meant there was a way out— to make it pleasurable.

Lysander looked at the vision of an elf sprawled on the bed. The lust in him screamed for this to happen. Before now, before the courtyard, he would have, but if he took Eroan here, like this, whatever tiny flicker of hope he had that they might one day be something more would be crushed. Eroan might have forgiven the lashings, but he'd never forgive rape.

Have his mother fuck him, probably kill him, or try to at least make it pleasurable? Whatever way it was dressed up, it was still rape, and he would still be gone tomorrow, leaving Eroan in his mother's grasp.

Lysander closed his eyes and breathed out. "If I do this, he comes with me to the coast."

His mother's purrs made his skin crawl. "On one condition. He must choose to go with you."

For anyone else, of course, they would choose to get away from hell, but not this elf. All Eroan had wanted was to be right here, close to the queen so he could kill her. This elf might like males, but Lysander had seen enough of the assassin's stubborn streak to know he wouldn't throw his life's purpose away to follow Lysander into another dragon-infested pit.

Eroan would choose to stay with the queen no matter the cost.

The elf blinked at him now, breathless and alert. Waiting, like Lysander's mother waited.

One problem at a time.

Lysander approached the bed, stripped off the swords, letting the weapons clatter to the floor, and bared his teeth at the loitering blond, summoning a throaty growl to warn him off. His mother groaned in delight behind him, and that only made Lysander's constant anger knot into a tighter barbed ball in his gut. Fuck her. And him. The blond was a leech, and the bitch-queen could get her rocks off watching. At this point, he was beyond caring.

Eroan's elegant elven eyes tracked him, and a sorry sat unspoken on Lysander's lips. He swallowed it, along with all the regrets and knelt on the edge of the bed. Prowling forward, his glare fused with Eroan's. Whatever was going on in the elf's head, he kept it from his guarded face. Lysander wanted a reaction.

Lysander placed a hand at Eroan's right side and a knee on his left, and prowled higher, keeping himself raised above the elf's panting chest, not touching. Eroan's widened pupils and slightly parted lips did nothing to rein in Lysander's raging desire. He lowered his head, looking deeper into the elf's eyes, trapping him, and whispered two words: "I'm sorry."

Eroan turned his head away, and the hollow ache in Lysander's chest grew larger. So that was the way it would be. What had he expected, really? That Eroan would let this happen? That he'd be okay with being shamed and disgraced, tied to his enemy's bed and fucked against his will.

Desire buzzed hotter, tighter, tangling all the wrongs with the few rights. Lysander pushed onto his knees and tore off his shirt. When he fell forward again and braced his arms on either side of Eroan's shoulders, the elf flicked his gaze back to Lysander's face and let it wander down.

Lysander felt that scorching look as though the elf had his chained hands on him, stroking him, and giving in to the sudden, urgent need to seal this moment in his memory, he brushed his mouth over Eroan's, nudging, teasing, testing. *'Please,'* Lysander's heart screamed, *'please want me.'* He might break apart if he was forced to do this against Eroan's will.

Eroan lifted his chin. The elf's eyes fluttered. Lysander stilled, heart pounding out a relentless beat. Eroan parted his lips, sighed out, lifted his head and darted his tongue across Lysander's lower lip. Lust clutched at Lysander's breaths, cutting them short.

"Don't be sorry," Eroan whispered.

Lysander breathed in those words and tumbled into a messy, plundering kiss. Eroan matched his fervor, so the kiss grew hotter, hungrier, like a fire alive between them. The elf arched beneath him, his heat like the warm, inviting glow of the sun on his wings. Lysander wanted to bask in it, to breathe in this elf and capture him forever inside. He cupped the elf's face and broke the kiss. Brightness filled Eroan's beautiful eyes. Brightness of need, of belonging, but of sadness too. He understood, this stubborn, stupid elf, he understood it all. And Lysander's heart stuttered. How could it be that now they shared this moment?

With a growl masking his wrought groan, Lysander crawled down, running his tongue over Eroan's right pec to where a tiny pebble-like nipple stood erect. He swirled his tongue there and heard Eroan's hiss. Lower, he kissed over the ripple of abs, rising and falling in a panting rhythm, and lower, into the dip at Eroan's waist where the tempting V lured Lysander's mouth.

Lysander flicked his gaze up the beautiful expanse of Eroan's body, and with a grin pulling at his lips, one that seemed to elicit an intensity to Eroan's face, he ran his tongue up Eroan's velvety smooth, hard erection.

Eroan arched again, this time throwing his head back, his hips tilting his arousal, his body seeking to fit itself into something tight. He uttered something smooth and foreign and Lysander happily answered by closing his mouth over the silken steel, tasting salty sweetness. He curled his tongue around the head and flicked, delivering a shot of pleasure that sent a cascade of tremors through Eroan's body. He felt the elf pant, felt his body strumming, and tasted the salty pre-cum. But this was just the beginning. How Lysander ached to bring Eroan to the cusp of screaming his name, only to switch it up and make the sweet anticipation all that more consuming. He could love this male for hours, and to know he wanted this too—

A sword touched Lysander's neck. His sword. He knew its song. He froze, mouth still molded around Eroan's cock.

"There's a good boy... thank you for warming him up. Now, if you don't mind... this one is mine."

Eroan's panting changed from urgent need to those of short, sharp fear. Lysander lifted off and turned his head, scoring his mother with a magic-laden glare. She narrowed her eyes and asked, "Will you fight me on this, Lysander?"

"He's mine." Magic beat inside him like a second heart. Magic and rage and power, fear, and hurt and shame. All of it beat like a drum.

"Get off him now, dear, before he loses the lust. I want to milk it out of him."

Lysander grabbed for the sword's handle. His mother twisted, but not fast enough. She lunged, but he pushed off the bed and sealed his fingers around her throat before she could get a hold of him. Lust and rage pumped power through his veins. He'd kill her, fuck her, tear her to shreds —all at once. His fingers dug into her neck. Oh gods, nothing had felt so right as this.

Breathless, Elisandra's mouth gaped, her one remaining eye flared.

Lysander slammed her into the wall. Bricks and cement buckled. Her beautiful face turned blue, and the rage inside broke open, spilling new strength into his veins. He leaned in, squeezed tighter, and whispered. "Die for me, Mother."

Her struggles slowed. He plastered himself close, still flushed and wanting, but hungry for death, not sex. "For so long, I've been under you." Her lip twitched, and his magic swelled outward, the shift crawling into his bones. "I've suffered your love, succumbed to your whims. No more, Mother! No. Fucking. More."

He held the magic back, damming it while at the same time using it, funneling it. He was stronger, so much stronger than he'd realized, and in her eye, she saw it too. Fear crackled. Real fear. It pulled on her shift, dragging her true form out of the dark.

Her neck snapped with an audible grisly *snick*.

Still, he pushed, crushing her bones into dust. It wasn't enough. Lysander roared and let the magic go, let it all go. Power flooded into the room, into him. He embraced it, took it, used it, shaped it, until he was made of scales and claws, and fangs and wings, and the fire inside of him churned and danced and blazed. He slammed a foot down on his mother's human carcass, curled her limp body into his claws and crushed it inside his fist. The roar didn't sound like his. Maybe because he didn't feel like himself either. Power danced through him, lit by the fury inside and fanned by years of her abuse.

She was dead.

He'd killed her.

His rampant thoughts stuttered.

He'd killed the queen.

Wind rushed from the room as though sucked out. Lysander whipped his head around to view the windows, and there, outside, night had molded itself into the shape of an enormous beast. Akiem. Golden eyes glowed like the fire glowing behind obsidian chest scales, building, churning, rising up his brother's throat. Lysander spread his wings wide, shielding the elf on the bed. His broken wing twitched and bent at an odd angle, but it didn't matter. He lifted his head. He had to protect the elf.

Akiem's fireblast poured in through the windows. Liquid flame spilled over walls, devoured the floor, and slammed into Lysander's chest and wings, washing over his scales. Eyes closed, he dropped his head against the onslaught and bore the weight of heat. On and on it rolled, until he was sure nothing outside of a dragon could survive the blistering furnace. When the fire collapsed, pulled back like a wave receding, Lysander whirled.

The bed, the ropes, it was... ash.

He raked claws through the debris, turning over cinders. No!

It couldn't be. After everything they'd been through,

Eroan had to live. Because if he hadn't lived, what was the point to all of this, what did it matter? The queen was dead...

But so was Eroan.

That fragile hope inside his chest shattered.

A growl rumbled up Lysander's throat, rattling his scales. He bowed his head and charged at the windows. The wall wouldn't stop him. He burst through bricks and stone and lunged, clamping his jaws around his startled brother's neck, sinking his teeth into scale and gristle. Akiem's thunderous roar shook the air. He clawed at Lysander's belly, at his wings, and they both tumbled. Pain, Lysander knew it all too well. They scrabbled, Akiem's wings beating, whipping up a storm, but Lysander had a hold of his brother by the neck and pulled, dragging him out of the air.

roan

EROAN PALMED both of Lysander's swords as he ran from the queen's chamber. The tower jolted, rocking sideways. Thunder ripped through the walls. Dust rained, and still, Eroan ran. When the fire poured in behind him, it licked up his back. He didn't stop.

Every footfall, every beat of his heart sang—*the queen is dead.*

He veered around a corner and plunged the twin swords into a dragonkin's chest, barely missing a step. On, he ran, and cut down more, letting the blades sing for him. In the confusion and noise, he plucked the dragonkin from their life-strings. One, two, three... Until he and the swords were soaked in blood.

Bursting out of the tower's base and into its courtyard, he looked up to see dragons filling the moonlit skies. Two of the beasts tumbled through the air, raking and clawing, teeth flashing. Down, they fell.

Lysander and Akiem.

Eroan watched them fall until smaller spires blocked the sight. Shudders trembled through the earth moments later.

He couldn't help him, not now.

The queen was dead. Freedom was moments away, waiting right outside the walls. All he had to do was pass through the gates while the beasts all gathered in the skies. He wouldn't be noticed.

A roar split the air. He couldn't tell which of them screamed their agony.

Protect him, Carline had said. How could he? This wasn't his world.

It was done.

Eroan turned his back on the tower and jogged toward the stone gateway. As their mangled bellows and screeches rolled into the night, he slipped silently into the dark.

CHAPTER 25

*L*ysander

FLAGS FLUTTERED ALONG PALISADE WALLS. Like snake tongues, Lysander thought. The wall stretched for miles, rose and fell with the hills, severed forests and cleaved through valleys. Lysander knew because he'd been following it for days now. One foot in front of the other, that was all he had to do. One, two, three, four...

Hot sweats and cold shivers racked his body, but he had to keep moving. If he fell, he wouldn't get up. The outside hurt had numbed days ago, the wounds dealt to him by Akiem. But the inside... the inside ached so badly he wanted to fall to his knees and let it consume him. He knew that need. It was the same need that once had him soaring toward the ground with his wing held closed. That voice, that need, it whispered sweet promises of freedom, but it wanted death. And Lysander wasn't ready for that. Not yet. He'd walked too damn far to die now.

"Halt! You there!"

He blinked into the misty rain and up at the watchtower.

"State your business in bronze lands."

My business... Lysander swallowed. *To live,* he thought. His legs buckled beneath him. His hands sank into the cold mud. It writhed through his fingers like Akiem's insides had. He hadn't killed his brother, though. Hadn't been able to...

A gate rumbled open and a stream of bronze soldiers filed out, all in their tarnished armor. The smell of metal and blood swirled around Lysander.

"Your name, visitor?" one barked.

Fog lapped around them, making them seem surreal. *Maybe I am dead,* he thought. *Akiem has killed me after all.* "Lysander Amethyst," he croaked, voice as broken as his body. "The queen is dead."

THE NEXT HOURS or days were a blur of hot and cold, of faded golds and the sound of clanging metal. None of it made any sense, but when he closed his eyes, he saw his hands around Elisandra's throat, felt her bones shatter beneath his fingers, and that didn't make any sense either. The only sound that made any sense was a voice he didn't know but liked to hear. Female. She spoke softly, murmuring in his ear and her touch fluttered lightly over his broken heart. Soon, her voice was joined by the rumblings from a deeper male, one he knew. Dokul. The bronze leader. They spoke of things he didn't want to hear. Of death and chaos. But like an approaching storm taints the air, the truth would soon be on him, and he couldn't hide from it forever.

"You killed the queen."

Lysander blinked into the mug of steaming soup and rolled a few possible answers around his head, tasting the sound of them first. He was somewhere deep inside the bronze stronghold, in a warren of underground tunnels. It had been days since he'd collapsed at their gates. They'd cared for him, fed him, dressed him in simple clothes. This room was warm and close with heavy, moisture-rich air. A table and a couple of chairs. No windows. They didn't have windows here. It all seemed mostly civilized. But then they would, until they got what they wanted out of him. Whatever that might be.

"Amethyst are demanding your return."

The female who spoke was all caramel skin and golden eyes. Lysander's thoughts stalled at the sight of her smooth, hairless head. Even her lips held a warm, bronze sheen like she'd been poured into a mold and hardened into the creature sat at the end of the table. Her rich, tantalizing voice had been the one he'd heard as he'd recovered.

"Who?" he asked. It might even have been the first thing he'd said to her.

"Akiem."

When he'd fled, the skies full of teeth and claw, his brother had lain still and lifeless at the foot of the tower. They had fought before, many times, but never like that. His kin had stalked him for days after, maybe longer.

And now the dragons had a new ruler. "King Akiem."

The name tasted bitter on his tongue. Something inside his shoulder sparked. He rolled it, working out the pain.

"Not our king, and not yours, I think."

Lysander sent her a sideways look.

The golden beauty answered with a smile. "The queen is dead. The tower and her lands are in chaos. We're readying our forces to attack."

The bronze were going to war on two fronts? "What of the frontlines?"

"We can manage. The humans build their machines and we tear them down. It's been like that for centuries. They have nothing new to assault us with. The lines are holding. Their numbers are failing. We haven't seen them in months. It won't be long now before they stop coming altogether."

The bronze were savage and had the numbers, but his brother's intelligence was a vicious thing. Akiem knew how to strategize. A war would be costly. Lysander personally knew every member of the flights who would throw themselves into battle. Many he'd trained and fought alongside. They were honorable, brave. And to think his actions might bring about their deaths. He hadn't wanted that. He'd just wanted the pain to end.

"You came to us... Why?" she asked.

"Perhaps I was fulfilling my mother's deal?" His mouth danced around a smile that never quite appeared.

"Or perhaps you were sent by Akiem to infiltrate our ranks prior to an attack?" The bronze's soft lips lifted at one corner, inviting him to admit the truth.

She was a slippery one, not as blunt as Dokul, with keen, intelligent eyes that had already read him several times. Lysander laughed and lifted his mug to his lips, tasting the rich, syrupy soup. It went down like sweet caramel. "He'd be a fool to attack you."

She leaned forward, jangling the strange metal jewelry around her neck, and spoke softly, "If we assume you came here to seek sanctuary, then I think you've underestimated your brother's pride. The jeweled ones want you back as a matter of justice and honor. Every moment you're free undermines his new rule."

"You have the wrong brother. I can't undermine anything of his."

The bronze's smile grew. She stood and perched herself on the edge of the table beside him. Draped in bronze lamé armor that contoured to her body, she looked as though she'd been dipped in gold.

Lysander allowed his gaze to roam over her powerful physique. She was no lithe, jeweled dragon, and could likely match him in strength as a man. As dragon, he had yet to see, but few bronze dragons were small. Gold glittered on her lashes. Whoever this bronze was, she was important. Dokul's daughter, perhaps? He'd never seen her, but he'd heard much of the warrior-female that mounted betrayers' heads on the stakes lining the palisade walls. Oddly enough, few bronze betrayed their own kin.

Did she count the queen's death as a betrayal?

"Should we start a war over you, prince, or is that exactly what Akiem wants?"

"Let's not fool ourselves." He leaned back in the chair, making the gesture seem casual, but had moved out of her reach. "You've wanted war with the amethyst since my mother killed your queen. My being here gives you a convenient excuse—"

179

ARIANA NASH

"Why did you kill Elisandra?" Delight flashed in her eyes and pulled her lips into an unsettling grin.

Lysander stroked the mug to keep from seeing the bloodlust warming her face. It only reminded him of how this brood operated from the ground up on violence. But he had walked here and surrendered himself to them. He'd known what awaited him. But why had he killed her? It wasn't because she'd threatened him. She'd twisted him around her fingers for years. Neither was it because she'd tortured Eroan, though that had played a large part in it. It wasn't any one thing but a mountain of them, pushed down on him for so long, it finally broke him open.

"I killed her..." he swallowed and ground his teeth, forcing the words up and over his tongue. "...because it was that or fuck her, and you probably know I prefer males." The bronze didn't care who fucked who, just that they did, graphically and in public, for them all to enjoy. He didn't think for a second he'd escaped that fate, but at least he'd earned their reverence. It would save him, buy him enough time to figure his way around this mess. For a little while.

The bronze breathed in, expanding her chest and flaring her nostrils. She dropped off the table and bent over, filling his vision with her glittery eyes. "We'll see, Lysander Amethyst." She spoke so closely, his name touched his lips, tasting sweet and metallic. "My name is Mirann, and you owe me a coupling." She padded away, barefooted, anklets chiming. "I'm the last line of defense between you and my father." She paused at the door and threw a look over her shoulder. "Get strong, prince. War is coming, and you're to be its beating, bloody heart."

CHAPTER 26

The bronze warren stretched along the coastal cliffs, to the end of the world as far as Lysander could tell. Tunnels interconnected, linking living domes with the areas allocated to workers. There were no towers here and no far-reaching views. Just long windowless corridors, torchlight, ventilation fans and the throaty sounds of the central forge bellows. Lysander had often wondered why the bronze wore chainmail mail and little else. Now he knew, the heat made him want to peel his skin off and pant out the excess as dragon.

He dressed in the supple chamois-style leather pants and vest that had been left out for him and found the firestarter buried beneath the clothes. He turned it over in his hand. He couldn't recall bringing it, just the memory in which Eroan had tossed it at his feet and asked him to light a fire—as though it were part playful insult, part wry joke.

Eroan had started a fire all right. One that hadn't burned nearly long enough.

And now the elf was dead.

He closed his fingers around it.

His mother was dead. Akiem was the dragon king. And what was Lysander's place now? All dragons outside the bronze would kill him.

He shouldn't have done it. But he hadn't been thinking about the after. He wasn't sure he'd thought at all, just acted, just closed his hands around her throat and squeezed. He hadn't known he was capable. He *shouldn't* have been capable. The strength that had surged through his veins... it hadn't felt like his at all. And the shift, when it had come over him... It had never been as raw as that before, as visceral.

He shuddered and set the firestarter on a shelf. He wasn't ready to throw it away. If his mother's words of savagery were correct, he might need a few good memories to cling to.

MIRANN WALKED him through the winding corridors, saying little with her words, but her looks were expressive. She ignored any lowers passing by and acknowledged any bronze worth her time with a curt nod. Lysander watched it all and soaked in the smell of hot metal, warm rock, and fire. In human form, all the bronze had a solid roughness he wasn't used to seeing. Jeweled dragons were slimmer, more agile, quicker, like snakes in the grass, but what the bronze lacked in speed, they made up for in muscle, and much of it was on display behind their minimal mail attire and chinking adornments. Anklets jangled. Earrings, nose-rings, arm cuffs glinted like treasures, advertising their wearers' assets, drawing Lysander's wandering eye.

Some of the bronze males looked as though they could crush him with a glance. Most ignored him, though he caught a few curious glances his way. They were made for soldiering, which was exactly what this warren had been created for. Battlements peaked out from the cliff face, drawing in salt water that was likely the reason for the bronze's constant tarnished appearance. Extended perches beat with the constant sound of dragon wings coming and going from patrols.

"Where are we going?"

"My father wishes to see you, now you're recovered."

It had been inevitable. He'd been among them for a few days with Mirann as his guide but so far had avoided Dokul.

"Don't worry." Mirann turned her head. "You're still mine."

Lysander made a mental note to better guard his expression. His mother's deal with the bronze likely still stood, but with Akiem king, and none of his brood old enough to fight to rule, that made Lysander a viable candidate should Akiem lose his grip on the tower. Dokul wasn't about to throw away an opportunity like that one. Lysander hoped. But the bronze chief had been known to throw reason aside to get what he wanted, like stealing the queen's elf because he could.

Mirann heaved open a set of enormous dragon-sized doors, freeing a blast of sweltering air. It rolled over Lysander, almost dropping him to his knees. Sweat plastered his shirt to his back and dripped down his neck. Molten iron churned at the center of a huge natural cavern. Great fans sucked in air, feeding an enormous forge, currently managed by a dozen lower bronze. Metal clanged and rang. Molten iron bubbled.

The dragon in him stirred, wanting to stretch out and bask in the heat. He breathed in, wondered if there was any air left in this place, and saw Dokul by one of many smelting molds.

"New barriers," the chief grumbled without lifting his head. "The armored boats can't breach our defenses, but it pays to be prepared." He finally looked up and regarded Lysander with a flat, unimpressed frown. "She should have known she had a viper in her brood. I saw it coming..." Dokul's gaze slid downward, assessing like a dragon does his next meal.

Lysander straightened his shoulders and shrugged off the sense of unease.

"I tried to get you out from under her before events turned, but she was determined to have one of her whelps in my brood, spreading her jeweled seeds." Dokul's hard mouth formed something of a smile, but before it settled on his lips, it twisted, turning into a leer. "And here you are, Lysander Amethyst. All ours." Dokul stroked at his chin and nodded. "Healed quickly, I see. I hope you left him in a worse state."

Lysander dipped his chin, politely acknowledging the words. Unsure as to what he was supposed to say, he figured no dragon could shrug off praise. "You have an impressive operation here."

"We are the machine protecting the dragonlands, its beating heart of defense!" Dokul boomed too loudly, the sound of it rang over that of clanging metal. "A fact your mother took for granted." Dokul dropped a hand on

Lysander's shoulder and turned him so he had no choice but to walk alongside the bronze chief. In the heat, sweat glistened on the dragon's brow and bare chest, absorbing the firelight, making him seem to glow from within. "Akiem wanted to divide us. Were you aware?"

"No." Lysander didn't strategize, that was his brother's role.

"He believed we'd become too strong a force and were a threat to Elisandra's rule."

Hammers clanged over and over, thudding like Lysander's racing heart. The heat was crawling beneath his skin, trying to unwrap him and spill the dragon out. He wondered how all these bronze could stand working in it without freeing their true selves. If he didn't escape soon, he'd struggle to keep himself controlled.

Dokul's fingers sunk deeper into Lysander's shoulder, verging on pain. He stopped and peered into Lysander's eyes. The bronze's golden eyes took the firelight and honed into something ancient and sharp, and that gaze burned into Lysander, traveling deep, scorching his soul.

"Elisandra's rule was weak," the chief sneered. "With you, we're going to take our destiny back from the jeweled pretenders, back where it belongs, in bronze claws."

"How?"

"Your brother showed us his wants too soon. You are his weakness. He'll do almost anything to get you back so he can demonstrate to his restless brood how he has the right to rule."

Lysander couldn't imagine Akiem would be so foolish as to bargain for his return. His brother should be glad to be rid of him. There had to be more at play here. "Few in

Amethyst will challenge him. My worth isn't so great as for him to make mistakes."

Dokul chuckled luscious rolling laughter and patted his hot hand against Lysander's cheek. "Her greatest achievement was making you believe you are worthless. Soon, you'll come to realize your worth. I'll help you with that..." Dokul chuckled as he walked away. He waved a hand and Mirann appeared by Lysander's side.

"Join me, later, Lysander *Amethyst*," Dokul rumbled. "We have much to discuss."

Mirann's eyes narrowed at her father's back. She cut that look toward Lysander. "You may wander freely but do not attempt to leave, you will be stopped. With force if necessary."

"I'm your prisoner then?"

"Oh," she purred, her smile slithering back into place. "Very much so."

CHAPTER 27

*W*hatever wine Lysander had in his cup, it was hot and spicy, and he was going to need more of it to get through this.

Mirann, her father, and half a dozen of his brood, discussed a breach in one of their defenses, what to do with a bronze who'd committed some heinous crime—the details of which Lysander didn't want to imagine—while Lysander listened, ate, and consumed enough wine to blur the hard edges of this suffocating place. He hadn't seen the sky in days, and while it normally wouldn't have bothered him, coupled with the heat and oppressive atmosphere of so many bronze all packed into their underground warren, he found himself wanting to crawl out of his skin and stretch somewhere outside. Only now did he begin to appreciate how Eroan must have felt shut away from the light.

A few bronze asked about the tower, about the queen, Akiem, his brood. He answered, keeping his replies vague and light. No doubt there were social hierarchies here he had yet to understand. He also watched them closely between wine refills. They touched often. A brush here, a hand there. Amethyst had been the same, but not for him, not for a long time, since they'd learned of his *failures*.

One of the lowers serving at the feast sparked a memory in his mind, but it wasn't until she refilled his drink for the fifth or sixth time that he recognized her. The lower from the amethyst feast. The one he'd tried and failed to fuck as a test.

He took his fresh drink with a tight smile in her direction, but something in his eyes must have tipped her off because instead of continuing to keep her distance, she leaned down, squeezed his thigh, and whispered, "I'm ready to try again when you are."

Mirann tore the lower away from Lysander's side and in a grappling rush that was over in a blink, she dropped the lower to the floor, then stepped over the motionless lower, returned to her father's side at the table, and fell right back into her conversation. It had happened so fast, Lysander could only sit in stunned silence. None of the others seemed to have noticed and certainly didn't care. He looked down at the fallen lower. She wasn't moving. He stared at her chest, waiting for the rise and fall that would tell him she was at least still alive.

He spent the rest of the meal acutely aware of the cooling body and found he'd lost his appetite.

"YOU'RE MINE NOW. She disrespected me by touching you without my permission, especially before the coupling."

So, *that* was still happening. Wonderful.

Lysander dropped onto the end of the bed and fixed Mirann in his swimming vision. She glowed in the doorway, a vision of metal and tawny skin. She'd killed the lower without blinking. It was a lesson he wouldn't soon forget. But as prime a bronze as she was, he would not be able to couple with her.

She strode toward him, planting herself between his knees, and tilted his head up. "I know this is hard for you."

Her hot fingers sizzled against his chin. This whole fucking place sizzled. He wanted to go home, to go back to where the skies were big and the forests sweeping.

"Not hard where I need it though."

She shoved him. Lysander threw a hand back, bracing himself upright, for all the good it did him. Her mouth met his. Her tongue pushed in. He considered blocking her but knew if he resisted, she'd still take him. So he kissed her back, trying to push some feeling into it and failing miserably.

Mirann straightened and stroked his cheek. "It's a shame, truly, but it won't save you."

He licked his lips, rolling them together. She tasted like metal. "It's not you."

"Oh, I know that." She laughed, drifted to the door, and kicked it closed. "But we're going to have to figure out a way to make this happen. Otherwise, our brood will use you up and throw you away." Reaching behind her back, she unclipped the lamé gown and let it slip into a puddle at her feet. Stepping out, she approached Lysander again, bracelets glinting. She wore a tiny diamond piercing in her right nipple. A green circle looped through her belly button, and she had another glittery gem between her legs, clearly visible beneath a neatly trimmed V of golden hair. As far as he could tell, it was the only patch of hair on her.

He should feel something, a stirring, a lick of desire, anything. "I, er... it's the drink."

"Oh, please. Don't insult me by lying." She pressed herself close and settled her hands on his shoulders. "We know all about your desires."

Lysander looked up. She gathered his hands and planted them on her thighs. "It's not the drink, it's up here." She flicked him on the forehead hard enough to sting. "And it's not wrong. You think we care how you prefer males? That's an amethyst hang-up, not ours. You can fuck all the males you like. I'll pick some out for you if you like. But we do care that you can't fuck females. That is a problem. One we need to fix."

"Fix?"

"We have some herbs that help. You'll be so high you won't care what you're fucking, but I'd rather avoid that. Dokul likes the couplings to be... pure."

High he could do if it meant he got it over with. Although, he was skeptical it'd make any difference.

"I can teach you." She reached down and cupped his balls. "This—" her fingers found his limp cock "—is just a blood vessel. Stimulated, you get hard. Males get you off. So think of a lover sucking your cock..." She stroked, applying just enough pressure to ignite something low in his belly. "There we go..."

Lysander opened his legs a little more, letting her hand ease lower. He closed his eyes, blocking her out so he could think around her. There were a string of lovers he could recall, and before Eroan, it had been about the blonds, but now... Now he pulled the image of Eroan spread on the queen's bed. The way his body quivered, not with fear, but with lust. *Don't be sorry.*

Mirann's mouth found his again, and this time Lysander took it, *hungered* for it. Her grip eased, a tug pulled at his belt, then his cock was free for her fingers to close around the head. She squeezed, delivering a glorious tightness that had his balls pulling tight and pleasure licking up his back. The things he could have done with that elf if his mother hadn't stopped him.

"Your problem is keeping it hard."

He fluttered his eyes open, not needing to look to know his cock was no longer playing this game.

She pinched. Pain shot through his dick. "Ah, fuck." Her hands slammed into his shoulders and he fell back, pinned beneath her. He let her crawl up him, his head a drunken mess.

"You have to get out of your head. It's screwing you up."

"It's not something I can just change my mind over or I would have! You don't know what she did—"

She grabbed his cock and balls and squeezed them together in her fist then crashed her mouth over his.

Blinding pain rocketed through him. He couldn't move, couldn't fight her off, and instead stayed frozen and pinned, his heart thumping in his ears.

She broke off, gasping. "You don't need to worry about the queen anymore. You need to worry about me. Only me. Because if you can't perform, I'll be the one who'll tear your throat out. Right after I tear this from between your legs." She yanked.

His teeth chattered as he bared them at her. "Get off me."

She finally let go—allowing Lysander to breathe again —and sat back on his thighs. "You're ours now. I will try to help you, but I can only do so much. I promise you one thing though. You only have to come during the coupling. After that, you can have any male here. None will pass up the chance to fuck Prince Lysander. But not before, you understand? And that includes my father. My claim on you is too important. I will not have it undermined."

His balls throbbed so damn hard he could taste them in his throat. "Fine," he hissed. "Get me those herbs, get me high, because there isn't any other way I'm doing this."

Mirann climbed off. "I'll bring you some."

Lysander cupped his bruised parts then wished he hadn't as they throbbed harder.

"I'm not your enemy."

Mail jangled.

He closed his eyes. "Do you tell that to all the males before you geld them?"

He heard her chuckling laughter long after she'd left.

CHAPTER 28

 roan

EROAN HAD NEVER IMAGED he'd return. None of the Order thought it. When they left the forest with blades clipped to their belts, wrists, and thighs, a righteous fire in their hearts, they left behind their lives and their futures.

He drifted down the winding village track, feeling detached and changed inside, as though he were a ghost and none of this was real. Children playing outside their village huts saw him first and stared, wide-eyed, at his blood-painted chest and face, at his torn trousers, at the stained blades crossed against his back. When they didn't move to greet him, Eroan was sure he had died and this was a dream, one that would guide him to Alumn's blessed garden.

He walked on, closer to the heart of the village. His people began to emerge from inside their homes. Emotion tried to choke him, trip him, rob him of all strength, so he fell, but he kept his eyes ahead, kept his thoughts in line. It wasn't over, not yet. A few more steps.

The village fountain burbled ahead—a natural spring bubbling over granite rocks into a pool. Sunlight sparked across the water, making it appear as though diamonds trickled over the rocks. He knelt and plunged his hands into the basin. Blood flaked off and dissolved, clouding the cool water pink.

Cupping his hands, he splashed his face, gasping at the sudden cold. His heart, so strong a thing until now, fluttered, suddenly fragile and light like it might shatter. Dozens of gazes rode his back. It might even be all the village. They were silent, so all he heard was his own heart thudding. He knew their thoughts: Order assassins never returned.

He rose slowly and lifted his head. Hundreds stared back at him, eyes full of hope, wonder, and fear. Young and old. The Order was here, smudges of dark on the fringes of the crowd, glittering with weapons. Every single one watched and waited for the truth.

He swallowed, unsure if he could find his voice. The crowd shuffled apart, revealing Elder Xena in her fine white robes. Behind her, a female hunter with a bow at her back. Her eyes wide and shining with unshed tears. Janna. He felt himself break. She *knew* him beneath all the blood and wreckage. So this was real, it wasn't some dream he'd buried himself in.

His chest tightened, and his flighty heart threatened to break free.

"You return to us, Eroan Ilanea?" Elder Xena spoke loud and true, lifting her voice so it carried over the sound of the fountain. The voice of reason, the voice of law. But even her gray eyes shone with fragile hope.

He nodded once and swallowed the great swell of emotion, so that when he spoke, it was clear and unbroken. "It is done."

Xena blinked and drew in a sudden breath. Relief flashed across her face. Relief and pride. She turned. "It is done!"

Cries went up, hands reached for him, closed around him, kisses, touches, so much adoration he thought he might drown in it. None cared that he was soaked in the blood. His brothers and sisters from the Order silently bowed their heads, and later, he would be among them, but for now, he let his people weep their joy. Eroan closed his eyes and lifted his head to the sunlight.

The Dragon Queen was dead.

A CELEBRATION HAD sprung and spilled out into the village paths. Drums beat, the elves sang and danced, and Eroan knew he should be among them but wasn't sure his legs would hold him a second more. So he watched them sing, listened to their sweet, feathered voices, and let the sound of it lull his frayed thoughts.

"Go." Xena's silvery eyes sparkled. Beside him, she bowed her head and whispered, "There will be time to celebrate again. They'll not notice your absence."

He tipped his head and forced his weary body from where he'd wedged himself against a wall. He could barely remember what hut was his—it had probably been given away—and stumbled toward one when a warm, soft hand slipped in his and firmly guided him on. Janna offered a smile, but he couldn't return it. A numbness had infected him since the fountain. Exhaustion, probably. Shock, too. He knew the symptoms but couldn't seem to organize his thoughts enough to pull himself out of it. He should be happy, should be celebrating with them.

Janna guided him through a low door into her hut. He took a step into the warmth, then another, but on the third, he went to his knees. The wall he'd built around himself had broken open, and now the flood of anguish was coming. He couldn't stop it, could only let it happen, and he buried his face in his hands. The pain of being trapped in the dark, drenched in fear, buried under his own self-loathing and disgust. He remembered the dragons on him, flashes of madness, the queen's claws, his bones withering to nothing without the light. What they had done... it was inside him, rotting him like a cancer. He reeked of dragon, of blood and death, of that tower and its dungeons, of the queen and her vicious intent.

"Shh..." Janna gathered him close. He buried himself against her chest. Silent tears soaked them both. He wanted to tell her why, tell her everything, but all the words choked him. Most of all, he wanted to tell her how he had returned but feared he shouldn't have. He wasn't like them now, wasn't as they remembered him. Eroan Ilanea, assassin of the Order. He didn't know who he was. Something inside had been lost or left behind in that tower, and now he was hardly here at all.

"Eroan," Janna whispered. Her hand stroked over his hair. "It's all right."

No, it wasn't. It never would be again. He couldn't tell her, though he wanted to. He ached to have the words out of him so they no longer festered. But it was too soon and too much, and all he wanted right now was to be held, so he knew he wasn't alone in the dark anymore.

"I'm sorry..." Her voice caught.

He heard another say he was sorry—Lysander—the only ray of light in that forsaken place. And he had left him there.

Eroan pushed out of Janna's arms and stumbled to his feet, fighting off her reaching hands.

"Eroan." She stood too, and came closer.

"Don't." He needed to think his way out of the dark, to take his thoughts from that terrible place and turn them toward some good. "It's fine. I just..." He fumbled with the swords. When the latch opened, he shrugged the sheaths off and gently rested the stained blades against the hut wall. *Lysander's* blades. Stained with the blood of the dozen dragonkin Eroan had cut down as he'd ran. The blood had dried, turning near-black, but some of the sharp edges shone through.

His thoughts stuttered.

"Where do they bury their dead?" he asked.

"What?" Janna crept closer, her steps careful and light.

"Their dead..." He looked up and blinked, clearing his swimming vision. Janna's long, green-hued white hair framed an innocent face, one he had seen in his mind and clung to in the longest moments of darkness. But here, now, she was too bright a thing, too innocent a thing. She looked at him with wide, doe-like eyes. His skin itched, dried blood cracking. The scars on his back tightened, then those on his chest. He rubbed over his heart. Then, to his horror, he remembered the collar. It was still there.

He dug his fingers into the thick leather. They had

seen... everything. The scars, the blood, the collar. Shame roiled through him, turning over his stomach. It was all he could do not to run from her gaze, from his people. He stepped back. The room twisted out from under him.

"A knife." He tugged on the collar, briefly choking off his own air and the memories rushed in. The bronze bastard's hands around his throat, his other hand on his arousal. The queen jerking him like a pet on a leash. "Janna, a knife!"

He reached for the wall and managed to prop himself upright. His stomach heaved, body trying to reject the memory. Janna plucked a hunting knife from her belt and approached with fear in her eyes, and that only made all this worse.

He reached out a hand, fingers shaking too much. "Cut it off me."

She didn't move, and his gut heaved again. "Janna, I'm not going to hurt you. Cut it off, please..." *Please, get it off, then cut out this wrongness inside of me.* He rested his head against the wall and closed his eyes. His heartbeat thudded too loud in his ears, and the darkness was flooding in, trying to swallow him. "Hurry."

The blade touched his throat, pushed down, and sliced through the leather with a gasp.

Free.

Janna's warm hand cupped his face. He opened his eyes and wondered how she could even stand to be so close to him. Then she was on her toes, her arms flung around him. "It's all right now. You're home."

He pulled her close, buried his face in her hair and breathed in the pine and cut timber smell of home. It hurt, it hurt so much that without her holding him up, he would have fallen and not stopped falling. He dug his fingers in, afraid to lose her, afraid she might turn to smoke, revealing this was all a dream, and he was still deep inside the bowels of the tower, still chained in the dark, waiting for death.

It wasn't over. Not for him. The shudders passed.

"I know how to kill them all," he whispered.

CHAPTER 29

The Order—what little remained of them seated around the table—regarded Eroan with wide-eyed awe that set his teeth on edge. They hadn't yet bombarded him with questions, but the barrage would come, better to deal with it now and get it over with.

He dumped Lysander's blades on the table and shoved, sending them skidding down the timber, so all twenty-two of the remaining assassins could get a good look at the vicious recurved design. He hadn't cleaned them. The blades were ripe with stale blood and dragon. All of the Order would need to become familiar with the smell for what he had planned. "At first, I thought these swords were forged steel, but take a closer look." They did, reaching out to touch and then recoiling at their tacky stickiness. "They're teeth, highly polished and shaped into that style." Murmurs drifted between them, questions bubbling. "And they're the only thing that can pierce dragonscale."

"You've seen it?" Hussan asked. "You've seen these blades pierce their scales?"

Eroan fixed the young assassin under his glare. He seemed younger than he remembered, but now he supposed they all looked young and too eager to die. "Yes."

The warriors picked up the blades and passed them around. "Why do they have these at all?" Seraph asked, the earring in the tip of her ear twitching as she arched her eyebrow. Before leaving for the tower, Eroan had told her to remove that gem from her ear, and there it was, still there. She likely believed he'd never return to know she'd disobeyed.

"When they shift into human," he explained. "They move freely about their domains. The one who had these..." He licked his lips, hoping they hadn't noticed the way his voice hitched. "He carried them with him at all times and used them effectively, either as swords or throwing weapons."

Memories clawed at him. It was too soon, just a day had passed since he'd returned. He straightened and moved about the table, hoping to temper the flutter of panic tightening his chest. Just so long as he could keep himself together in public. The only alternative was to sit and rot in Janna's hut. This was too important to wait.

"You killed him then," Seraph said. She handed the blade off to Kaja beside her. "Else he wouldn't be without them now." Her smile was an innocent thing, but it still sliced deep into Eroan's heart. "It must have been glorious," she went on. "I wish I'd been there to see it."

The others all grinned and murmured their agreements.

Eroan closed his hands into fists. "My pride was slaughtered. Lyel, Reese, Kine, Brend." The names of the dead rang likes bells. All assassins. All who had been seated at this table, just like they were now. "Slain before we reached the tower walls." His tone shut them down. "There is no glory in death, Seraph. When it comes, there's no epiphany, no sudden realization or justice. It's brutal, it's drawn-out, you might die clutching your insides, trying to shove them back where they belong, or you might feel the pull of a blade across your throat and taste your lifeblood spilling over your tongue. Death is not a celebration of life. It's cruel and uncompromising and a bitter waste."

Seraph bowed her head, the tips of her ears turning pink. "I didn't mean to speak so lightly of it."

"Clearly, you did."

"I'm sorry, sassa," she mumbled, adding a term of respect.

"Don't be sorry, be smarter." He folded his arms and straightened to regard the rest of the Order. Only Curan and Nye were older than him, and they watched silently, warily, likely remembering how their hero had returned to them painted in blood.

Eroan rubbed at his neck. "There's a dragon graveyard two days' hike from here, near the borders. I want four prides to go there, dig up their teeth and bring them back."

"We're making new weapons?" Hussan asked.

"Yes. But not just for us. There aren't enough of the Order left to stop them."

"Then who?"

Curan narrowed his eyes. The older assassin had likely been in charge before Eroan's return. Eroan returned his gaze now. "I'll tell you when you return."

The group filed out. "Seraph," Eroan stopped her before she could slip through the door.

She turned and seemed to straighten as though lifting her shoulders could make her seem bigger. She wasn't the strongest here, nor was she the brightest, but she was fast and lethal. Traits he'd honed into her before his leaving.

"Take the earring out."

She blinked rapidly and reached up to touch the gem. "Sassa, I—"

"I don't want excuses. Do it, or I'll tear it out myself when you least expect it. Do I need to explain again why it's inappropriate? We must always be ready."

"Of course, sassa." She unclipped the earring, tucked it into her pocket, and hurried after the others, leaving Nye and Curan behind, seated at the far end of the table. Thankfully, they didn't wear the awe-struck gazes of the young ones. Curan and Nye knew him too well to place him high on a pedestal. Shame tried to heat Eroan's face. He turned his thoughts to the blades instead and caught Nye looking them over too.

Nye's black mop of hair and dramatic sloping eyes contrasted with most of the elves in the village. He had never cared to dance around his words and wouldn't now. Eroan didn't have to wait long for him to make his thoughts known. "The last time we partnered with humans, they betrayed us and left us on the wrong side of their ocean." And there it was, Eroan's plan right out in the open.

"But they also suffered enormous losses, rendering them almost extinct."

Curan glanced between them both. Bigger, broader, the scar running down the right side of his face regularly frightened the children. In truth, the scar was the hardest thing about the male. Inside that guarded exterior was a heart that cared too much. "Shouldn't you take some time?"

"What for?"

Curan raised an eyebrow as though asking if it was really necessary for him to spell it out. "To recover... from your *ordeal*."

Eroan folded his arms crossed. "Xena has given me the all-clear. Are you going to argue with her?" Luckily, Xena hadn't seen him come undone in Janna's arms last night or the elder would have ordered him to rest up. He'd lose his mind *resting*. He needed to be *doing*.

Curan sniffed. "You could tell her the sky is purple and she'd agree with you." The assassin rose and bridged his fingers on the table-top, eyeing Eroan in the same way he imagined he'd appeared to Seraph. The older elf had never challenged Eroan's authority, until now. Eroan wouldn't have much of an argument either. The others had missed all the signs, too wrapped up in the mystique of his return, but neither Curan or Nye were so easily fooled. Eroan's fingers still trembled when his gaze wandered. He looked at them behind crossed arms now, but they saw. They couldn't miss the raw grazes on his neck either.

Curan pushed upright. "Your sacrifices haven't been ignored, brother. Nobody is going to blame you if you take some time to recover."

"Time?" he laughed. "Amethyst are in chaos. The dragons are in turmoil. This is our opportunity. We won't get another like it in decades, if ever. We need to move on this now."

Curan stilled, considered it, and nodded. "Do what you

must, but make sure your judgment is clear." He left, leaving only Nye behind like a shadow simmering in the corner.

"No sage words from you?" Eroan asked.

Nye stood, scraping his chair back and squared up to Eroan. The elf's gaze flicked to Eroan's grazed neck—the pattern of the collar clearly visible—and back up to his face. Eroan waited for the scorning words, words that would strip his flimsy barriers and reveal the raw wounds behind, but Nye said nothing, and left moments later, which somehow felt worse than if he'd said what they were all thinking... that Eroan was walking the fine edge of reason and gambling with the lives of too few Order elves.

He collected Lysander's blades and hesitated. The twin blades weighed less than a single elven one. Their design was art and function. Had Lysander made them himself, fashioned them from amethyst teeth? No other dragon had possessed anything like them. There was surely a story behind them, one Eroan would probably never know. And now they might be the key to unlocking the solution that would see the dragons fall back into the earth from where they came.

He ran a hand down the sweep of one, brushing his fingers over their filthy roughness. He should clean them, free them, make them his, and he knew exactly where to do that.

CHAPTER 30

*E*roan waded toward deeper water where the surface churned and the noise from the White-lady waterfall drowned out the thoughts in his head. Soaked through, he shrugged off one sword and plunged it beneath the surface. After a few brisk strokes, it came up clean and smooth again. He plunged the second sword in and scrubbed it clean.

If only it were that easy to clean their taint off me.

He'd washed last night in the near darkness, not long after weeping in Janna's arms, but he still felt the sting of the dragons' invasive touches on his arms, his wrists, and around his neck. It hadn't mattered in the prison, or even in the queen's bed. He hadn't expected to survive, to come back, to live with this knotted wrongness inside of him.

Movement near the water's edge caught his eye. He lifted his gaze from the blades and found Nye standing on the pebbled bank. And there it was, Nye's raw look, the one that betrayed Nye's thoughts. More shame knotted inside, tightening into an acidic ball, leaving him with a sickness he couldn't shake.

Wading back to shore, he set the swords carefully down on the stones.

"I thought you might be here last night." Nye's cheek fluttered. He looked at the crossed swords, probably considering the best way to launch into all the questions on his mind.

Wrapped in all black, he looked like the shadows he preferred to move among. Had this been night, Eroan wouldn't have seen him on the riverbank. It made Nye an effective hunter and a ruthless assassin. But in stark daylight, he seemed sharper, harder, like a piece of cut flint.

Eroan wrung out the damp ends of his hair and squeezed water from his shirt. "You shouldn't be here. Do you not have patrols?"

Nye's shapely eyebrow arched. He glanced behind him, where trees lined the bank, knowing they were unlikely to be disturbed. Few came to the falls. The roaring waters made it risky should anything bigger be out hunting.

"I thought you were gone." Nye's gaze tracked past Eroan to the plunge pool.

"I was." *A part of me still is.*

The elf's mouth twitched but not to find a smile. "We're not supposed to care," he said softly.

Eroan could hardly chide him. He'd cared too. But he'd let it all go when he'd walked away, his pride of elves walking to their deaths beside him. They weren't supposed to feel because it made leaving easier, but they *could* feel. If it hadn't been for the memory of Janna, Eroan might have lost his mind in the prisons.

"What were they like?" Nye asked. He tucked his thumb into a hip pocket and leaned to one side but still looked down, or out at the water, anywhere but at Eroan.

He didn't look at him because he knew what the dragons had done. Eroan felt unclean. Like he should turn and dive into the pool, and maybe the water would cleanse some of his soul. "You know."

Eroan was done here. He couldn't stomach the questions that would follow, not from Nye, not from anyone. He scooped up the swords and trudged up the bank, but when he turned back, Nye had waded into the water. The elf clasped his hands together and fully clothed, dove under, disappearing from sight.

Eroan scanned the surface, more curious than anything else.

When Nye resurfaced mid-stream, water plastered his black hair down his face. Treading water, he shook his head and ran both hands back through the locks, pulling them back from his face. The falls swallowed all sound, so all Eroan saw was the ludicrous smile on Nye's lips. A smile that tugged at his own.

He should get back to the village before Xena worried, or Curan came looking for them both. Or worse, Janna tracked him down here. But he was already soaked, so what were a few more minutes in the water? It was the only place his thoughts didn't bother him.

Nye was gone again, vanished beneath the surface.

Eroan set the swords down and strode into the water. When Nye broke the surface, Eroan stood at the edge of an underwater shelf. If he took a step farther, he'd plunge off the edge. Water lapped around his waist, tempting him closer. But he couldn't seem to bring himself to take that final step.

Nye saw him and swam close, but kept enough distance between them to leave questions hanging. This close to the waterfall where the water clouded the air and the falls thundered about them, there was no point to words, the roaring water would eat them. Eroan looked on, wondering too many things.

Nye's eyebrow arched, tilting his smile with it. Treading water, he crossed his arms over his chest and submerged. When he kicked back to the surface, he tossed the shirt behind Eroan, revealing the smooth roll of water-lapped dark-skinned shoulders.

Eroan wasn't supposed to be here, this wasn't supposed to happen. Janna and he... But Nye's long looks through the years had left Eroan wondering if the elf felt more than Order camaraderie. And then it had been Eroan's turn to take a pride to the tower, and he'd been gone with those things in Nye's gaze left unsaid. Nye kicked backward, and Eroan admired the contrast of hard muscle and smooth skin. Sunlight kissed at Nye's arms, down his chest, and into a narrow waist. A long, tightening pleasure started down low, enough for Eroan to adjust his trousers. Nye couldn't see how Eroan's body responded beneath the waterline. Although, from his smirk, he had likely guessed.

Nye rolled over and swam long-form to the opposite bank. He climbed out, and Eroan lost his thoughts in how the water glued the trouser fabric to Nye's hips and thighs. Nye reached up and ruffled his wet hair, knowing how Eroan watched. And when he padded along the bank, Eroan's gaze fell shamelessly to where Nye's trousers peaked.

It wouldn't have been right to entertain these thoughts before. Things had changed. Against all the odds, Eroan had returned. And now he had a second chance to explore the possibilities he hadn't allowed himself before, like the reason for Nye's long glances and heavy silences.

Eroan dove in and under. Warm water swallowed him whole. He kicked hard and remerged gasping, near the opposite bank, sweeping his hair back and searched for Nye. He must have vanished along the rock path where it wove its way behind the falls. There was nowhere else for him to go. Eroan waded from the pool, short, sharp breaths betraying a renewed sense of anticipation and perhaps a little fear, though he quickly dismissed it and balanced along the narrow path to push through the curtain of water.

A memory tried to sink its claws in.

Water falling, pummeling his torn back, his fingers on the metal grate, blood swirling down the drain. And then Nye was there, propped against the rock wall like he had all the time in the world to wait for Eroan to take the bait.

This didn't have to mean anything. In fact, Eroan preferred it didn't. He stepped in, cupped Nye's face, tilted it up and almost fell into the kiss. But the male he imagined wasn't Nye. He let his eyes flutter closed and imagine another in his hands, a male with eyes of green and lips curved in a cocky, teasing smile. This male Eroan dreamed was a different kind of killer, not an elf at all, but his enemy, making his desire a forbidden thing. Eroan kissed Nye like he needed to breathe him in. He tasted all wrong, all elf, not dragon, but Eroan discarded that thought. His memory filled in the blanks and painted over the wrongs. Nye's smaller frame was replaced by the larger, more muscular design that Eroan had so wanted to touch but with his wrists bound, he'd never had the opportunity.

Eroan drove his tongue in, exploring Nye, taking the kiss, and Nye gave it all back, nipping and nudging, wanting more, coming alive in Eroan's hands. This heated kiss—this alone was worth the risk.

Eroan maneuvered Nye back against the rock face. Nye hissed, either in pain from the rocks or pleasure. His dark eyes said pleasure, and reckless need strummed through Eroan, notching the raw lust higher. He eased Nye's thighs apart, just enough for him to ride his hand up Nye's thigh and knead his hand against Nye's erect member through the trouser fabric. Nye let his head fall back, and Eroan ran his hand higher, pushed his thumb in and over. Nye bucked, growled a curse, and Eroan leaned in, pinning him still, his own desires coming undone. The sounds of Nye's panting matched his own. He bowed his head, brushing his chin against Nye's cheek, and imagined it was Lysander's jaw he ran his tongue along.

The prince had roused a sleeping beast in Eroan. A beast of want that had always been there but was only now stirring to life, stretching, filling him and breaking free.

"You've no idea how long I've wanted this..." Nye gasped. "Wanted you." He palmed Eroan's rigid arousal, molded his fingers and thumb around it and worked it slowly. Sharp, desirable tingles darted through Eroan, stealing his breath, stealing his thoughts, almost his strength too. "I wasn't sure..." Nye went on. "You were untouchable, like wildfire."

Eroan listened, let the words sink in and shiver through him, but in them, he heard more than careless lust. Nye had cared. Eroan did too... but every touch was

Lysander's hand, every breath on his neck from Lysander's lips. He remembered Lysander's mouth on his arousal, his tongue working its magic, and even though it had been so wrong at the moment, so twisted and dark, by Alumn, it had felt so right.

Nye's gaze fell on Eroan's face, and guilt stabbed him in the chest. Eroan braced an arm against the rocks, suddenly ashamed that he'd think to use his friend like this. "I can't do this..." *for you,* he wanted to finish. *Because you want more and I... don't.*

Nye's hand tightened and pulled. Blinding pleasure jerked Eroan's hips toward the source of that delicious friction. "This says you do." Nye locked a hand around the back of Eroan's neck and pulled him into a fiery, plundering kiss.

Between Nye's hand and his hot mouth, Eroan thought he might be losing his mind. But he knew one thing. He didn't use people. He had more honor than that. The dragons hadn't taken that last shred of decency from him.

He tore free of the kiss and breathed, "Nye, stop."

"Don't—" Nye let go but threw that arm around Eroan's neck and held him close, so all Eroan saw was the fierceness in his friend's eyes, one fractured with fear. He hadn't meant to do this to Nye. "Don't push me away when I've just found you again."

The falls still raged behind Eroan, blocking out everything but Nye and Eroan's own messed-up thoughts. Thoughts of a dragon he couldn't have, thoughts of the very cruel and sharp desire cutting through him. "I can't do this, Nye. It's not... right." He tried to pull free but Nye's arm tightened, and Eroan's paltry efforts fizzled to nothing.

"It doesn't matter what was done to you. Nobody cares, Eroan. They love you for who you are. I..." Nye stopped, tripping over what came next.

Eroan kissed him to cover the words. He couldn't stand to hear them. He wasn't ready for this. He wanted Nye, but only because he was here, because Eroan could forget the horror he'd endured and make up some forbidden fantasy in his head that would cover it all.

"You don't have to pretend with me," Nye breathed. He arched his hips, giving himself to Eroan's hand. "Don't think. Just... just be here, just do this. The rest... the rest needn't mean anything. Please..." Nye growled out the word like he hated it. "For so long I didn't act and then you were gone. I need this. We both need this."

Those words, they released him of guilt. His blood ached for this, ached for him to lose himself in someone. Anyone. Just so he could forget who he was supposed to be and who they had made him into.

Eroan gritted his teeth and tore at Nye's belt, flicking it open, freeing the male's taut erection. He had it hot in his hand in the next breath and had the male panting moments after. Harder, he pumped, feeling something ugly swell inside him. A hurt, a want, a muddle of things that didn't make any sense.

"Wait, wait!" Nye brushed him off, shoved at Eroan's shoulder and marched Eroan back against the rock face. "Take it slow, sassa..." Nye drawled.

Hard, cold rock sank into Eroan's shoulders, reminding him of another wall, one buried deep within the bowels of the dragon's tower. Old scars sizzled awake. His biceps burned from the strain of holding his arms above his head, wrists too, where the chains cut in. The chains were gone now, but in his mind, they were still there, weighing him down. Fresh, bitter panic fluttered in Eroan's throat. "Nye, I can't, not now—"

Nye plunged his tongue in, swallowing Eroan's denials. Eroan couldn't breathe. Couldn't think. He heard the door rattle, saw the lantern light, saw the queen smile her slippery serpentine smile and felt his wrist shatter. She laughed. Hot hands on him. The bittersweetness of dragons on his tongue. Carline's words to protect a lost prince. A severed cock forced down a bronze's throat.

"Eroan... sassa...hear me?"

He blinked back to himself, back to the now and stared at the stranger searching his eyes for something that seemed to frighten him. Water roared, and the same cold, wet rocks cut into Eroan's back. But no, this wasn't the same place. Light played through the water here. What was this place?

"I'm sorry... " Nye said, blinking water from his eyes. "It's too soon. I... Eroan, did I hurt you?"

'I'm sorry. Don't be sorry.' Eroan blinked and Lysander was gone. Of course he was gone. He'd never been here. Nye was here. His friend. He was home again. He rubbed at his wrists, surprised to find them chain-free. "No. I'm well. I just..." He looked down between them, at his limp member, at Nye's still proud and wanting and knew this couldn't happen. Not yet, maybe never.

Eroan rubbed a hand across his mouth and tucked himself away. What had he been thinking? "This was a mistake. Don't talk of this again."

Nye moved in, crowding too close. "It's too soon, that's all. I'll wait—"

"Don't fucking wait, Nye. Just get on with your life. I'm

not back, I'll never be back. Get off me." Eroan shoved Nye aside and stepped to the ledge's edge. The waterfall raged in front of him, a rushing white wall... falling, falling, never-ending. "Get *over* me." He stepped off the ledge and plummeted into the pool.

CHAPTER 31

*A*fter changing out of his wet clothes, Eroan was met with the formidable sight of Janna and Xena seated at Janna's main table. Cups of tea steamed in front of them. Xena's half-finished. He hadn't heard them at all while he'd been changing, but then he'd had other things on his mind.

"This looks like an ambush..." he drawled, adding a smile in hopes it would ease the tension.

They both smiled politely. Janna moreso. Xena had heard it all before. The lines around her eyes crinkled but that was all he was getting from the elder.

Eroan didn't feel much like sitting across from them. Restless energy still buzzed through his veins. He'd planned to head to the Order and see if anyone would take him up on some sparring sessions, but nobody dismissed Xena, not when she clearly had come for a reason that involved staying long enough to drink tea.

Eroan planted himself against the wall. "We haven't heard back from the prides yet. It'll be another day before they return with the teeth. I don't know what was used to shape the enamel, but I have some ideas..." He trailed off. Xena's soft smile somehow chided and patronized all at once. His gut told him he wasn't going to like why she'd come.

"That's not why I'm here."

He figured he knew why, especially when Janna suddenly found her tea so fascinating. She'd told Xena about his breakdown.

Eroan's mouth twitched. He rubbed at it. "You want to take me out of the Order?"

"Temporarily," Xena confirmed, so careful and quiet. But therein lay her power. She didn't need to argue. Whatever she said, whatever she wanted, it happened. Her word was law.

If he didn't have the Order, what was he supposed to do? "I'm fine. There's no need to remove me."

"Take some time, Eroan."

Time. What was time supposed to do? Somehow magic all the past away? Why did everyone keep telling him time would help? Time would do nothing but make the rot in him fester. "Time changes nothing."

"Eroan," Janna chided, nipping off his sharp tone.

Xena merely smiled and sipped at her tea. "Few here will understand what you're going through. We live a sheltered life, protected behind the Order. Many don't consider the sacrifices you make. They don't like to think about the horrors beyond the village. Horrors you protect us from."

And that was fine. He didn't want everyone knowing what he'd done. He folded his arms over his chest and resigned himself to listen to the elder. Whatever she said, though, he wasn't leaving the Order.

"Curan has offered to step up."

So Curan had been speaking with her too.

"In your absence, he made a fine leader."

"My absence?"

Xena's eyes hardened. "When we experience terrible things, our instincts tell us to block it out and move on, but soon, there's nowhere left to run and those memories catch up with us, usually at the worst possible time."

"I said I'm fine."

"It's been less than two days, Eroan," Janna said.

"You'll be stepping down as the Order's leader with immediate effect," Xena went on. "I have another role for you. I would like you to be a part of the ruling council alongside me."

She was retiring him. "An elder?" He couldn't keep the scorn from his voice. "You want me to govern, to settle menial arguments, discuss border and harvests?" He snorted a dry laugh. "I'm not you, Xena." He'd lose his mind if he had to stay in the village for the rest of his days knowing what awaited out there. No. He couldn't do it. Wouldn't do it.

"We need a strong warrior on the council."

"You don't need a strong warrior on the council, you need one out there." He flung a hand at the door. Outside, the sounds of children laughing rang like distant celebration bells. Children he protected. A village he had spent his whole life protecting. He could not stop now.

Xena let the words settle, let the sounds drift into the hut. "And we need fathers."

Eroan glanced at Janna and saw the flush creep up her

pale cheeks. They'd already been discussing this. Over tea. She flicked her eyes up. "Children, Eroan. A family."

The hope and desperate need in her voice only made him feel more wretched inside. Not only was he to be cut out of the Order, he was to be retired to some fatherly role he didn't want.

"We haven't heard from the East since you left," Xena explained. "We know Cheen has lost its prime males. Their numbers are dwindling. Our numbers are dwindling. We need children, Eroan, or there will be nothing left for you to protect."

Him? A father? He was barely in his prime. "Curan is ten years my senior. Have him retire."

Xena blinked. "Curan has declined."

"He gets a choice but I don't?"

"Yes, of course. But not on the Order. You're not to return to your role there until I am convinced you've sufficiently recovered from your trauma. Our warriors are too important. Perhaps, if you were to consider becoming an elder, you'd have the power you feel I'm taking from you now."

He laughed and didn't care that it sounded ugly. "Maybe you should tie my wrists to the wall? I see little difference."

"Eroan!" Janna shot to her feet. Her cup toppled, spilling tea across the table. "Apologize immediately." She turned to Xena. "I'm so sorry, he didn't mean—"

"I meant it." It had felt good to bite back, to watch the careful and polite rules come undone. He wanted to upset it some more, but then he caught Xena's kind, understanding look and the spite deflated, leaving guilt and self-loathing behind.

"It's all right," Xena said, directing the words toward Eroan. "Your anger is perfectly normal. There will be more of it. It leaves you vulnerable and unstable, and you know it, Eroan, so do not stare back at me as though I am your enemy. I have seen terrible things, just as you have. You and I have more in common than you realize. I know what those dragons are capable of. If you wish to talk, I am here for you."

"I don't need to talk. I need to act!" he snapped. "We need to build alliances with humans and share what I've learned regarding the new weapons. I can't do that if you're cutting me out, Xena. You need to reconsider this. I'll not be retired to some menial role fathering children I don't want." Janna flinched. Eroan felt the words twist in his gut. It was too late to take it back now. "I can make a difference."

"Yes, you can, as an elder. Now, if you'll excuse me. We have an infant girl born just last night, and I'd like to meet her. Perhaps you should come, Eroan?"

He stared at the elder, his heart squeezing into something small and hard. "I can't be what you want me to be."

"You must. It's your duty."

He stared at the door long after she'd left and Janna cleared the spilled tea away. His duty? He'd given everything, his whole life, to the Order. He'd lived every second perfecting himself into a weapon. One to protect, one to kill, and in one normal, friendly conversation over tea, Xena had taken it all from him.

"I should have died."

Janna gasped, shocking him into realizing he'd spoken aloud. The words were out now. He almost apologized, but what good would it do? It was true. He couldn't be an elder, a father, that wasn't his life, not now... before, maybe.

He looked around him, at hopeful Janna, at her modest hut with its neat little tables and chairs, quaint fireplace and bed. How could he ignore the monsters outside? Was he supposed to just pretend they didn't exist? "I can't do this."

"Eroan, no." She reached for him, tears shining in her eyes.

He backed away, feeling betrayed. "You know I can't be a father to your children. You know this! You've always known this..."

He left her weeping, hearing her sobs long after he'd entered the Order's long meeting hut. The flights hadn't returned. It didn't matter. He took two daggers from the racks, unbuttoned his shirt, giving himself room to move, and stood in the center of the training floor. It was quiet here, and with the blades in his hands, his mind was a quiet place too.

He started the familiar motions, sweeping the daggers through the air, his muscles remembering each stance without him having to think through it. Like a dance he'd known his whole life, he fell into the rhythm. The ache in his wrist made his right hand stiff. He worked with it, using the pain and the memory to make each thrust fatal, each slice vicious. He practiced until his arms burned and his shirt clung to him, but anger was still there. If anything, it was worse, like a demon on his back.

The more he tried to fight it off, the more it sunk its claws in.

He straightened back into a neutral pose and tried to

channel the rage into something cleaner, something he could use.

"Xena spoke with you," Curan grumbled behind him.

Eroan tightened his grip on the daggers and tried to steady his breathing. "Lead the Order if you want, but I'm not leaving."

"I didn't want this, but you must see it's for the best."

Eroan flicked the blades in his hands and returned them to the rack, placing them firmly home, only then could he meet Curan's gaze. The pity in the older elf's eyes felt like betrayal, like they'd seen him return with a collar around his neck and thought him weakened or changed. Tainted. Clearly, they didn't want that rot in the Order.

Curan brushed a hand over his hair and down the back of his neck. "You'll see, eventually, that we're trying to help you."

He could see that. And this wasn't Curan's fault. Had Eroan been the one standing there and watching their leader fall apart, he would have done exactly the same. The Order was too important to allow its weakest link to hold it up.

"You're right," Eroan sighed.

Curan lifted his head.

"The Order is my life. I'll protect it at any cost, including removing myself from command." Eroan approached until he stepped inside Curan's space. "But I won't be set aside like a broken blade."

"Xena's orders were explicit—"

"I've seen their inner workings; how weak they are together. With the queen gone, they're in turmoil. It will take time for them to pick a new ruler and settle. There will be power struggles. While they're focused on their own ranks, we can strike as a united force. Humans and elves, and we do it for the first time with weapons that can bring them down from the skies."

The older elf frowned. "With swords?"

"Not swords. Arrows."

"Arrows? We'd need a thousand to bring down a single dragon. We don't have a thousand archers left."

Eroan smiled. "Not a thousand. Just two. Tipped with dragons' teeth."

"Two?" Curan frowned and mumbled, "I can't decide if you've lost your mind or if you're a genius."

Eroan patted him on the shoulder and headed out. "A little of both, my friend."

Nye jogged into the main hut, Eroan's dragonblades in his hand. "Three of the prides returned early. They were ambushed by a stray. One is missing." He handed out the swords.

"Which one?" Eroan asked, throwing the swords on. Xena be damned. He wasn't sitting back, not for her, not for anything.

"Seraph's."

Nye collected a brace of daggers and nodded at Curan. The older elf locked his questioning sights on Eroan.

Eroan waited for the words that would shut him out and push him aside. Curan was the leader now, and Eroan obeyed the Order above all else, above even Xena. Always had. If the elf said the word for him to stay behind, then Eroan would be faced with breaking his oath to the Order, and that was not something he could take back. It would be over for him. Curan, not Xena, held Eroan's destiny in his hands.

Curan nodded. "Let's go."

CHAPTER 32

On approach, draped in dusklight, the huge bones arching out of the ground looked like bent trees leaning into the wind. But there were no trees here. Nothing larger than moss and brush grew where dragons left their dead.

Eroan climbed lightly over a half-buried hip bone and dropped down the other side, weaving between the enormous ribcage and a tumble of boulders. The source of the great huffing he'd heard from over a mile away became clear as he vaulted over a ridge of tail bones. A dragon lay on its belly. A small one, although still large enough to swallow an elf in one bite. Its enormous lungs heaved, expanding its chest, and cool, flinty eyes found Eroan, then skipped to Curan and Nye behind him. Someone had tied its snout with vines, hence the huffing. Its wings, clamped to its sides, had been bound in much the same way. On closer inspection, the vines holding its legs and neck had frayed and would continue to unravel.

Eroan scanned the barren landscape of rock and bone

and spotted the pride of five elves tucked inside a depression in the earth. He was about to wave Curan on and hand-signal Nye to stay with the dragon when he remembered he wasn't in command and this wasn't his call.

Curan nodded at Eroan, reading the obvious commands anyway and Nye dropped his chin and maneuvered toward the trapped beast.

"We're losing the light," Curan said. "Best make this quick."

Eroan had noticed. There were more dangers in the dark than pinned young dragons. He hesitated a few yards from the pride and frowned at their hushed bickering. Hussan's leg had been fixed inside a makeshift splint and they seemed to be arguing over whether to leave, split up, or stay. None of them had seen Eroan approach. "I'm tempted to leave them out here all night just to see who survives," he said quietly to Curan.

Curan huffed a dry, subdued chuckle. "Survival of the fittest only works if one lives."

The pride saw them then and stopped their bickering. Seraph, proud thing that she was, stepped up to Eroan's approach first. "We were dealing with it," she told him, her chin up, eyes fierce.

He leaned around her to get a good look at the shamed faces. "I can see that. And what would have happened when the dragon broke free? Do you think it was just going to fly off and forget all about the pride of elves that ambushed it?"

"No, I—"

"Or do you think it might have come back with five of its bigger, hungry brood?"

She winced. The twitching in her flushed cheek

betrayed her anger. Her face was all scratched up and the earring he'd told her to remove had clearly been returned to her ear because now it was missing again, along with her ear tip. A dried dribble of blood marked her face and neck. She'd fought here, and well. All of them had. But without the kill, it wasn't over, and could easily have ended in their deaths. Still could. A dragon was at its most dangerous when pinned down.

"What were you going to do with it exactly?"

"Kill it," she hissed like he was the fool for asking.

Eroan glanced behind him at the panting beast. "So why haven't you?"

"I'll move the others on." Curan gathered up the others and organized the best way of carrying Hussan over the rocks.

Satisfied Curan had their survival in hand, Eroan returned to Seraph. She glared up and through Eroan, reminding him so much of himself, he almost laughed aloud. Instead, he freed one of the dragonblades. Her eyes fluttered at the sight of it and again when he planted the handle in her hand. "Come."

He led Seraph back to Nye at the dragon's trapped head. The beast's big eyes, glassy and bright, didn't blink, just observed.

"Your restraints are lacking," Nye said, flatly. "Another hour and it would have wriggled free."

"They held this long," Seraph growled back.

"This is the part where you listen," Eroan said, hiding the smirk at hearing her backtalk.

The dragon huffed harder, blasting them with dust. At the lower section of its neck, where the scales met its chest, an orange glow throbbed like a second heartbeat.

The firepit, where their liquid flame churned. The second this one got free, it would have turned the graveyard and Seraph's pride to ash. And it wouldn't have stopped there. More dragons would have come, searching for the village.

"You want the kill?" Eroan said. She nodded, losing her smart remarks. "You've earned it."

Her eyes widened, that infamous elven pride swelling. But it would all be for nothing if she couldn't end it.

Eroan roamed his gaze over the beast's snout and face. This one had a narrow, long nose, but like all the others, it had a crown of smooth, hardened scales atop its head. Those scales brushed together now, sending a loud warning rattle. It wasn't very old, Eroan considered. Its crown was small, not fully developed. The shimmering scales implied it was a jeweled dragon, likely from the amethyst brood.

"Behind the horns, you see them," he pointed at the beast's head.

Seraph nodded.

"There's a weak spot beneath that crown, where they raise those scales to rattle. It leaves their skin unprotected. There was little we could do before beyond annoying them, but now..." He dropped his gaze to the sword in her hand. "You need to thrust it in strong and true. You won't get a second chance."

Pride glittered in her eyes. She set her lips into a firm, determined line and started the climb up the creature's forelimb. The dragon panted harder and strained against its restraints. Its eyes narrowed on Eroan. Topaz eyes, Eroan saw. What had it been doing out here alone? Were they in such turmoil that this one had gone hunting on its own?

228

The beast's lips rippled and a growl bubbled up its throat.

"Do you think its mother will come looking?" Nye asked.

Seraph clambered along its ridged neck, her approach awkward with the sword in her hand. Eroan felt his own heart stutter in anticipation. "No," he said. He heard the queen's wicked laughter and met this beast's glare. "They don't care for their young like elves do."

Who was this dragon kit? Just another scrambling infant trying to survive its siblings? Was that why he'd fled? To survive? Eroan found he couldn't care less. This dragon's death would be the first of many to come.

The vines groaned. He swallowed the urge to tell Seraph to hurry. This was her kill. A long time ago he'd been an eager assassin too. Too eager, too confident, thought he'd known it all. His first kill had almost killed him, but she'd decided to play with her prey instead of just swallow it down. It was a mistake that dragon paid for with her life.

The beast bucked, and a vine snapped. "Now!" Eroan pulled the second blade free, and Nye freed his daggers. Vines unraveled from its forelimbs and snapped from around its snout. Fire burbled up its throat. It lifted its head, scales rattling.

Seraph punched her blade in, clean and surgical. The beast jolted, slumped, and collapsed forward with a heavy *whomp*, blasting up dust and stones, throwing Seraph clear.

Eroan ran to her side and pulled her to her feet. She spluttered, wheezed, and saw the fallen beast. Fire spilled from between its teeth and simmered over rock. Cold, dead eyes stared at nothing. It didn't seem so frightening a thing now all the fire had snuffed out of its eyes.

She smiled, and Eroan grinned back. "They're not invincible."

"Come," Nye urged. "Wolves will smell the carcass."

Seraph offered Eroan the bloodied sword.

"Keep it. We're going to make more."

Her smile grew, and the steel armor Eroan had clamped around his heart to keep it safe broke open just a little.

ANOTHER DRAGON dead and with the village safe for a little while longer, the people celebrated. Eroan admired their ability to dance and sing like all was right in the world. The younger Order members fawned over Seraph who delighted in showing them her bandaged ear. Hussan hobbled out to join in with the revelry. Curan managed to both scold and praise them all in equal measure, and Eroan watched it all from the sidelines.

Janna had avoided him since his return. And Nye acted like nothing had happened, just as he'd asked. He should have felt relieved, joyous even, so why then, did Eroan feel like he was going through the motions?

He ducked into Janna's hut and found her hanging her bow and quiver, both freshly cleaned. The hut smelled of wood oil and leather. "Not celebrating?"

"I will..." she stretched onto her tiptoes and adjusted the quiver so it wouldn't slip off its hook. Her slip of a shirt sat lightly on her hips, hugged her waist, and cupped her breasts. Lightweight and dark, it made for good, silent camouflage when moving through the trees.

She dropped to her feet, smiled carefully, and tucked her hair behind her ear. "You?"

He'd often accompanied her hunting and admired her stealth. Few could match her patience at stalking. She'd once waited a day, from dawn 'til dusk, for a deer herd to roam close enough for her arrow to deliver dinner. In all that time, the herd hadn't sensed her in the grass.

"I owe you an apology." He helped spread her stack of arrows across the table and watched her examine each tip, checking for damage. Lithe fingers stroked down each shaft, her touch slowing under his gaze.

"I'm trying to think around these things in my head, trying to make it right and it's not as easy as it should be," he admitted.

"I understand."

"I know you do." The music started up again outside, tugging on Eroan's heartstrings. He couldn't remember the last time he'd danced without a blade in his hand. "You should be out there."

She took his hand suddenly, planted it on her hip and lifted the other to her shoulder. "Or we could dance right here?"

They had danced before, and sung, and gotten tipsy on grape-wine, explored and tested, hunted and ran, tumbled in leaves, laughed in the rain. In all the years since the Order had found him abandoned, Janna had been a constant. His friend.

She swayed against him and flattened her hand against his back, drawing him close.

"Janna..."

"I know, but don't spoil it."

He closed his eyes and bowed his head, breathing in *home*, and together they swayed as one.

"You think I didn't know all those years, Eroan?"

"Know what?" He liked it here, in her arms, listening to her heart thump, feeling her curves pressed close, feeling her soft, warm and alive beneath his hands.

"That you and I would never be more?"

"Then you figured it out before I did, because I didn't know until—"

"I remember. The messenger from Cheen. I knew it the second you laid eye on him. You've never looked at me like that. I wasn't surprised."

"I was." Eroan fought with a smile. "He taught me some interesting things that night."

Janna laughed and thwacked him on the arm. "Eroan! I'm trying to be earnest here."

"Sorry, please continue being earnest. Tell me more of this messenger. I'm not sure I remember correctly—"

"Oh, you!" She tried to pull away, perhaps to go and join the celebrations, but he caught her arm, reeled her in so she fit perfectly against him, and gently kissed her smile. They had always played like this, but while Eroan knew they'd been fooling around, he'd also known, for Janna, it had been different. Her smile opened, lips parting like soft petals. He tasted their sweetness, letting it sit lightly on his tongue. She was a gentle thing, a fragile thing in his rough hands. He didn't want to break her. His thoughts weren't gentle, not now. They had been, but not anymore, not since he'd returned bathed in blood.

She fluttered her hands against his face, scared to touch and her eyes shone with all the wonder and hope he now lacked.

"I want to kill them all for what they did to you," she said. So fierce, his Janna, even as her tears fell. He loved her, always had, but it was a soft, friendly affection.

He kissed a tear away. Her hands dropped to his shoulders, and he kissed another tear from her cheek. Shifting onto her toes, her mouth met his, tongue nudging deeper. Heat simmered low, leading Eroan's thoughts and hands astray. He slid his touch down her arms, around her waist and pushed over her rear, clutching her ass tight enough to bring a gasp to her lips. Pulling her in, he ground his hardening arousal into her hip. Now her eyes shone for a different reason.

"Don't tease," she warned, her voice carrying a sharp, warning tone.

Eroan gathered her hair to one side and kissed the curve of her neck where her pulse fluttered. "Why not? When you seem to like it?"

"*Alumn*, I missed you," she breathed, sinking her hands down his back to pull his shirt free. "She told me to move on, that you were dead."

"I'm impossible to forget," he whispered into the corner of her mouth while his fingers unbuttoned her shirt.

She chuckled. "Maybe I did?" She pushed on his chest, leveraging some room between them, and unbuttoned the fastenings he hadn't gotten to yet. "Maybe I found your messenger from Cheen and asked him to show me what he'd shown you."

Now those memories were ones Eroan welcomed. The dark-haired delight from Cheen had been a vision of a male. One who had opened Eroan's eyes to many, many possibilities. He willingly recalled the male's tongue on him now as Janna's sweet face turned serious and wicked and wanting. His trouser fabric tightened over his erection like the messenger's teasing fingers had. But now it wasn't the messenger Eroan imagined, but a green-eyed prince who had looked at him as though he held the world in his hands. Eroan recalled precisely how the messenger had spread his thighs and clamped his ass in rough hands. He imagined it differently now, imagined it was Lysander's hands on his hips, Lysander's erection pushing in close.

Eroan fell on Janna, his mouth a tingling, buzzing thing that needed more. She squeaked as he tore open the shirt and claimed her waist. Then her deft hands were tugging his belt free, shoving his trousers down, finally freeing his hot, aching erection. Her hand went around him, light but tight. He imagined it was the prince's hand and felt his thoughts spiral. His body became a single, straining knot of want. He shouldn't be thinking this and didn't care as the thoughts came faster, thoughts of Lysander's velvety want pushing into his center.

"Turn around," he hissed.

Janna twisted to face away. She sent the arrows scattering from the table and fell forward to clutch at its edges and ground her ass against him.

Eroan was losing his mind. He pushed her trousers down, took his arousal and stroked with his left hand while sliding his right between Janna's legs, over her silky entrance to the tiny, tight button. Janna spat a foul curse, one that had a smile tug at Eroan's lips and a bead of precum leak from his head.

"Eroan," she begged, his name a breathless gasp. *"Please."*

He angled his head at her wet opening, delaying as long as his mind could stand, until she jerked back, taking him in and then he lost it all. Lost control, lost his thoughts, lost his mind. He thrust deep, filling her up until his thighs met the backs of hers. She mumbled something, making it sound a lot like begging. There was no holding back, no restraint. Deeper, faster, he pumped, skin on hot skin. Pleasure knotted harder, tighter, singing through his whole body. Hate was there too, feeding the ugly, twisted thing inside of him that wanted more hurt, more pain. But not here, not with her. He'd known she'd wanted this for a long time.

Her knuckles whitened at the table's edge. She said his name, ground it out, screaming it.

Eroan clutched her hips, adjusted the angle, and pounded himself deep until it wasn't about the feel of her or the memory of a prince, but had become a blinding all-consuming madness. He tried not to think of Lysander's mouth, of the dragon's flicking tongue, and failed spectacularly. The crescendo built, cresting, coming. More. He needed it. Deeper. Harder. Janna cried out, panting and clutching at him like an animal and he filled his thoughts of Lysander rising behind him, Lysander coming deep, his teeth and fingers digging into Eroan's back. He wanted that male on him, in him, in all ways. And the fact it was wrong only made him want it more. The kiss. He remembered that one, careful, drunken kiss while he'd hung in chains. A kiss that had lit a fire in Eroan's belly that had never stopped burning.

Pleasure burst. A ragged cry slipped from his lips. He stuttered, his solid, sensitive arousal releasing, freeing, spilling electric shivers through his veins. Pleasure crested to the tip of pain and then rolled back again, freeing him to breathe again.

Janna turned her head, her lips full and face flushed. She tilted her hips, smiling her delight as Eroan gasped, the pleasure too sharp, too much. He fell forward and mouthed her shoulder, tasting her shudders.

"Eroan Ilanea, you are a wicked, surprising thing."

Bracing a hand against the table, he leaned close, sinking into her gaze. "Give me a minute and I'll surprise you some more."

CHAPTER 33

Sunlight streamed in through the windows, and the pine-scented breeze fluttered the drapes. Outside, the village lay soft and quiet.

A pile of reclaimed dragon teeth waited in the Order building, but Eroan couldn't bring himself to move from Janna's arms. Maybe last night had been a mistake. But Janna wasn't Nye. She wanted only what he was willing to give. She loved him like he loved her, as friends, didn't she?

She might think differently after last night.

He stretched, naked beneath the sheets and trapped under Janna's carelessly flung arm and leg. They'd fooled around over the years but had never let things go that far.

Did it matter? Wasn't this how it would be now anyway if Xena had her way? His mood shifted, his chest tightening.

As the sun brightened, lifting over the village, he heard chatter from outside. Normalcy. He hadn't been sure he'd ever feel it again.

Janna's fingers circled a nipple. He looked down at her

sleepy face and mussed-up hair. She pulled her hand back from the circular scar around his nipple. She'd seen the scars on his chest and back last night. It hadn't mattered in their madness, but now, in the sleepy morning light, he could feel the questions building.

"I need to work on the weapons..." He threw the sheet off and planted his feet outside the bed. She plastered herself to his back, nuzzling his neck in that spot she'd found last night. The one that yanked him out the moment and dumped a ton of lust in his veins.

"Don't go. Spend the day here, with me." Her morning voice turned sultry and dark.

He breathed in and held that breath, sorely tempted to lie back down and lose himself in her all over again. "You need to go hunt."

"Then tonight?"

She trailed her tongue over his bare shoulder, sending a cascade of shivers down his back. "Janna, this... this doesn't change anything."

And she was gone, withdrawing, dragging the sheet with her. When he looked, she leaned against the wall and blinked at the ceiling.

"It's fine."

It clearly was not fine, but he knew better than to argue. Dressing quickly, he preferred to escape now before this descended into an argument he didn't want and wouldn't win.

"Maybe I should have moved on," she said.

"Xena was right." He shrugged on his shirt and laced it up. "You should have. I'm not the only handsome male here, you know. Although, you'll struggle to find someone who'll compare. What about the elf who follows you around like a lost puppy? What's his name? Rand... No, Ross? He clearly doesn't compare to my effortless perfection, but I hear he has stamina."

Her lips twitched. She gathered her pillow and tossed it at him with a laugh. "Get out, you rat. Go play with your teeth. I'm going to trek to Cheen and find the messenger."

Eroan avoided the flying pillow and ducked for the door. "If you do, make sure you bring him back with you. I'm not opposed to a threesome—"

"Go! You fiend!"

He slammed the door on her laugh and chuckled, crossing the village yards. Children scattered, chasing one another with green ribbons tied to their belts. A hunting party had gathered near the grand hall, readying their weapons and discussing their route. An elf he recognized but couldn't recall her name carried a bundle of logs. Normalcy. The Order didn't see much of it, just enough to know it was worth protecting at all costs. Assassins of the Order were forever apart from the community. Guardians. Soldiers. Anything the village and Xena needed them to be, but not part of it.

And now Xena needed him to stand beside her.

His mouth twisted. How could he set aside his entire way of life? He wasn't ready, but after last night, he imagined he might be one day. A future. He'd never allowed himself to think of it. A life, a real life, as part of the community, not skirting its fringes. Would it be so bad a thing?

He pushed into the Order house to find Curan and Nye already inside examining and sorting bundles of dragon teeth. Eroan counted fifty teeth. It wasn't enough. "We need more."

"I thought you said we only needed two?" Curan's smirk held its own playful humor. Eroan hadn't missed the way he'd handled the teeth, admiring their curves and structure. The older elf was impressed.

"Two per dragon, if we don't miss. But how many dragons are there? We get one shot to hit them hard. I'm not prepared to blow it because we've run out of teeth." A few hundred thousand dragons infested the lands, at least, he figured. By Curan's scowl, the male figured the same.

"All right," Curan grumbled. "I'll organize the prides into retrieving more."

"All of the teeth. Every single one. And if we can, we go to other graveyards and get those too."

"We'll need help..." Curan rubbed at his chin, turning his thoughts over.

They'd need more than just help. All the Orders from every village would need to act on this. "Contact Cheen. See if they can spare some hands."

"What for?" Nye finally asked. He'd been silently scrutinizing each curved tooth and set one of the larger ones down among the pile. "How are we going to shape these teeth into weapons? I've tried to scratch them; steel blades slide right off. They're as hard as granite."

"We can't shape them, we don't have the means, but humans can. They had forges. They once created iron-tripped war-machines. These teeth just need to be softened enough to carve into shape. They can do it."

"But you don't *know* it's possible. We don't even know if there are any humans left?"

Eroan recalled the conversations he'd overhead between the queen and the bronze chief. "There are. They continue to assault the bronze lines. They're still fighting."

Nye's expression opened with curiosity and awe. Eroan waited for the questions to begin—exactly how he knew these things—but Nye just wet his lips and looked down at the teeth.

"You know this will work. You saw Seraph use the blade to kill the kit. We can strike back for the first time since it all began. Elves haven't fought them in force in generations. The queen is dead. We can do this." *I can do this.*

"It's a risk." Curan lifted his gaze. "If we start mobilizing, the dragons will notice. We've survived this long by staying small and quiet, keeping to pockets hidden in the forest—"

Hiding was not living. "And how long do you think we'll survive like that? The queen is dead, but a ruler will rise and again we'll be sending assassins to their deaths. We're killing our best. It's fruitless. We need to hit them hard or not at all." Eroan wrapped his fingers around a tooth and lifted it between them. "This is the only way. Humans have the means to shape these, to use them. They just need the knowledge."

"And you're going to take it to them?" Nye asked, eyes glinting behind long, dark lashes. "You're going to break through the bronze line and cross the ocean, give them these blades, and then what?" His friend's tone deepened. "Come back through the bronze line again? As easy as that? Just cross an ocean and back again, just stroll on through a thousand dragons because you're Eroan Ilanea and you're what, invincible now?"

"Nye..." Curan warned.

"He has a death wish," Nye snarled. "He'll charge into

anything, not caring if he lives or dies. Even hoping he dies..."

Eroan quenched his own rising anger and tossed the tooth into the pile. "I'm an Assassin of the Order. It's what we do. Or have you forgotten?"

Nye laughed. "You make it an obsession and I'll play no part in it." He stormed through the door.

Eroan waited until he heard Nye's boots stop thumping in the dirt and turned to Curan only to find their leader with a single eyebrow raised. "I need his head clear," Eroan said. "He was always focused. Like this, he's useless to the Order. What by Alumn happened to him?"

"You did."

Eroan winced and leaned against the table, turning his face away from Curan's glare. "Don't put this on me. I'm carrying enough already. He just..." He closed his eyes and rubbed at the back of his neck, scratching over healing sores. Opening his eyes again, Curan was still watching and looking at him like this was all his fault. "I get it, I do. The queen is dead, the Order succeeded, he gets to live. We all get to live, but for how long? Just because she's dead doesn't mean it's over. You see that, don't you?"

"I do." Curan rumbled. "But you don't need to do this. I can take it to the Ashford Higher Order—"

"The Higher Order are all full of air." Taking it to Ashford would just delay things. They couldn't afford to wait for council members to discuss and argue and vote. "This must happen now."

"You can have a life *now*. Do you even understand what a gift that is? Because I don't think you do. Xena gave you a way out."

Eroan gritted his teeth and hissed through them, "I don't want a way out."

Curan sniffed and straightened. "You don't want to hear it, but you need to. You're so desperate to leave. It's easier than staying." Curan saw Eroan flinch. "We've sent hundreds of assassins into the night and none thought they'd ever return, though we prayed to Alumn for it. *You* came back."

Eroan dragged a hand down his face, trying to clear the fluttering anxiety beginning to turn his insides over. "You sound like Xena."

"Then maybe you'll listen? You've done enough, Eroan. We'll do this, we'll get you the extra hands, we'll find a way to get this knowledge to the humans, I'll send a messenger to Ashford, but it's not your fight."

Not his fight? Eroan shot the older male a raw glance. "You're the one not listening to me. I need this." He gestured at the teeth piled high. "I have to do this. It has to be me."

"Why?"

How could he tell him, his oldest friend besides Janna. In the absence of parents, Eroan had admired Curan as he imagined one admired their father, and now even he was trying to shut Eroan out. He glared at the closed door and ground his teeth. "I can't stand the way they look at me like I'm some returning deity. Those people out there, my people, I love them, but they think I'm something I'm not."

"They love you."

He knew that and hated it. "They love the *idea* of me, Curan. I came back. I killed the queen." He sighed, and whispered, "Only, that's not what happened."

Curan opened his mouth to argue or brush off Eroan's words, but he'd asked Eroan why this meant so much, and the Order leader was getting the truth. All of it. Eroan needed this wretched thing out of him before it ate his insides and turned all of him dark.

"I didn't kill the queen." The words were out now, and he couldn't take them back. Needling anxiety prickled his back. "Her son killed her. Do you want to know what I did while that was happening? Why I'm so heroic? I lived. That's all. I survived." His words trembled now, but it didn't matter. The truth was coming, and it was time he set it free. "They chained me to a wall, carved into me, kept me from the light. I thought I was dying, for so long, I thought I was a dead thing."

Curan turned his face away. "Eroan, you don't need to tell me—"

"The night the queen died, I was tied to her bed about to be violated by her and her son." His voice cracked like the thing inside split open and spilled out its darkness. "Do you have that image in your head now, because I do."

"Eroan."

"No. You want to know why? I'm telling you." He straightened and squared up to Curan, watching the male's throat bob around a gulp. "A flight of bronze stole me from the tower, in chains, threw a bag over my head. They had some plan to take me to their brood on the frontline, only one of them decided he'd like to try to fuck an elf before they got there."

Curan's mouth twisted downward in disgust.

"I only lasted as long as I did because her son kept..." Eroan growled a stammer clear. "Because he kept saving me. I'm not a hero, Curan. I'm not a returning triumphant assassin who did the impossible and felled the Dragon Queen. I just didn't die." Curan opened his mouth to speak, but Eroan's next words cut him off. "And to make it worse. *I liked it.*" Gods, he'd said it. He'd said the vicious truth and the sickness was back, and that ugly thing inside of him was awake and hungry again. "I wanted the prince to fuck me because it meant I'd feel again and it was all I could focus on. Nothing else in that wretched place made any sense."

"Eroan, stop," Curan growled. "I can't hear these things from you."

"You can't? I don't care whether you can hear it or not. It happened. I need to take these teeth away from here because I can't be your fucking leader, I can't be Janna's mate or a father, and I can't be some elder you all look up to. I'm just another assassin thrown at her walls. Only for some reason, this time, her son saved me."

Curan's mouth twisted. "Don't." He tried to turn, but Eroan found himself sinking his fingers into the elf's shoulder, pulling him back, making him hear.

"You were right, Curan. I'm not fit to be here." The next words burned his tongue. "Because I *liked* what they did to me."

"Alumn, damn you, Eroan!" Curan grabbed Eroan's shoulders as though to shake, shove or hit him, but did neither. "Get out of this Order house and do not return."

Eroan's chest heaved, his wounded heart breaking. "What did you think the collar was for? Decoration?"

Curan yanked him close. "You are dismissed from the Order, and you will not return to its ranks. Do you understand?" The older male shoved Eroan toward the door, almost knocking him off his feet.

Eroan caught the wall to wedge himself up. "Perfectly," he muttered. Then he was gone.

THE WHITELADY FALLS GROWLED and hissed, drowning out the thoughts in Eroan's head. He sat on the bank and threw pebbles into the pool until daylight faded and shadows stretched far and long. Returning after dusk when the village was quiet again, he bundled an armful of dragon teeth, threw on a fitted fur-lined trekking coat and the remaining dragonblade sword, and crept from the village, into the night.

He hadn't gotten far when a whisper of movement from behind pricked his ears. "Go back, Seraph."

"You're leaving again." She hopped down from a branch above, landing in a crouch and marched at him like an arrow, direct and full of determination.

"Some things have to be done, and sometimes, there's only one person who can do them."

She frowned. "If you're trying to sound like Xena, you're awful at it."

He smiled and nodded at the sword handle peeking over her shoulder. "Wearing it on the back, huh?"

She shrugged, jolting the sword. "Makes it easier to carry through the trees. It kept getting snagged when I had it at my hip."

He nodded and glanced at the path he would be taking ahead of him. Looking back, Seraph toed at the leaf litter. She saw him watching and said, "I want to come with you."

"No."

"I can help. You're going to the humans. While you

rest, I can stand watch. You've always told me we travel in prides of more than two. Always." The words fell out of her in a rush.

"Seraph, I'm going through bronze lines. If anything were to happen—"

"I'm an Assassin of the Order. This is what I do, Eroan!"

Her words struck at the hard stone inside him. Words so much like the ones he'd said to Nye. She'd overheard his conversation in the Order. Probably been listening the whole time. "Well, I'm not with the Order, not anymore." He turned his back on her and started on. "Go back. I'm not handing the dragons another elven life."

"You can't go alone."

"I can."

"You'll die." She caught his arm, yanking him to a stop.

He looked down at the small hand on his sleeve and up at her face. Maybe if he'd stayed, maybe if he'd had it in him to settle with Janna, he'd one day rear a feisty, defiant daughter like her. But that was not to be, not for him.

He kissed her quickly on the forehead. "Protect them."

"Until you get back? You are coming back?"

"Until I get back." He gave her a small smile, hoping it might ease her mind.

She took his hand and dropped a tiny green earring into his palm. "Take it. So you know you're not alone."

A knot tightened his throat. He swallowed, trying to clear it, but didn't quite manage it, and whispered, "Thank you."

She flicked her own stubby ear and smiled shyly. "It's not like I can wear it anymore anyway."

He backed up. "Don't tell them I've left. By the time they realize, I'll be days away."

She nodded. "I know I'll see you again. This isn't goodbye."

With a sad smile, he nodded, turned, and plunged into the brush.

CHAPTER 34

$\mathcal{L}$ysander

THE DRUG WAS MADE from plants, Mirann had said. And some other shit Lysander couldn't remember. All he knew was how, when the grainy powder touched his tongue, it took him far, far away from the stifling heat, the constant sweet smell of sweat, and filled out the hollowness inside.

In the weeks since he'd collapsed in the mud outside the bronze line, Mirann had been a constant. When she didn't have her hands on his cock, she was in his head, directing his thoughts. And it worked, in as much as he could fuck her hand and finish, but he couldn't bring himself to care. He was stuck in a downward spiral, and just when he thought he might be climbing out of the dark, Mirann was there, the drug touched his tongue, and the spiral kept on moving down.

"Dokul will know if you're drugged during the coupling." She had told him the same over and over, but the more he let the drug numb him, the more he needed it. With it, he was a creature with simple needs, needs she kept meeting, but without it, the world got complicated and the memories tackled him all over again. His mother's murder, his brother's attack, Dokul looming, Mirann pulling his strings... That reality wasn't somewhere he wanted to be.

Until now. With a day left until the coupling, Mirann hadn't come, and Lysander paced his room, ready to tear his skin off to rid himself of the crawling need. "I can't stand this." He needed out. He needed to breathe. He needed to *fly*—great gods he ached to fly.

He flung open the door and strode from the room. There had to be somewhere he could go, somewhere he wouldn't be watched or guarded and leered at.

"Lysander..."

Mirann. Fucking Mirann. She blocked his retreat and reached to touch him like all the bronze did. Constant touches. Fingers stroking, digging, gripping.

"Don't..." He pushed her off. "I need to shift, okay? Somewhere outside. Is there somewhere I can go where I won't be seen?"

Scorn darkened her face. She looked at him like that when he'd failed to do something for her, to say the right things, to release his seed at her command.

He grabbed her wrists and shoved her against the tunnel wall. "Unless you want a fucking dragon filling this corridor, tell me where I can go now!"

She twisted her wrists under his hands and smiled —*liking* the pain. Lysander jerked away from her and carried right on walking. There had to be somewhere. He didn't care where, just so long as it wasn't this tunnel. He needed space.

"Don't." She caught up with him.

"Don't what?"

"Don't shift. Use it."

"Use it...?" he laughed. She made it sound like his anger was a tool, like something he could wield. "The last time I used it, I killed my mother. Do you want to die tomorrow while we fuck for your whole nightmare of a brood to see?" Wild magic spritzed through his veins, twitching his fingers. All of this felt wrong. The bronze brood, Mirann, the drug in his veins. He didn't want this, had never wanted it, but somehow here he was, underground, buried among dragons he despised.

"Wait... when you killed her, what were you doing?"

Her question jolted him to stop. *I'd been doing an elf*, he thought with a sharp grin. "I told you. It was kill her or fuck her."

She circled around and blocked his path again, sizing him up with slitted eyes. "Then that's it."

"Get out of my way, Mirann."

Her grin was a horrible, slippery thing. "I just need to make you rage, prince." Her fist hit him like an oar.

LYSANDER CAME TO, blinking into flickering torches—like the bastards didn't have enough heat in this place already. A pointed ache numbed his shoulders. He tried to lift his hands to discover he couldn't. His hands were tied behind him, to the upright pole grazing his spine. He tugged, but the pole had to be a foot thick. It wasn't going anywhere and neither was he.

Then the murmurs soaked into his broken thoughts.

The bronze were here. A lot of them. All of them, maybe. A sea of tarnished bronzes, golds and greens around a staging area, he was currently fixed on. He hoped to the gods he was still high and this wasn't real. What was it his mother had said? The coupling was a sexual cele-bration?

Lysander didn't feel much like celebrating.

But he'd had a day left. Or a few hours, at least. Mirann, the bitch, had knocked him out. His jaw still stung where her ringed knuckles had stuck. Well, wasn't this just perfect.

He pulled on the chains and strained forward, trying to break a link or two. The pole groaned, his muscles screamed, but the chains held. Gasping, he fell back. And now his audience had noticed him. They admired him with golden, hungry eyes. Just a few near the stage. Lowers, he figured, from their scant attire. Lysander noticed he'd been dressed in a thin lamé vest, a low-slung belt barely clinging to his hips, and leather chaps, and felt a laugh trying to claw its way up his throat. He grinned, making sure to show some teeth, and watched the lowers' gazes darken with lust.

Fucking wonderful. He was the main attraction. If he couldn't fight his way out, then better to get it done and over with. Where in the hells was Mirann? Maybe she wouldn't show and the whole thing would be called off, though he doubted it. He'd never been that lucky.

The minutes dragged. The crowd swelled, and heat beat down in waves until finally Dokul and his naked daughter climbed the steps onto the stage. The chief wore a crown of forged iron and shimmering ceremonial armor. He'd thought amethyst had enjoyed the dramatic, but these bronze were pretty, self-centered fools. He fought the laughter back into its box. No use in getting his throat cut for lacking respect. Though he was sure he'd be dead soon enough anyway.

Mirann draped her gaze over Lysander. Gold paint swept around her thighs, up her waist and circled over plump breasts. In his drugged stupor, he'd had his mouth on most of those parts during the last few weeks. But he wasn't drugged now, and her curves did little to rouse him.

"Today marks the union of two great lines," Dokul began, silencing his horde. "But also sends a message." The chief turned toward Lysander and not for the first time, desire blazed hot in his eyes. For a moment, Lysander stilled. He'd seen that look a long time ago when Lysander had told him no. Dokul hated to be defied, to be told he couldn't have something he wanted. He'd tried to take Lysander by force then, and now had the perfect opportunity to make it happen where all the bronze could see how amethyst bent over for them.

Lysander worked to his feet and ran his tongue over his top lip. Dokul's eyes flared.

You can't have me, asshole, Lysander mouthed.

"Weakness will not be tolerated!" Dokul boomed over the crowd.

"Weakness?" Now Lysander did laugh. "I wasn't the one groveling at the bitch-queen's feet for scraps at her table."

Fury flashed across Dokul. He thundered across the stage. "Watch your tongue, *prince*, or I'll rip it out."

"Fuck. You."

Dokul fell on him, trapping Lysander against the pole so it dug into his back. The male's thick chest and heavy armor scratched through Lysander's clothes. It had been like this before. The male's body too big, too heavy, a grappling of hands as Lysander had fought him off. He'd been younger then, and he'd still managed to best the bastard. But he hadn't been tied. And he hadn't been buried among bronze-kind with no escape.

Trying not to pant out his fears only made his breaths come harder. Lysander brought his gaze up and looked the ancient dragon in the eyes, looked into his soul. "You want me?" he whispered. "You can't have me. Or will you steal me away like you did the elf? Remember him?" Lysander pushed in and whispered against the male's whiskered cheek. "I killed your ill-fated flight that night and set the elf free."

Dokul shuddered, forcing out a sigh. Lysander smelled the male's spicy lust. Refraining from taking him was taking every ounce of strength the bronze had in him.

"Take me here," Lysander whispered. "Undermine your daughter and she'll shred you in your sleep." He could see Mirann over her father's shoulder and by the fire in her eyes, knew she'd make her father pay if he stole this moment from her.

Dokul caught Lysander's jaw and squeezed. "Survive this and you'll have to survive me."

Lysander smiled around the pinch of the male's fingers. Dokul wanted him. He wanted him so badly he'd do almost anything to have him. Lysander was his weakness just the same as Dokul had assumed Lysander was Akiem's weakness. A weakness Lysander knew how to exploit.

The bronze chief tore his hand free, leaving Lysander's face stinging, and stomped off the stage. He caught one of the nearest males and pulled him close. Whatever he said, the male flicked his gaze to Lysander. Plotting, perhaps. Lysander was beyond caring. They wanted a show. He was going to give them one.

"Untie me," he snapped at Mirann, forgetting the crowd as anger sizzled through his veins. "I'm not your pet."

"Aren't you?" She crossed the stage, skin shimmering, nipples pert, that little V between her legs already slick. "You act like one." She stroked his cheek, pulled at his lips, and with her other hand, dragged her nails up his crotch.

She leaned too close, and he snapped his teeth together in warning, feeling the shift stretch through his skin.

"Are you going to kill me, Lysander, like you did your mother?"

He yanked on the chains, biceps straining. "Free me and find out."

"Is that how you planned this would go? You're not weak like you led your brood to believe. Nothing weak could kill the queen." Her nails scratched down him again, making his balls tighten. The pain felt good, felt clean. It stoked his anger, and the anger chased away all the nonsense witterings in his head. This bitch pulled on his strings and knew exactly what she was doing, his cock responding to the desire to fuck or kill, or both.

She knew it too. She *wanted* it.

"Break the chains." Her hand squeezed him and her eyes flashed. "I can't, but you can."

The restless building, aching, burning writhed beneath his skin, power crackling and coming alive. The last time he'd felt this rage, he'd let the dragon pour into his skin, but not here, he couldn't here. He'd shape it differently and use it.

The chains bit into his wrists, skin tearing.

Mirann sauntered backward, hips swaying. "Or will the little amethyst prince fail again?"

He'd kill her, then eat her, bones and all. He hadn't come here to be treated like a toy. He was a gods-be-damned amethyst, finest warrior in all the queen's flights. He'd survived it all, and she was not beating him now for some mockery of a ceremony. Lysander funneled the raw fury where it was needed, through his arms. He pulled on the chains until his body burned and trembled from the exertion. Metal snapped. Chain links flew. He lunged, caught Mirann's throat, and squeezed. Her quick hand dropped to his cock, striking lust alight and setting the madness ablaze. And it was a madness, he realized, because nothing in his head made any sense.

The hollowness swelled, eating him whole, only now it wasn't a hollow thing anymore, but pure ravenous, power. Mirann's lashes fluttered, her eyes closing. Her hand loosened. He could kill her. The beast in him wanted it, wanted to tear this whole place down and go on destroying. The fire in him burned so high it blinded and became an all-consuming force. There were no thoughts now, just heat and rage.

He threw her against the pole, clutched around her waist when she almost fell and dropped his hands to her hips, and then he was inside her, his cock a raging, thumping, heated thing. Hate. Gods, so much hate. It stoked him alive, turned him inside out and made him wild and free. Mirann panted. Screamed. Sinking his fingers into her back, he fucked her deep, fucked her until he'd lost his mind in her, until she screamed his name, and then he locked his hands around her neck and pumped, driving into her, riding the wave of pleasure, hating her, hating what this was, what it took from him, until he felt the tightness swell and pleasure twist into a maddening, devastating point. She clawed at his arm, trying to reach back, to fight free, and it only made him rage more. They thought him weak, thought him a failure. If he killed her here, they wouldn't think that anymore... gods, he lusted to kill her. Pleasure snapped up his spine, dumping out all reason. He thrust, briefly lost to the fire, to the light. His seed burst, hot and free, freeing ripples down his back and pooling them beneath his balls until slowly, finally, he came down from the madness to find Mirann slick and limp between him and the beam. He jerked his hands free of her neck and for a few terrible silent seconds he thought he'd killed her.

She gasped, coughed, and clutched ahold of the pole like it was the only thing keeping her alive.

Don't...

Lysander's thoughts cascaded.

Don't think...

Could have killed her.

Wanted to...

He looked at his hands, felt the buzz of sex shiver off him, and slid his softening dick free. This wasn't who he was. He felt exposed, disgraced, like he'd sold some part of him for nothing.

Mirann was moving, staggering. Blood wept from scratches on her legs and back. He couldn't even remember touching her there.

She swept her hand between her legs and lifted it, dripping with cum, to the whooping crowd. Half of them were too busy succumbing to their own rabid desires to give a shit about the entertainment on the stage or to notice how Lysander staggered. Mirann licked the creamy seed off her hand and turned on Lysander. She kissed him, long and slow, holding him up so he couldn't collapse in front of them all. He tasted his seed on her tongue and nipped at her lip, deliberately drawing blood, mixing the two, falling into the horrible sense of wrongness.

When she drew back, her eyes glowed. She whispered, "Now, prince, you're ours."

CHAPTER 35

roan

EROAN SLIPPED through the bronze lines like thread through the eye of a needle. Torchlights haloed the watchtowers, marking where to avoid, and with a quick scrabble over the palisade walls and through an array of steel spikes, he was through. Getting back in would be much, much harder.

He crouched at the clifftop edge to minimize his silhouette and leaned forward to peer into the muted dark. The wind breezed through his hair, cooling his face. Three hundred feet below, foaming breakers crashed against jagged rocks. And that was where he needed to be. Ahead of him, the horizon disappeared in the gloom of an inky black ocean. He'd have preferred a moonlit night, but he hadn't fully expected to leave so soon. And alone. But he was here now. There was no turning back.

Shifting the bundle of teeth over his shoulder, he threw a leg over the cliff's edge, tested his footing in a ridge, and began the long climb down. Salt dried the frigid air, cracking his lips and tightening his throat. The waves crashed and rumbled like snarling, hungry beasts waiting to swallow him should he fall. This was simple, like climbing through the tree canopy. Nothing he couldn't handle. Just one well-placed grip at a time.

The wind teased through loose locks of hair, tickling them against his cheek as though whispering for him to let go, to fall. He dug his fingers harder into the stones and dirt and kept on climbing. Dragon calls peppered the quiet, their screeches piercing and sudden, but distant. They wouldn't see him, not plastered against the rocks. Closer to the foot of the cliffs, the sound of the waves drowned out their calls, though he still caught their sweeping silhouettes against the twilit sky.

He preferred the forests. The cliffs provided little cover, just a few gorse bushes clinging to vertical slits in the rocks. Finally, arms and legs aching, he reached the beach, adjusted the bundle of teeth and sword again, and made his way over fallen boulders, farther down the narrow strip of beach.

Debris barred much of the way. Tangles of wire and great chunks of rusted metals. Strange mangled wreckage from human machines, so rusted they didn't resemble anything. The remains seemed bigger out here, exposed on the rocks, unlike the buried monoliths dotted about the forest floor, but the strange, twisted monuments offered good cover.

Resting on a rock, he scanned the horizon. Flickers of

light occasionally flashed far out to sea. He'd heard the straights were twenty miles from coast to coast. Messengers had once boated across. But none had come in decades.

He eyed those distant winking lights. They seemed closer than twenty miles. Human vessels perhaps?

If he paced himself and followed those lights, he could make it by morning.

A dragon's roar shook the air, so loud Eroan pressed his hands to his ears and ducked himself into a tiny crevice, tucking himself in tight. Rocks and pebbles bounced with each footfall. Closer, it came. The snout came first; an enormous whiskered nose cut with a grinning line of sharp teeth, bigger versions of the ones he had strapped to his back. Its eyes were narrowed as though it had something in its sights. It prowled by him, green scales so close Eroan could almost reach out and run his hand along them. The saltwater and seaweed likely masked his scent, and even if the dragon had smelled him, he'd mistake it for pine. Although, Eroan couldn't hide his thudding heart. Hopefully, the sound of the waves did that.

The beast was huge, with a proud, fully-developed crown and towering back ridges. Higher on its back, where the scales were table-sized, color shimmered like the inside of a seashell. The one's colors suggested jeweled. Not a bronze, and a long way from the tower. Then they truly were all stirred up after the queen's death.

Eroan waited a while for its tail to slither out of sight and the rumbling breathing growls to fade before leaning out of his hiding nook. The beast could have been curled among the rocks, waiting. He wouldn't have seen it until

ARIANA NASH

he was almost upon it. The crashing waves and how the sound echoed about him made the beach a dangerous place indeed.

Shifting the bundle higher and checking his sword, he started down the beach and paused, glancing back to the cliff face where a curtain of vines and weeds rippled in the wind. Almost completely hidden, the cave-mouth gaped. At high tide, it would disappear altogether. A way in and likely where the dragon had come from. He'd be a suicidal fool to venture inside. If the dragons didn't find him, the tide would flood him out. Still, he marked its location in his mind as a possible access point and made his way down to where the breakers slammed in, splashing the air and him with salted water.

An entrance like that, right into the heart of the warren? If he could reach the humans, expose the entrance... Frigid water lapped around his knees and then withdrew, trying to drag him out.

A blast of warm, wet air hit him from behind. He froze, ears pricked, only now picking up the sound of a thudding heart.

The lights out at sea winked, mocking. *So close...*

The wind turned, brought in by the waves now shoving at his thighs, and with it, came the overpowering stench of dragon.

It was behind him. So close his skin prickled. If he turned, he'd see only his fate looking back at him with eyes of fire.

Eroan bolted. He made it three strides before the foot came down, slamming him under the water. He gasped, drawing water down his throat, and grabbed for the rocks, for anything to hold on to. A wave struck him, or maybe a

262

foot. His head cracked against rock. He gasped again, pulling more water into his lungs. Then the weight was gone from his back. Spluttering, he broke the surface, twisted and saw it, its huge face inches from his. Its golden eyes studied him, slitted pupils swelling as though they alone could draw him in. They were large enough to. A bronze. Bigger than the jeweled, with scales like polished disks.

A wave hit Eroan in the back, shoving him closer toward the rows of teeth. His thoughts scrabbled for escape. If he could somehow find deep water, he could get away, but the pool he stood in was inches. Enough to drown in but not enough to hide in. And still, the dragon watched him.

It reared up, puffing its chest, and cocked its head quizzically.

Run!

He pushed his boots into the silt and shoved backward, hoping to fall away, but the waves shoved at him again, driving him closer, and the movement seemed to spark delight in the dragon's eyes, widening them farther. Its jaw dropped open, teeth sparkling, and Eroan saw the view of its gullet, the same view Nylena must have seen in her final moments.

A rogue wave breached the boulders and poured in from the side, its sudden power slamming into the bronze, tearing it clean off its feet.

Eroan blinked.

Not a wave.

Another dragon. It locked its jaws around the bronze's neck and dragged it, thrashing and groaning up the beach, away from Eroan.

The bronze screeched, jolting Eroan into a run. He didn't stop, didn't look back. Just ran, sinking into deeper water until the waves crashed over him and dragged him away from the sounds of snapping jaws and wounded howls.

CHAPTER 36

$\mathcal{L}$ysander

LYSANDER PINNED Mirann under his claws, trapping her neck between his teeth. He was a twitch away from breaking her. She whimpered like a scolded kit, and some forgotten instinct in him pulled him back from the edge of that rabid violence. The second he let off, Mirann snapped her jaws inches from his nose, but she wasn't rising, and when he withdrew, her scales rattled low against her head and neck, signaling bitter defeat. It briefly occurred to him that her submission seemed too easy, but his thoughts drifted from her and back out to sea, searching for a streak of white hair among the surf. Snuffling, he caught the slightest scent of forest. But that was impossible. Everything here smelled of salt and rot. A tiny flicker of a memory brought to mind the elf, but it couldn't have been Eroan. Not here. The elf was dead.

Mirann shifted, trying to roll and cover her vulnerable belly. He swung his head back and rippled a snarl across his lips, warning her to stay down. She opened her jaws, panting. He lifted one great foot and spread his claws on her chest, holding her still, feeling an unfamiliar thrill at pinning one of his own. He'd rarely had the strength to best any of the amethyst, but things were different now.

Mirann averted her eyes, another sign of her submissive stance and Lysander's lips pulled back, drawing her scent through his teeth and over his tongue.

He'd asked her for somewhere to shift right after the coupling, before he tore his own skin off, and she'd brought him down here, among the surf. The last thing he'd expected to find was an elf. Or maybe that had been wishful thinking among the madness still clawing at his thoughts.

He lifted his head to admire the swirling flights overhead. Mirann bumped her head against his neck and purred. Disgusted, it was all he could do not to cover her snout with a foot and push her away. But at least he had her under him now. And soon, if he played it right, he'd have Dokul under him too. It had cost him much. Too much of his mind, too much of his soul and most of his body, but then, what else was left? His life was surviving. It always had been. And now he knew how to survive these beasts too.

He let the fire churn low in his throat, tasting acid and nursing it into flame. Spreading his one good wing, keeping the broken one pulled close, he let the fire build, let it bubble and spit, and then roared it out, sweeping flame across the rocks, turning water to steam. Light flooded the beach and blasted farther out to see where Lysander gazed now.

If it had been Eroan, then maybe the stubborn elf had finally learned to run away from death instead of toward it.

He turned and plodded back into the cave, each step on firmer ground, but leaving his heart behind in the surf with the last dregs of hope that he might one day be free.

roan

"Found him... washed up..."

"Get... warm."

"...scars..."

Humans had round faces, big eyes, and stubby ears. Eroan had never seen a real one outside of sketches—the severe-looking dragon kind didn't count. Humans seemed so soft, almost alien.

The female who'd been given the task of watching him poked at a fire, sending hot sparks up the chimney. Her cropped hair stroked her jacket-covered shoulders. Eroan shifted uneasily beneath the bedsheet, realizing he was virtually naked but for a slip of underwear. His clothes on a window seat, dried and folded, along with the opened bundle of dragon teeth.

She said something in a language he didn't understand,

her accent smooth and lilting. But her smile was friendly. He understood that.

"You're awake." This time she spoke in a language like his own. "And you've stopped shivering, *quelle folie!*" She tucked her thumbs into her trouser pockets and shook her head. He wasn't sure of the meaning to her strange words, but it sounded as though he'd just been fondly chastised.

Her eyes weren't unlike elven eyes, a little rounder, and their colors more of a muddle of hazel and green than an elf's intense eye colors. She didn't seem very old, but he wasn't entirely sure how humans aged. Had she been an elf, he might have assumed she was his age, but humans sometimes aged faster... at least, he recalled they did from his early teachings, but he hadn't paid much attention back then.

He shuffled backward and sat up, noting how her gaze began to flick from his face to his chest. She probably hadn't seen man elves before either. "May I have my clothes?"

She collected the pile and set it on the bed, then stuck out her hand.

He took her hand in his, found it warm and soft, if a little small, and gently gave it a shake in greeting. "*Je m'apellee* Chloe," she said.

"Eroan Ilanea."

Her smile grew. "When you're ready, Eroan, join us outside."

After she'd left, he quickly dressed and rewrapped the bundle of teeth, but there was no sign of his sword. It could have fallen off during the swim, or the humans had taken it. He couldn't recall much of anything after the first few hours in the water. He'd drifted, the current had taken him off course, then the cold had set in. The last thing he remembered was a string of lights getting closer. He likely owed these people his life.

Gathering his hair in a long tail, he knotted it around his knuckles and tied it into a loose bun, touching the earring high in his left ear before lowering his hands. He'd made it this far. The rest should be easier.

The human dwelling was made of thick stone walls and windows set into those deep walls. The straight walls, set at right-angles, reminded him a little of the tower rooms, only warmer, softer and smaller. Drapes fluttered behind an open window. Outside, maize swayed in far-reaching rolling fields. He couldn't hear the ocean, just the squawk of birds. They must have brought him inland. No trees, bar one spindly looking thing that was barely any taller than him.

The wide-open space beckoned.

He was here for a reason. He could do this.

Venturing outside, he followed the line of dwellings lining a road, toward a small gathering of people. They seemed to be focused on some kind of wheeled-vehicle. Its hatch was open, and two of the humans leaned inside the machine like they might be eaten by it.

Chloe was among the group. She waved him over.

They spoke their language quickly, rattling it off so the words blurred into one long string. He waited, listened, and watched. The machine they were huddled around appeared to be able to carry five grown people. Its wheels, although chunky, wouldn't get far in his forests, but out here, on the flat plains, they could likely travel many miles in a day. Flat, black glass panels covered the roof. He'd thought them armor at first, but up close they looked too fragile to stop much of anything. He touched one and found it warm.

"Solar panels," Chloe said.

He blinked at her, unfamiliar with the words.

"It takes the light from the sun and converts it into power."

Alumn! He pulled his hand back. The *solar panels* fed off light, like he did?! "Are they magic?"

She laughed softly. "No, but I suppose it might seem that way."

But humans didn't have magic. At least, they hadn't in the past. They were, however, ingenious. The reason why he was here. "I need to speak with your elder."

"Of course, right this way."

More machines lined the road. Some bigger, some more armored, all likely had a different purpose. People watched him, nodding when he caught their gazes. They weren't so different from him. Some were shorter, some rounder, some darker, but elves varied too. And the people here were all younger men and women. Hard lives took the old and young too soon. Eroan knew that all too well.

He entered a long, single-story building, likely used for storing the grain but was now for storing guns. Stacks of them. It was often said that when the humans fled, they left behind metal and guns. Everything else, nature reclaimed.

Beyond the stacks, an enormous sheet hung half over what appeared to be an unfinished cage. It had to be as big as the largest Order houses. Large enough to accommodate a small dragon.

"Unfortunately, producing bullets is slow," Chloe was saying, walking him right by the cage. "And we've run out of the necessary components. Plus, guns never did work against them, not effectively."

Eroan stopped and peered up the long, narrow spaced bars. "Have you ever caught one?"

"We tried." She regarded the cage. "But we can't contain them for long. They shift, always finding a way out of our restraints. But this cage—" she grabbed a bar and gave it a testing tug "—once finished, should solve that."

Their cage had narrow, closely welded bars. A fully grown dragonkin could not slip through them, not even wearing its human skin. He tried not to gawk like an outsider and instead kept his gaze measured, like all of this was routine, when inside hope and delight sent his thoughts reeling. Elves could never have built such a thing, not on such a huge scale. "Where am I exactly?"

"Outside what used to be called *Le Touquet*." She saw the name meant little to him and added, "Northern French coast. One of few remaining strongholds. A brood of dragons took the Paris ruins when I was small. They've been spreading outward ever since. They don't bother us so much as the bronze across the channel. I assume you came from there?"

"I did."

"How did you get through their barricades?" she asked.

"Getting out is easier than getting in."

She studied him, likely wondering how he'd survived the crossing. Eroan bowed his head slightly. "Thank you, for saving me," he added.

"You were lucky." She left the cage and beckoned him along behind her toward a closed door. "A few weeks later and the ocean temperature drops considerably. You would not have survived long in the water." She knocked on the door. A deep voice barked *Enter!* and she pushed into a room full of maps. The walls were papered in them and the table strewn with the largest, a flattened map of the world.

A man got to his feet and beamed at Chloe. They exchanged quick words in French, then Chloe gestured at Eroan. "The elf we found on the beach."

"*Oui, oui!* You recovered quickly." The man grinned, crinkling his tanned face. His hair had faded to silver in places, the same as his peppered chin. He had eyes the same as Chloe's hazel ones.

"I am in your debt."

The man clapped his hands together and exclaimed, "*Ça alors!* It's been so long. We assumed you had all been killed, *je suis profondément désolé.*"

More French fell from the man's lips, and all Eroan could do was smile at the man's glee. "We believed the same of humans, but you are clearly thriving and inventing traveling machines."

"Thriving? Hm, not so much. And the cars, well... we have adapted some, but they're prone to faults and parts are scarce. We've all but scavenged anything of use within two hundred miles." He ventured around the table and tapped the large world map. "For all we know, Europe is all but desolate. The far east may have held on, but anything on either side of the Atlantic suffered the most. We have not heard from the Americas in decades now. They would send messengers across the seas, but their ships stopped coming when I was a boy, so that should tell you how long they've been silent."

Eroan scanned the map. The epicenter of the rising was marked high up in the center, just below the continent he knew as simply the Whitelands. And from there, the dragons had spread like an infection. He brushed his fingers over the dark stain. Similar dark blooms swelled all over, making the map appear as though it were rotting. His ancestors would have wept at this sight. It had been their responsibility to hold back the rising. Eroan felt the urge to apologize for the failure of his people. He swallowed the words. "I did not know…" he said instead. "I haven't seen it drawn like this before." The map painted a stark picture of a world lost to dragons. To see it laid out so clearly, it made the reality of his missions all the more daunting.

"I imagine not." The man offered his hand beside him. "I'm Gabriel… Gabe."

"Eroan Ilanea."

Gabe gripped Eroan's hand tight and clung on. "Are there any of your elders left?" he asked softly.

"Some. But we are scattered and small in number."

The man cupped Eroan's hand in both of his and squeezed. "That, in itself, is a miracle. I promised myself if I ever saw an elf again, I would apologize for the sins of our past. It should never have happened."

Eroan didn't feel qualified to ease this man's guilt. The events of the past were more myth than memory now. As far as he could recall from his childhood tales, both humans and elves had made mistakes. "It was a long time ago. I'm here to forge a new alliance." He gently pulled his hand free and set the bundle of teeth down onto the table, untying the straps so the teeth spilled out. "I recently learned of a weakness we can all exploit. It's why I'm here."

He told Gabriel and Chloe all he knew of the dragon's

teeth, including a slimmed version of how he'd come to realize how the teeth could penetrate dragonscales, but also how they might be weaponized with the help of the humans' huge machines.

More humans joined the meeting. Some clearly warriors from their lightly armored clothing and hard eyes. And Eroan answered their questions until the shadows outside had turned to night. The meeting moved from the map room to another building where a handful of families gathered to feast. More questions came his way, but also tales of how the humans had lived, how they had fought back by scavenging the remains of their old-world and created armored ships. Even the armor they wore, small steel plates over a black mesh-like fabric, specifically repelled dragon-fire, was an ingenious invention. They shared it all, so eager to bring him into their fold. The news was not as grim as he had feared. Humans were still alive, and they were fighting. Their enthusiasm warmed his blood and hope swelled in his chest. He had done the right thing by coming to them.

"Tomorrow," Chloe said. She leaned against the wall beside a generous fireplace, lit by the fire-dancing flames. "There's a team going to the nearest dragon pit to dig up their teeth and we'll put this idea of yours to the test."

He stood beside her, soaking up the warmth while watching the people. "I could show you if I hadn't lost my sword—"

"We have it," she said. "We weren't sure whether to let you keep it, but it's safe. You'll get it back when you leave."

Unease slithered beneath his skin. "I would prefer to have it with me."

"I'm sure you would," she laughed lightly. "But there are many here who feel safer with you unarmed."

"You don't trust me?"

Her friendly smile lost some of its softness. "It would be foolish of us to trust a stranger washed up on the beach."

"Elves are honorable..." He left the sentence hanging, and by Chloe's arched eyebrow, she had caught what he left unsaid.

"Yes, well... You've also been living among dragonkind for a very long time. I'm not suggesting you're anything but honorable, just that we don't know you or where that honor lies."

"Are you suggesting elvenkind might have formed an alliance with dragons?" It was enough to make his blood boil, though he kept any emotion from his face. To insinuate such a thing was a grave insult.

Another shrug. "We've all done things we thought we'd never do to survive. I'm sure elves are no different."

He studied the gathered people instead of letting her see anything unguarded on his face. "If I were so untrustworthy why would I risk my life to bring you this information?" He felt the sneer lift his lip and let it. Perhaps these humans needed a reminder of who it was they were dealing with.

"Why indeed?" Her smile softened, and he wondered if her human senses warned her that she was treading on thin ice. "Don't take it personally. We just... we have to be careful. There aren't many of us left. You would be no less suspicious of a human suddenly appearing in your camp."

That was true, considering what he knew of humans, but he had come for an alliance, and he wasn't about to let his pride ruin it. "I'd like to go with you tomorrow." He would get a feel for their warriors and what they were made of, and perhaps they would learn to trust him some more.

She nodded. "I'll ask Gabe. I'm sure he'll agree."

Good. This felt like progress, despite a few cultural frictions.

"How *did* you get through the bronze line?"

"Carefully." Eroan smiled. "I almost didn't. A bronze saw me on their beach. It toyed with me, would have killed me had another not attacked it."

"They fought? You saw it?"

He nodded, recalling the beast's face inches from his. "I escaped while they were distracted."

She chuckled. "Then luck is certainly on your side, Eroan. Let's hope you are a good omen. We're sorely in need of one."

Eroan felt his smile grow and the tension ease. The beach attack had been close. He would have been eaten if the emerald hadn't fought off the bronze. It had been wounded too, he recalled now. Instead of stretching its wings, it had tucked one in close. The bronze likely tore into it. His thoughts wandered to another dragon, his wing also damaged, and the last time he had seen him, tumbling through the skies, locked in combat with the black dragon, Akiem... Thinking of Lysander wasn't going to help him now, and yet he couldn't seem to be rid of the prince's memory for long. It stalked him often. He'd dreamed of those green eyes before waking here.

"How *do* you plan to return to your village?" she asked quietly, pulling Eroan's thoughts back. Before he could answer, she'd already seen the reply on his face. "You didn't plan on returning, did you? This is a one-way trip."

Until it is done.

He had told himself he'd return. He'd said the words to Seraph, but it had been a lie. There was no place for him among the Order, and after everything he'd admitted to Curan, there was no going back. Ever.

Chloe chewed on her lip and sighed. "You're a brave man—a brave elf. Are all your kind like you?"

"I used to think so." Now he hoped they weren't. Bravery led to foolishness, and there weren't enough elves left for their lives to be carelessly tossed away.

"Perhaps, if this works, I'll meet more elves one day. Gabe used to tell me stories when I was little of how the elves were a kind and caring people. *Hidden guardians,* he called them. He admires you, I think. Like you're a mythical creature come to life. He sees you as a new hope. If you can survive, then so can we."

Pride and warmth swelled in his chest. "We've sacrificed much of our kindness to protect ourselves, but it's still there, hidden. I would like for you to meet more elves too." It was unlikely in their lifetime unless the bronze wall fell, but he could hope. After all, blind hope had gotten him this far.

CHAPTER 38

*L*ysander

LYSANDER COULDN'T REMEMBER the name of the bronze in his bed. He wasn't even sure if he'd been told it, they'd barely said three words. The lower had appeared outside his room with a bring-it look in his shining eyes. Mirann had likely sent him as *fodder* and Lysander had been in no mood to turn him away. Things escalated from there and for a few blissful hours, he'd lost himself in the feel of the male's mouth taking him on deep. The freedom of not pretending, that was all he'd wanted, and the nameless bronze had given it to him. Or rather, Lysander had given *it* to the lower. Repeatedly.

Mirann had sent the lower as thanks for not forcing her hand in killing him, or for him not killing her. He wasn't entirely sure, but this gift would probably come with caveats. Lysander was too far gone to care. Fucking a nameless bronze emptied out all the messed-up shit in his head and that was enough. He could return to being the prince afterward. Here, with a lower, without his mother watching, without the entire dragon brood judging, the freedom he fell into finally made the hell he'd endured the last few weeks almost worth it.

He had quickly discovered the bronze had a piercing where his cock met his balls and had spent a great deal of time investigating it with his tongue, delighting in how the bronze groaned. After that, he'd flipped the male over and rimmed his spread ass with a wet finger, and for the first time in forever, he didn't feel that ugly, vicious shame of being wrong or different or a failure. Or the pressure of having to spill his seed in a female just because the bitch-queen needed to sell her numbers. Thinking of her sent him into a frenzy, and while the bronze panted beneath him, Lysander fucked the hate and pain away.

He rather liked Mirann's gift, he considered now, with the male sprawled beside him.

The lower stirred, finally waking. He lifted his shaven head and tried to reach out, to draw Lysander's into a kiss. Lysander pulled free and shifted out from under the male's warm limbs, hoping to avoid the awkward morning after. By now, in the tower, he would have had to pay an amethyst male off for his silence, making the whole act feel dirty.

There was none of that here, and yet it still felt as though he was being tugged by someone else's string. Mirann's.

She would appear soon.

He swallowed and dragged a hand down his chin and

around his neck. Thoughts from yesterday began to pile in. Thoughts of how he'd almost killed Mirann in full view of the bronze brood. Word would no doubt get back to his brother. That thought more than the others made the ugly hurt return with a vengeance. Would Akiem congratulate him or would he see Lysander as the enemy? *You're ours,* Mirann had said.

The bronze lower knelt behind him, pressed his knees on either side of Lysander's thighs, and brushed the silken softness of his hardened cock against Lysander's lower back. He purred and licked behind Lysander's jaw, at the sensitive spot below his ear, and tingling heat tightened Lysander's balls, reawakening lust.

This bronze—slimmer than most, which was probably why Mirann had picked him—was made of pure muscle. As dragon, he probably outsized Lysander, but the male's mind was a submissive and willing one. Lysander had explored much of the male's impressive design with his tongue, losing his fucking mind to the salty thrill of it. He was having a hard time thinking past it now.

The male rubbed against Lysander in an easy, rocking motion, and reached around the prince's waist to capture his straining erection. Fuck it. Lysander lay back, let the male thrust into his back, and dropped his head against the lower's shoulder. The male's mouth was on his neck again, his tongue swirling, and his hand pumped faster, lifting Lysander's lust higher and higher, making it crackle in all the right ways. He could feel the spooling, unraveling sensation, and shifted his hips, making the angle just right. Then the damn bronze was gone from his back but quickly dropped to his knees in front and between Lysander's thighs, his mouth and hand now working in a symphony.

Pleasure snagged somewhere inside. Lysander gasped and fell back onto his elbow so he could peer down himself at the bastard pinching his tip.

"Tease me at your own risk," he growled, low and deep, letting dragon slip through.

The bronze's mouth twitched. He parted his lips, pressed his tongue beneath Lysander's glistening head, and worked his fingers and thumb, pumping that pleasure higher all over again. Lysander kept him locked in his sights and watched his cock flush, felt the release coil low, gathering all the nerves into one sweet, tight ball that dumped him in mindless ecstasy the second the pressure broke, and his seed pumped onto the male's tongue. Once, twice more. Fucking diamonds, the bronze knew his way around a cock better than any amethyst he'd paid in the shadows.

The bronze pulled a few more times, tearing a curse from Lysander, then swallowed, his face flushed with glorious mischief. Lysander fell back and blinked at the ceiling. Yeah, he was going to have to pay Mirann for this.

He didn't hear the door open but smelled Mirann's metallic scent and heard her fingers snap together. The bronze hurried out, naked, sweat-soaked and erect.

"We weren't done," Lysander grumbled, propping himself on his elbows.

"You're done." She peered down her nose. "Get cleaned up. Your brother is here."

The afterglow fled, filling the pit of his stomach with dread. "He's here? What does he want?"

"To talk. Something about elves." She flicked a hand. "It's a ruse. He wants *you*. So let's show him you, shall we?"

Lysander stared at the closed door long after she'd left.

The way she'd grinned chilled his blood. Anything the elves could do wouldn't have been enough for Akiem to leave the tower and visit the frontline, not at a time when his rule was so fragile. She was right, his brother was full of shit. Akiem was scheming.

FAT, black clouds hung low in the skies over the lands behind the bronze palisades. The bronze flags still fluttered, only this time the wind had them pointing out to sea.

Lysander climbed the scaffold to the central watchtower and was met with Dokul's heated glare plus two other mute guards. The chief's tarnished armor was the battered and bruised kind, not the flimsy ceremonial garb he'd worn on the stage—the last time Lysander had seen him. In comparison, Lysander had thrown on something made of cotton, so he could at least breathe without clinking, and added an over-jacket. He couldn't bring himself to wear all their plates and chainmail. He wasn't built like a bronze. That armor just looked ridiculous on him. Dokul noted his lack of bronze attire with a grunt. "You look like something I'd chew up and spit out."

Nice. Lysander threw him a bright smile, and the male's lips twitched around a sneer that died on the way to his lips.

The bronze's threat sizzled in his memory. *Survive this and you have to survive me.* It had only been a couple of days since the coupling and Lysander had spent much of that mindlessly fucking the nameless bronze. Dokul knew where he'd been, of course. The chief likely knew everything that happened in the warren.

"You're ours now," Dokul said as Lysander took in the sight beyond the bronze line.

So you all keep saying...

Akiem had brought five flights, at least fifty dragonkin. Enough to turn this from a friendly chat into a clear threat. Lysander gripped the wall and scanned their numbers, recognizing many among them. They all wore their human masks—a strategic choice—and wore the typical amethyst plate armor, smooth and matte, so as not to reflect any light, but lightweight. Akiem could click his fingers, and that force would spill over the palisades in seconds. Had they been sprawled across the land as dragon, their numbers would have been a clear show of force. The bronze would have knee-jerked in response, but as human, they posed less of a visual threat.

The citrusy smell in the air reminded him of home, and he briefly wondered how he had found himself on the wrong side of a war he hadn't wanted. But it was done. Lysander was a traitor. And Akiem was here for him.

He spotted his brother among them, front and center of their loosely formed gathering.

"I will not give you up," Dokul declared.

Lysander arched an eyebrow at the chief and saw the male's broad cheek flutter as he regarded the amethyst force. Dokul would go to war on two fronts to keep him. Why? It had to be about more than the man's lust or his desire to have what he had been denied. Had Lysander's mother been the one bargaining with his life, he'd know why she didn't want to relinquish him. Breeding more amethyst. But Dokul hadn't mentioned offspring. Dokul didn't want Lysander because he was amethyst. There had to be another reason.

Movement among the amethyst drew Lysander's eye downward. Akiem strode forward. Behind him, four of his flight broke from the ranks, bringing with them two figures both tied at their wrists and dragged behind them like pets on a leash. Their pale skin, shapely eyes, and pointed ears were unmistakable. Elves. Lysander narrowed his eyes, sharpening his focus. Two females. Both wearing stubborn, blank looks, like all of this couldn't touch them. They should have been groveling and submissive. By diamonds, were they all as stupid and as stubborn as Eroan?

"Why does he bring elves to my door?" Dokul mused aloud. The big male gripped the wall, clenching it so tightly his caramel-skinned knuckles paled to a wheat color.

There was no reason to bring elves here, none that Lysander could imagine. He looked away, down the palisade walls and then above. Heavy cloud-cover hid the skies.

"Do you have flights in the air?" he asked.

Dokul turned his gaze on Lysander.

"Or are they all out patrolling the coast? Because if I were Akiem, I'd want all of your attention on the unnecessary elves and not on the skies if I were planning to steal back my traitorous brother."

Dokul nodded at a sentinel guard. "See to it immediately."

"Dokul!" Akiem called. The wind threw his familiar voice at them. "Must your king wait all day for an invite?"

"Or..." Lysander looked down. Akiem was close enough

now for him to see his mildly amused expression. "...he could just be here to speak of elves and gloat about his new role as reigning monarch." One of those options was a lot more likely than the other.

Dokul dropped a hand onto Lysander's shoulder, knowing it would be seen by all. "There was a time these things were settled beneath teeth and claw." Dokul kept his voice low so that only Lysander would hear. "I preferred those days." He nodded at the waiting Akiem and spoke aloud, "Of course, you are welcome, *Prince* Akiem."

His brother's amused expression cracked and fell away.

"Open the gates," Dokul told his guards. "Let him and his escorts in, but only them. Monitor those that remain. Any break from their ranks and I'm to be informed immediately."

Lysander knew that any attack wouldn't be as obvious as to come from the front. If Akiem had come here to fight, then there would be a force somewhere else, somewhere hidden. And the bronze would never see them coming.

CHAPTER 39

*T*he cavern carved from solid rock was easily large enough to accommodate half a dozen dragons in their true forms, but today, the vastness of space served to remind the amethyst how small they were inside Dokul's warren. At least, that's what Lysander assumed from reading his broods' quick glances and solid jaws. He knew all too well how an amethyst preferred to be above ground, not below it. The heat would be fucking with them too, although Akiem appeared immune, standing proud in his armor and cloak. His brother always had been immune to everything. Always above it and untouchable.

Lysander had to admit, Akiem looked like a king, even without a crown. A stern king. He had their mother's fierceness. Seeing him here, now, after they had both tried to claw each other to pieces, reminded Lysander of exactly why he'd killed her, and why he'd left, and why even this gods-awful place—with their twisted mind-fucks—was better than the tower. Akiem would have killed him. Still might.

The amethyst guards forced the elves to their knees on the polished stone floor. The right thing for those elves to do would be to drop their heads and act meek, so of course, they both knelt like they were about to be honored, not executed. The younger one had a fresh face with wide, emotive, darting eyes. The tip of her ear was missing. Had she been dragon, he would have assumed it had been bitten off, but elves didn't seem the sort to bite chunks out of each other. In truth, Lysander had no idea how elves lived. Maybe they were all vicious. Eroan had certainly been able to handle himself.

The older elf had a calmness about her, as though she had resigned herself to this and accepted what would happen with grace and honor. He saw some of Eroan's defiance and pride in them both. Not that it mattered, they'd be dead within the hour.

"Gifts?" Dokul asked. His rumbling voice echoed deep into the empty space around them.

"Of a sort," Akiem replied. "They have information." His gaze flicked to Lysander but he schooled his expression, keeping his thoughts far from his face.

Dokul took a long look at the elves, his smile growing with every passing second. "If you're hoping to trade them for Lysander, they had better shit iron. I have no use for them otherwise."

Akiem's jaw worked. "Lysander is an amethyst."

"You know he's not." This came from Mirann. She marched into the cavern, armored from her bronze boots to her shaped shoulder pauldrons and drew alongside

Lysander. "Your mother's deal was binding. He is bronze now."

"My mother is dead." Another flutter in Akiem's jaw. "Any recent deals she made were rendered void upon her death."

"Prince Akiem," Dokul stepped forward. "You have no authority here. We will not be giving up Lysander, and so, if there is no other business—"

Akiem withdrew a sword from inside his cloak and threw it to the floor. It sang against the stone. "I found this on the younger elf."

Lysander knew that sword, knew every recurve, every nick in its blade, every notch in the handle. It was his. How in the hells had the elves gotten it? His heart thudded too loud. He scoured the elves' faces. The elder one hadn't reacted, but the younger one... She looked at that sword, her chest rising and falling too fast. She knew it too.

"My brother knows what this is," Akiem said. "And what it means."

All eyes turned to him, all but the young elf's.

"It's mine," he said.

The young elf jerked her head up and met Lysander's gaze, failing miserably at hiding her emotions, although he couldn't read them all. Fear, certainly. Intrigue too. He didn't understand why this sword would mean anything to her, why the fact he owned it seemed important.

"Who are you?" he asked her.

She bared her teeth, showing two tiny little canine teeth. Eroan had often bared his teeth in the same way. Of course, she didn't answer him. Gods, he could feel it happening again. What was it with him and stubborn elves

291

and their stubborn silences? He wiped the smile off his lips before it had fully formed.

"Why did an elf have my sword?" he asked Akiem, splitting his glances between them.

"I was hoping you could tell us."

"I have no idea. The last time I saw my swords, they were in Elisandra's hands, right before I killed her. "

Akiem winced as Lysander had known he would, but his brother's discomfort paled as he thought back to that night in the queen's chamber. He'd dropped the swords by the bed right before he'd begun to seduce Eroan. She'd picked one up and pressed it to his neck, and then... Those blades would have been left in the rubble and ash, surely?

"You let elves into the tower?" he asked Akiem.

Akiem growled. "Don't insult me. Only one of us has let an elf live long enough to steal from you."

"That elf died."

"Clearly, it did not." Akiem gestured at the sword. "Unless you gave your swords to the elves? Did you? Are you in league with the elves, brother?"

"No... I..." Dokul and Mirann were observing all this, reading their own assumptions into it. "The elf died, Akiem. You were there. Your flames killed him."

Akiem huffed. "I saw you kill Mother, nothing else. It really doesn't matter. This sword is yours, and now the elves are disturbing our remains, digging up our dead and stealing our teeth."

"That has nothing to do with me—"

"He didn't die!" the young elf blurted. "He survived, he came back to us, and now we're going to kill you all!"

Akiem backhanded her from behind, sending her sprawling close to Dokul's boots. The bronze snatched a fist full of her hair and jerked her off the floor, so her legs kicked. She hissed and spat, snapping her teeth at the bronze. Dokul laughed and grinned at Lysander. "I like this one."

Lysander needed to know more. The sword being here was important. That elf was important. She knew Eroan... and impossibly, she said he lived. His carefully guarded heart fractured and a splinter of pain cut into his chest. Eroan had survived. That damned fool of an elf had escaped that night and stolen Lysander's sword, maybe both of them. Did he wear the other blade? Lysander's mind ran free with the possibilities.

Mirann was watching this all unfold with too much fascination. Dokul, too, waited for Lysander's reaction, and Akiem knew Lysander could not let the young elf leave.

"What do you want?" Lysander asked Akiem.

"You."

"No," Dokul answered. "Ask again and you'll never leave this warren."

"If I do not return, my flight will rip through your defenses," Akiem replied.

"Our line has stood for hundreds of years."

"Yes." Akiem smiled. "Against forces attacking from the sea. Your internal defenses are weak. You've never needed to fight off a force from the north."

Dokul's chest broadened. "You'll never get inside the warren."

"We don't need to get in, we just need to limit your efficiency. The humans will do the rest."

Dokul's laugh turned dark. "Without our defenses, you're exposed."

"No, without your defenses, we're free to advance beyond the coast, to spread farther. We don't need you, Dokul. We never really did. The queen kept you here, kept you working away to keep you occupied on the humans, to give you bronze something shiny to distract you, so you didn't bother her."

Dokul dropped the elf and squared up to Akiem, dwarfing him in bulk. "You need to withdraw, or I'll take your pissy flight and tear them to pieces."

Akiem's guards reached for their weapons.

Mirann reached for hers.

"A new dawn rises and the age of the dragons will soon be over," The older elf said, her quiet voice cutting through the thick violence with scalpel precision. She looked at Lysander—looked through him, and in one sudden lunge, grabbed the blade off the floor, her wrists still bound together, and thrust sloppily toward Dokul. Mirann was between them in a blink, her bronze dagger punched through the elf's chest, lifting her off her feet.

Lysander grabbed at Akiem's shirt and yanked his brother close. A swell of crackling magic darkened Akiem's aura. "Get out of here or they'll kill you and your flights. Go!" He shoved, hoping it would be enough to jolt his brother into action.

But it was already too late. The tension that had been building suddenly snapped. Akiem's human outline shuddered and sloughed off. A rush of power filled the space between them, sweeping Akiem up. His body split apart and scattered in a cloud of darkness, like stars, only for those pieces to find the edges of an enormous bulk and twist it, shape it, building dragon from the nothing space. Akiem's wings flung outward, blasting them all with a storm of dust, consuming everything from floor to cavernous ceiling, painting the space in black scales, and there stood Akiem in all his dragon-glory.

Lysander bolted, grabbed the young elf and ran. Deafening roars chased him down. The push and pull of air shifting briefly tripped him, then a second roar blasted and bronze wings burst open above like golden fireworks exploding.

Terrible sounds of claws raking on scales, of teeth snapping, broiled behind him. He didn't look, couldn't look, and ran for the doorway. The ground dropped, sending him and the elf sprawling. Rock tumbled, and one of the dragons screeched like the very earth was opening to swallow it. Lysander saw then. The bronze chief and his daughter—both enormous—had his brother against the cavern wall, pushed into the rock, shattering the wall and the ceiling above. More boulders collapsed. Teeth flashed. Then, as an orange glow burned through the clouds of dust, Lysander twisted, launched off his feet and sped from the room with the elf in tow.

LYSANDER BUNDLED the elf into his room, slammed the door closed, and flung himself against it as though he could hold back the inevitable. Whoever won that fight would come for the elf and him. What had his brother been thinking attacking the bronze in his warren?

The elf gingerly lowered herself to the edge of his bed and gripped the sheets as though hoping they could keep her safe. "By Alumn..." she whispered, "by Alumn, by Alumn..." over and over, a prayer to her goddess.

If Lysander was in trouble, she was dragon feed.

"We don't have long." He crouched in front of her, hoping to make himself small and less threatening. She was a little thing, all long limbs and darting eyes, reminding him of a startled deer. He lifted a hand to sweep her bangs out of her eyes.

She sprang, turning into a screeching, tearing, clawing thing.

Lysander stumbled backward. Her teeth sank into his neck. Punches thumped his ribs, trying to pummel him into submission.

He tore her off and flung her down. "Gods damn it, elf. I just saved your life back there!"

"For your own uses!" she spat, scrabbling backward until she bumped against the bed.

He dabbed at his neck. "Don't flatter yourself." His fingers came away bloody. "I don't do elves." She was a fiery one, and with passion like that, he'd bet his scales she knew of Eroan. "Who gave you my sword?"

"I'm not telling you beasts anything!" She tucked her legs under her, turning her long limbs sprawl into a careful, wary crouch, ready to spring again at any second.

"That was *my* sword." He clamped a hand over the bite to stem the flow. Bitten by an elf. By the great gods, what was next? "If you elves are so honorable, why did one of your kind steal it from me?"

"He didn't steal it from you." She stuck her chin out. "The person he got the sword from is dead."

"No, that's definitely not the case." He gestured at himself. "Definitely not dead. You, however," he pointed, "will be."

She blinked those big, emotive eyes. "You're not going to kill me after saving me."

"You'll live a lot longer if you don't argue with elf-eating dragons." Damn her. Of course he wasn't going to kill her. She had a mind as sharp as her teeth. "It was Eroan, wasn't it? The elf who gave you my sword?"

She shrugged, and even that little gesture was defiant. "I don't know any Eroan."

He narrowed his eyes. "Liar."

"A dragon's calling me a liar!" She laughed. Climbing to her feet, she frowned back at him. "Let me go and I'll tell you."

She had to be a whole two feet shorter than him, but for what she lacked in size, she made up for in pure rage, defiance, and stubbornness. So much so, when she started to stalk toward him, Lysander straightened and planted his feet, holding his ground.

"Let you go?" He brushed his bloody hand on his thigh and dabbed some more at his neck. The blood had clotted, at least.

She stopped outside his reach. Her constantly shifting gaze and tense stance suggested she'd bounce off the walls at any second or bite him again the first chance she got. "Get me outside and I'll tell you everything."

"You'll tell me everything about Eroan? He truly lives?" He tried to hide the breathless hitch in his voice and failed. At least she couldn't hear how his heart rattled.

"Maybe." She shrugged a shoulder again.

Insolent, foolish elf. "I could torture it out of you." He took a step closer. She wasn't backing down. If anything, his threat had sparked more fire in her bright eyes.

"The others would," she said, "but not you... I know who you are. Prince Lysander."

He spat a laugh. "You've heard my name, so you think you know me? You, little elf—" he poked her in the chest, risking her wrath "—have no idea what I'm capable of."

She pressed her lips together. "I know one thing, you saved an elf before, and you'll do it again now."

He knew one thing. Eroan *was* alive, for sure. He hadn't expected it to mean so much, for his heart to soar when his wings could not. Just knowing Eroan hadn't burned up on that bed cleared some of the fog that had been smothering his thoughts since that night.

If only he still had both his wings, he would take to the skies and find him, bronze and amethyst war be damned.

"Like I said," the elf grinned, reading her victory on Lysander's face, "let me go and I'll tell you what you want to know."

LYSANDER SCANNED THE BEACH. The tide had pulled back, revealing countless nooks for an elf to hide in. The thunderous sound of the waves hid any sound they might make, but bringing her down here was still a risk.

She had fallen quiet. The shivering had started minutes ago. Shock, probably. If the bronze found her, she'd feel worse than those tremors and then nothing at all.

"You'll have to climb those cliffs," he said, lifting his voice over the crashing waves. He nodded at the vertical cliff face. "I can't do any more for you."

The faraway look in her eyes made him wonder if he was just delaying the inevitable. If she didn't stop shivering, she'd never make the climb. Eroan had taught him that elves were tough bastards and this one was tougher than she looked. She'd make it. But once at the top...

The skies churned with dragons. He had no idea if the fight still raged or if his brother had gotten away. When the chaos died down, her chances were slim.

"What's your name?" he asked, starting the climb over a chunk of rusted wreckage.

The elf looked at the twisted metal like she'd never seen human machines before, then started gingerly climbing after him. "Seraph."

He made it to the top of the wreckage and spotted a bronze half a mile down the beach. The dragon eyed the waters, not the skies. It was too far away to hear them and the salt water would mask their scent, but its eyesight was sharp, especially in low light. "We should stay here a while, see if it moves away."

Seraph gasped and almost lost her footing. Lysander snatched at her sleeve and yanked. She looked at his hand. Then, wide-eyed, looked up at him. Raw fear showed in the whites of her eyes. Where was her fire from earlier? And then, Lysander realized, she knew if the cliff didn't kill her, the bronze flights circling above would.

"You know Eroan?" he asked, distracting her. They both crouched low and huddled against the brisk, sea-soaked wind.

"Eroan is—was my t-teacher." Her teeth chattered. She pulled her arm from his grip and hugged them around herself.

"Was?" Was this the part when she told him Eroan really was dead? He couldn't take it if she did. That tiny flutter of hope would shrivel up and die, sitting like a kernel of poison inside. Strange, that he'd pin so much on an elf he barely knew, terrifying even, but he couldn't pretend he didn't feel.

"He left." She sniffed.

Not dead. Lysander sighed. "Why?"

"The Order kicked him out. He... He said some things to our leader." She briskly rubbed her upper arms. The salted wind ruffled her hair and nipped at her cheeks, turning them pink.

So Eroan had gotten kicked out of the assassin club for his smart mouth. That sounded like Eroan, but even Lysander knew the Order wasn't something an elf walked away from. It was Eroan's life, his reason for breathing, the fire that had kept burning in the darkest of nights. Only now did Lysander realize what that kind of devotion might have felt like. "Must have been some words."

"Yeah, well... He came back from killing the queen all wounded inside, but the others couldn't see the scars," her lips twisted. "We *thought* he killed the queen. Turns out, that was you."

Lysander's cheek twitched. He watched the bronze again, keeping the elf in the corner of his vision.

"He thought..." she went on. "He thought he'd failed so... I don't know... I think he needed to do something to prove he deserved to be alive when all the others had died."

Pride. When Lysander had first seen him, strung up by the wrists in the dark, pride had burned in his gaze. It was Eroan's strength and his weakness.

"Where did he go?" he asked.

"He had the teeth and he said he'd..." she hesitated and bit her lower lip. "I shouldn't tell you."

"Akiem already did. Eroan figured out dragon teeth are effective at getting through scale." Eroan had seen him stab Elisandra with the sword, it was the only way the elf could have known. And now he was alive, free, and making more swords to kill dragons with. It wasn't a surprise, and Lysander should probably have felt more guilt for handing the elves a weapon, but he couldn't bring himself to care. Eroan was alive, and he was out there, still fighting, winning for his people.

"Where did he go?" he asked again. "After he was kicked out?"

"Here."

"What?"

"To the bronze line. Then he was going to the humans."

Lysander's heart stuttered. The elf on the beach, the one he'd stopped Mirann from toying with. That couldn't have been Eroan?

"What—what is it?" Seraph asked.

He sat back and switched his gaze over her shoulder and out at the gray seas. Eroan had been here, right under his nose? It didn't seem possible. Then he remembered Eroan's seemingly never-ending determination, his strength and how he'd survived for so long on will-power alone.

"He made it," Lysander whispered.

Her lashes fluttered. "You know for sure?"

"I know he made it through this line and I doubt he's the type to let an ocean stop him."

"Alumn..." Seraph sighed as though breathing out a great weight. "Xena would have liked to have known..."

The elf's frown cut deeper, and her eyes took on a glassy sheen. "Xena was with me when they came…"

Lysander winced inside. She looked tough, and her bite was definitely worse than her bark, but this little elf was on borrowed time. Climbing the cliffs in daylight would expose her, but if she stayed on the beach until nightfall, the cold would finish her off. Her simple leather clothes were thin and ill-suited to weathering outside. If he let her go now, she was dragon bait. How could he leave her?

"You can't do this."

"What choice do I have?" A tear fell. She swiped the offensive little drop away.

If he let her go now, and she died, he'd never forgive himself. If he ever saw Eroan again, he wanted to tell him how he'd met an elf and how Seraph survived, not how he'd sent her to her death when he could have saved her. After everything Lysander had seen done to Eroan, after every lash of the whip he'd dealt him, the least he could do was try to save this elf's life.

"I can protect you."

She swallowed.

"It means going back inside and choosing a time to escape when you can get through the line. But this here… trying to climb the cliffs, it will get you killed."

"You would help me?"

"I can't guarantee they won't hurt you, but I can keep you alive. I give you my word."

"A dragon's word? How can I trust you not to just hand me over?"

"That's the odd thing about trust, you either do or you don't." He offered her his hand. "This won't be easy,

Seraph, but you'll live, I promise you. And I'll get you out when the time is right."

She looked at his hands and his face, searching for deceit. "Did you really save Eroan?"

He pulled his hand back. "I tried, but he's... difficult. He would never have left if I hadn't killed the queen, no matter the cost. He didn't fail. He killed others. He would have killed us all eventually."

She tucked a dancing lock of dark hair behind her pointed ear. "But not you?"

Lysander remembered how Eroan had lifted his head to the sun and smiled like everything was right with the world. He remembered too how he'd wanted to kiss his jaw and run that kiss along Eroan's sun-blushed lips. But that moment hadn't changed the past or the whip lashes Lysander had dealt him. Someone like Eroan wouldn't ever forget that. Lysander wouldn't blame the elf if he one day took his revenge.

"He needed me to get to Elisandra." And that was an ugly truth he hadn't let himself admit. Eroan was a dragon-killer, and Lysander had been an easy target. He'd fooled himself into making up some fantasy that could never be. "Once it was done, Eroan would have killed me." *And I'd have let him.*

"So, why are you helping me? Why are you different?" she asked.

He shrugged and dragged a smile out of nowhere. "I've no idea. If you figure it out, let me know, won't you." He offered his hand again. This time, she took it.

∼

"DON'T FIGHT BACK, don't give them any reason to notice you. Be meek and obliging."

Seraph listened, her face paling. Lysander wasn't about to pretty this up for her. If she was anything like Eroan, she knew exactly what awaited her in a bronze warren. All he could hope was that he might save her from the worst of their *affections*.

Dokul's private receiving caverns were empty of dragons. He likely had them all out hunting down amethyst. And as the warren wasn't heaving with amethyst dragons, Lysander assumed Dokul had won the brawl. He'd soon know for sure.

"What do we do?" the young elf asked, absently eyeing the strange sculptures of twisted metal propped about the room.

"We wait."

Hanging tapestries covered doorways leading to other, more private areas of Dokul's chambers. Lysander had gone no farther than this room in the weeks he'd been in residence, and he had no wish to. He watched Seraph drift around, her dark clothes and little frame at odds with the enormity of this place. She reached out a hand to stroke some monstrosity of mangled wreckage.

"Don't touch anything," he snapped.

Seraph snatched her hand back. "What are these things?"

"Bits of the old-world. He likes to collect metal, anything that shines... it's a bronze thing." Collect it, wear it, some of them even ate the stuff. Lysander had tried not to think too hard on the bronze idiosyncrasies.

"How did you come to be here?" she asked him while eyeing the strange sculpture instead.

"My brother witnessed me kill Elisandra. He would never have let me live. I had no choice but to come here. It was that or go wild and..." he hesitated, "never mind, I was due to come here anyway."

She looked him over from head to toe. "Can't you go anywhere you want?"

He dropped into one of Dokul's tall-backed chairs and smiled at the elf's innocence. "You don't know much about dragon hierarchy, do you?"

She looked as though she might sneer something, likely an insult, and then tore her gaze away and fixed it on the tall, ugly metal thing in front of her. "They taught us some... in the Order."

"Tell me." This should be interesting, and it would keep his mind off what was about to happen.

"You have lowers who hunt and provide daily services for those at the higher end of the pecking order."

"Pecking order?"

"Oh, you know..." she waved a hand. "Like chickens."

"What?" He bristled.

"Chickens." She planted her hands on her hips and flapped her elbows. "Flightless birds."

A smile tried to break out across Lysander's lips. "I know what a chicken is, but I'm struggling to see why you would compare me to one."

"Well, not... you, not a direct comparison. I mean," she trailed off when his glower darkened. "Anyway, I suppose we don't know much about dragons socially. What was your point?"

He'd forgotten he had a point and stared at the elf, concern fraying his nerves. The bronze were going to eat her alive. He could protect her for a day, maybe a week, but it would happen eventually. Had he lied when he'd told her he'd protect her?

"The, er..." He cleared his throat. "I could never just leave. For one, the amethyst tower was my home, but the times I did try to escape, she always found me. Trying to leave is seen as a betrayal and swiftly dealt with. As Elisandra's son, I suffered... more than most."

"And now your brother wants you dead?"

"Broods, huh." His lips twisted. "How do elves discipline those who want to leave their flights?"

"A group of elves is called a pride." Seraph's smile bloomed.

"A pride of elves?" She nodded, and Lysander grinned back at her. That was ironically accurate.

"We don't discipline anyone for leaving," she continued. "Most don't. Why would they leave the safety of the village?" Her smile snagged on a memory then faded from her lips.

"Akiem took you from your village?" Lysander guessed.

"They tracked us from the air. We... had traps, we even brought one down, but there were too many." Her arms folded around herself again.

Lysander could only imagine the destruction his brother would have wrought upon finding an elven village. He wouldn't have held back, not after finding those elves desecrating dragon bones. Seraph and the other one—Xena—were lucky to survive at all.

Seraph's face had paled again. She looked at the strange sculpture and turned away. "Eroan doesn't know. He left before it happened—"

Grumbling barks drew Lysander's eye toward the door. Seraph heard it too. She threw a panicked look his way.

"Come stand behind me," he said. "Do as I say. If anything alarms you, just..." he wet his lips and gripped the chair's arms. "...just don't show it. Pretend like you're stone —or steel."

Dokul breezed in moments later with Mirann in tow. They both saw Lysander sprawled in the chair at the same time and failed to mask their joint surprise.

Mirann's predatory smile cut deeper into her cheeks. "I told you he wouldn't leave."

Her father tore off his breastplate and dropped it like it was trash. His heated glare fixed on Lysander. "Your brother's foolish actions weakened our defenses. We have a gaping hole in the warren!"

"Then you should have better defenses." Lysander made sure to wear the same blank look he'd perfected for his mother over the years.

Dokul blinked and frowned as though he couldn't have heard correctly, then barked a laugh. "You have some gall, princeling." He approached Lysander in the chair, his gaze burning hotter with every stride. "*You* brought this trouble to my door at a time I can ill afford to be distracted."

Lysander casually leaned to one side, it happened to be the side Seraph quivered on, as the bronze stalked forward. The elf's nervous energy crackled. She could act proud all she liked, but her fear betrayed her, and would likely arouse Dokul's instincts. Lysander was close enough to intervene, but he hoped it didn't come to that.

"All over elves and swords." Dokul veered from Lysander, reached out and cupped Seraph's face. She did well to look him in the eyes. "And one lost prince." His gaze slid to Lysander. He dropped his hand. "What brings you to my chambers, Lysander? What do you want?"

"War is inevitable, let us not pretend otherwise. And while Akiem's rule is legitimate, I trained the flights under him. A few discreet messages here and there, and I could take the tower right out from under him."

"You want to rule?" Dokul asked, measuring his tone carefully.

"No. I am... I am not a leader," Lysander's smile was coy, "but you are."

Lust and want sparkled in the bronze's eyes. Lysander was saying all the right things to an old, hungry dragon.

"All dragons will be stronger under you," he added.

Dokul swallowed with a click.

"Lysander—" Mirann began.

"Leave." Dokul snapped.

"Don't do this," Mirann growled. "You can't trust him, you know. But I can control—"

Dokul turned, "Leave, daughter. Lysander and I have much to discuss."

"He's protecting the elf." Mirann's too-sharp glare cut straight to Seraph, marking the elf for later.

Dokul narrowed his eyes at Lysander. "Is that true?"

Lysander's leisurely smile ticked. He rose from the chair and looked Dokul in the eyes. "This elf is not to be touched, harmed or harassed in any way."

The old dragon bared his teeth behind a leering grin. "And who are you to make demands in my warren? After the damage your brother left behind, this elf is surely mine."

Lysander pressed a hand against the bronze's cheek. His chin felt rough and leathery beneath the sweep of his thumb. He resisted the urge to shudder.

This had been coming for years, ever since Dokul had

tried to rape him and learned Lysander wasn't an easy catch. But if Lysander wanted Seraph kept safe, if he wanted to gain control of more than Mirann, if he wanted to rise up and teach them all what it meant to be wronged, then this had to happen—for now.

"You have a far more desirable prize at your fingertips." Lysander deliberately wet his lips, drawing the bronze's wide-eyed gaze downward to his mouth.

"Lysander is mine," Mirann growled a territorial warning low in her throat.

Lysander ignored her and peered into Dokul's gaze, keeping the male firmly under his spell. His mother had once said, long ago, after the third or fourth time she'd tried to kill him, how entrancing his gaze could be, like two pools of emeralds no dragon could resist. He used that gaze now, luring the ancient bronze in deep.

"Father!"

Dokul's temper flared. He swung its heat on Mirann. "Get out!"

After she'd left, he looked again at Lysander. "I could take you anyway. By force, if necessary."

"You tried that once. It did not end well for you." Lysander flopped back into the chair and deliberately twisted so he could prop a leg over the chair's arm. He dragged his knuckles down his jawline. "Wouldn't you rather have me willingly?"

Lust flushed heat up the male's neck and face. He glanced at the silent Seraph. "And you can take the amethyst's tower without a battle?"

The bronze chief had always been so easy to read, and this arrangement was no different than the one he'd performed with Mirann. In many ways, it was easier, and knowing Eroan was alive somewhere, knowing that foolish elf was out there, full of defiance and pride. It was enough to shore up Lysander and lend him the strength he needed to see this through.

Seraph caught his eye while the bronze peered at him. The elf's wide eyes were full of fear, for her, and perhaps for Lysander too. She was learning now what it took to survive as dragon among dragons. Especially a broken dragon prince.

Dokul braced an arm on the back of the chair over Lysander's head and leaned in so close his wet-metal scent filled Lysander's head and laced his throat. "You have no idea the beast you tempt... but you will."

Lysander swallowed. "Agree the elf is not to be touched."

Dokul locked his large, hot fingers around Lysander's throat and peered so close Lysander saw how the fire burned in his golden eyes. "When you play a foolish game with an ancient, do not expect to win, princeling."

"Agree..." Lysander wheezed. Instincts screamed at him to fight the male off, but it was too late to fight. It had to happen this way or not at all.

Dokul squeezed. "My bronze and I won't touch your elf, prince. Let it rot for all I care. But to make up for it, I'm going to own you in every way, until you can't breathe without tasting me, can't move without feeling me inside you. You have no idea what it is you've agreed to, but you will... " His grip loosened. He dragged his fingers down Lysander's panting chest, pulling the lamé shirt with them, making it cut into Lysander's neck. "You've just sold yourself for one pathetic little elf."

CHAPTER 40

 roan

BRISK, salty air dampened Eroan's cheeks and lashes. He closed his eyes, opening all other senses, and tilted his face toward the spray. Sunrays blazed today, soaking into his soul and warming him through. The ship hissed through the waves, its bow occasionally thumping against large swells. He tasted salt on his lips, felt it tighten his skin. This was freedom.

Bellows and calls sounded around him as the crew managed the enormous sails, harnessing the wind. These vast ships were ingenious, and the human fleet even more so. Opening his eyes, he spotted the three other ships carving through the waves to his left. To his right, two more thundered on, sails full. Their armored cladding shimmered in the sun.

"You look as though you were made for this." Chloe grinned, clutching the rail beside him.

He adjusted his sword slung against his back, and regarded her own armaments. A selection of short-bladed cutting daggers bristled at her hips and ankle straps. The arms of a modified crossbow peeked over her shoulder. Each bolt was dragontooth-tipped. She wouldn't have looked out of place among his Order.

"I am made for this..." He breathed in and held that breath, thinking of home, of all the times he'd dreamed of fighting back in force.

"A penny for your thoughts?"

He let the breath go and regarded her with a raised eyebrow.

"Oh, it's a human saying... You just... you seemed to be thinking so deeply."

"I was thinking of a dragon."

Her gaze thinned as it often did when the topic of dragons came up. "Just one?"

"Without him, none of this would be possible." Eroan swallowed hard. Had Lysander not persisted in saving him, Eroan wouldn't have made it this far, wouldn't have known to harvest the teeth. Without Lysander, Eroan would have fallen outside the queen's chamber just like the rest of his pride had.

"You never said how exactly you learned about the teeth..."

He tried to smile under her scrutiny and wasn't sure he managed it. "One dragon insisted on saving me. Without him, I would be dead. Several times over."

She huffed. "Likely for his own nefarious purposes. They never act out of kindness."

"Perhaps..." Lysander seemed to have no motive other than trying to make sure one of them lived. Shaking his head free of the prince, Eroan glanced at the shimmering deck. "You're not concerned they'll see the sun reflected on the cladding?" he asked, eager to steer the conversation in a direction far from the prince.

Chloe fondly smiled at the question, losing some of her rigid tension. "No. The sun is behind us, we're in its glare. They won't see us approach. And as it dips to the west, we'll shift to the east, low on the horizon."

Eroan wasn't entirely convinced. They seemed exposed on the flat of this great ocean. But this wasn't the first time the humans had assaulted the bronze defenses, and he was no seaman.

His gaze wandered back onto the deck where the enormous ballista sat proudly at the bow, its heavy-duty spear —the size of a lance—lay wedged against its side, ready to be nocked. A polished and shaped dragontooth glistened at the end of the hardwood shaft. Each of the ships carried one just like it, and each of the hundred or so humans carried dragontooth weapons.

There were many human lives relying on his discovery.

"It will work." Chloe shielded her eyes and squinted at him.

They trusted him. It had taken time to get this far. Time and patience. But with each mission to collect the teeth, and with Eroan having helped bring down a dragon scout, putting the blades into action, they'd come around enough to give him his sword back. A few weeks later, one had asked him to teach her how to swing a sword and was quickly joined by more, and somewhere in all of that, he'd started feeling like he belonged.

Eroan had hoped to return to the bronze line with a stronger force, one combined with his own people, but there was no messaging them, not until the bronze line fell. This human fleet with its new weapons would have to be enough.

He gripped the rail tighter and squinted into the sun. "Aim for their eyes," he said. "Blinded, they're disorientated. The boats must get close. We can't afford to miss."

She settled a hand on his. "We know. We're ready."

He looked at her human hands. Pink and warm. Then up into her kind face. The salt air had nipped at her cheeks, brightened her eyes and mussed up any loose strands of hair, making her seem wilder than her usual steady calmness. "Perhaps we should run another drill..." He gently withdrew his hand and closed his fingers into a loose fist. She had begun to look at him differently in the last few days. It reminded him of how his people had looked at him in their unguarded moments like he could deliver them from darkness. They hadn't known how he'd carried that darkness inside of him, a darkness he hoped he would soon wipe clean.

Chloe arched her eyebrow and leaned against the rail to admire the bustling crew. "If they don't know it by now, one more drill isn't going to make a difference. The sun is shining, the ocean is kind. Let them have this moment."

Because it may be their last...

This had to work. He'd lost too much for it not to. *Alumn, guide these humans and their aim.*

He didn't often pray—Alumn was always listening—but today they would need Her grace. *Make their faith in me be true. Make my survival mean something.* If the bronze line fell, the humans would message their prides and more would come. Without the bronze line, the amethyst were exposed. He hoped it hadn't been too long since the Dragon Queen fell, hoped they were still in turmoil.

If he could get through the line and return to his village, the Order would come, they'd rally more elves. This could be the beginning of the end of the dragons' reign.

He breathed in and felt the winds of change root him in the moment.

A glimmer far ahead caught his eye. He shifted position to the bow. The white cliffs, from this distance, looked like teeth rising from the waves. And there, above them, dragons circled. Too many at once. "Something is wrong."

Chloe lifted a spy-glass. "I see them... They're a long way off."

"You see how they're clustered over one spot, riding the thermals to the east?"

"Yes, we've seen them do that many times. They're patrolling, perhaps looking for something."

"One or two, but not so many. Look to the west..." He breathed slow, trying to steady his racing heart. They couldn't have hoped for this. "Their lines are scattered. They're exposed."

"Why would they...?" she wondered aloud. "Do you think it's a trap to lure us to the west?"

"If they knew we were approaching, yes. But you say we're hidden inside the sun's glare." He watched them soar again. From this distance, they were little more than beetles in the air. "Something has them distracted..." He couldn't imagine what would draw the dragons away from their posts but knew they likely wouldn't get this opportunity again.

She lowered her spy-glasses and for a moment, stared ahead, her glare determined. It was a risk, heading toward the west as the sunset would put them on the horizon line. But this was an opportunity to get close, to possibly make-land, to perhaps even breach the bronze line and bring it down.

Chloe turned her back on the wind, swept her hair back from her face and cast her gaze across her crew and those of the other ships. Any doubt vanished from her face. "Hard to port!"

The crew sprang into action. Rigging clanged and jolted, shouts went up, and it all seemed to work in glorious harmony to tilt the ship beneath Eroan's feet and turn the vessel leftward. The other ships responded, and within minutes, the fleet was heading parallel with the distant cliffs.

Eroan caught Chloe's eye and offered her a comforting smile. "It will work."

She nodded and swallowed, concern hiding in the tightness of her eyes.

CHAPTER 41

ℒysander

LYSANDER WANDERED the damaged section of warren where his brother had laid waste to its construction and torn a hole in the ceiling to escape. Much of it had been dismantled and carted off but work still progressed. Bronze lowers bustled through the tunnels, focused on their tasks, while those as dragon circled above, searching for any signs Akiem might return.

It had been weeks since the scuffle, but time meant little to his brother. He would return again and again until he secured Lysander back under amethyst wing. Which was likely, Lysander assumed, why Dokul hadn't yet called in the deal they had made. The bronze chief had largely ignored Lysander, besides a few long looks from across a room, and that made the wait worse. At least Seraph was safe, for now. Plenty of bronze had eyed the young elf like she was to be their next meal. Only her association with Lysander and his with Dokul had saved her. It wouldn't last. None of this would last, and the itch in Lysander's blood made him wonder if today was the day Dokul would call in the debt.

"Tell me more of Eroan," he said, drawing Seraph closer with his words. From his position on a walkway slug over the pit, they could talk privately and weren't likely to be disturbed. Bronze lowers fetched and carried stone and metal. Tools clanged and commands were barked.

The young elf had at first been reluctant to speak of her mentor, but as the days had gone on and Lysander had pestered, she'd slowly opened up.

"He was due to be an elder. We all knew it. He didn't, and I don't think he appreciated the decision being made without him."

Lysander could imagine Eroan pushing back against a decision like that. The elf had pushed back against *everything*. "Isn't he a bit young to be an *elder*?"

Seraph raised a dark eyebrow. "No more than you are too young to be a prince."

He chuckled. "All right, point made."

She fell quiet for a few moments "There are too few older elves left. We do not live long. Not anymore."

He had never killed an elf, but knew, before his time, his brood had almost wiped them out. "I am sorry."

"Are you?" she snapped and then softened with a sigh. "How long must I stay here?"

"Until we can slip you away unnoticed." He watched her face fall. "Is my company so hideous?"

"No, it's..." She clutched at the rope keeping them

from dropping the hundred feet or so into the pit below. "I don't know how he survived among you for so long."

Lysander breathed deeply, drawing the hot metal smell into his lungs. It didn't burn like it used to, but the heat and dust had worn Seraph's edges away. She'd been a bright, fiery thing when she'd arrived, but in the past few weeks, she'd lost her spark. He had seen the same happen to Eroan, though it had taken much longer. Elves needed light and freedom, but Lysander could not give it to her, not yet.

The air tightened, and below, a tension spilled through the workers. Dokul had arrived.

Seraph said something but Lysander's thoughts had wandered as he watched the bronze stalk through his brood. There was a whole world of pain coming, and soon.

"I still don't understand why you're protecting me."

"Because, as you said, there aren't many of you left, and that is a crime. You were human protectors once, I think?"

"Yes. Our ancestors were their silent guardians for thousands of years."

"Well then. Someone should repay that service."

She scowled. "But you're a dragon."

"I'd noticed."

"You're not like any dragon I've known."

"Known many, have you?"

"I've known *of* many. Bronze, Silver and Gold, were the first. They came from fire and ice in a faraway land. They were different from the jeweled ones of today. Elven history says humans helped make the second generation by using some terrible weapon full of fire and power, but instead of killing the dragons, it made them evolve. The jeweled are worse than the metals. More vicious, ruthless, they spread like a plague. Elves had warned of using such a weapon, and after it happened, they split from humans. A divided force could not hold the dragons back. We have been fighting to stay alive ever since. We are not a war-loving people, but we soon realized we could not survive alone. The Order was formed. Our own protectors. Not for humans, for us. We learned all about dragons from our ancestors, but this time, we learned how to survive them. So yes, I know enough."

She reeled it off as though she'd heard it many times. He imagined how elves would sit around a roaring fire in their villages and tell tales of the past and how things had come to be as they were today. Of course, nothing like that scene existed for him. Elisandra had been the knowledge-keeper, hoarding intelligence like gems. Now Dokul was the only history-keeper left.

A bronze lower slinked onto the walkway, bronze jewelry glinting. "Dokul has requested you both meet him in his chambers."

Lysander nodded, dismissing the bronze, and gritted his teeth under Seraph's concerned glance. The moment was upon him. How bad could it be, really? Looking up through the hole in the earth, he remembered soaring for what felt like forever on those thermals, like the dragons circling high above. "Steel yourself, elf. And know, whatever happens next, I'll survive." She blinked large eyes at him. "And so will you."

CHAPTER 42

 roan

THE CLIFFS WERE ferocious on approach. Ocean waves churned at their base, whipping the water and air into a foam and mist frenzy. Had Eroan seen the wall of rocks from this side first, he might have reconsidered climbing down them. The fleet was still some distance offshore but close enough to hear the occasional thunder of breakers pummeling rocks.

"Easy now!" Chloe yelled into the sound of flapping sails and clanging rigging. "Not too close!"

The fat sun lingered low to the west, behind them now, casting the deck in an eerie flame-orange light. He hoped it wasn't an omen. With one eye on the skies, he examined the crew's weapons and answered any last questions they had before the battle began. The ballista was armed and ready, pointed toward the east for the attack when it came.

Now all they had to do was get close enough to safely launch the skiffs.

He shielded his eyes and looked toward the sun. Their window of opportunity was a small one. Wait too long, and the ships would be silhouetted on the horizon instead of sitting beneath it.

"Ready the skiffs!" Gabe's bellows sailed on the salted wind.

"Ready the skiffs!" Chloe echoed. The command continued on the lips of the crew until all the ships were filling their small landing boats.

One last time, Eroan eyed the ballista with its barbed dragontooth arrow. When those weapons let their arrows fly, dragons would fall. Anticipation had his heart galloping, and for a few seconds, he allowed himself to dream of returning to his village with the knowledge that the bronze line had fallen. *That* was a worthy victory he would claim with pride. He could take that back to his people without shame, back to Janna and Curan and have them look at him with honor, not pity.

A shadow clipped a cloud. He saw it the moment the call went up. "Dragon!"

He dashed to the block-and-tackle ropes lowering the landing boats into the water. "Get the skiffs in now!"

A glance behind him revealed the dragon banking, tilting its broad wings side-on as it tried to sight them below. At that distance, the ships would look like rocks scattered close to the shore. There was a chance it might dismiss the fleet as just that.

The landing craft thumped onto the water, and its crew extended the oars. They had half a dozen boats in. Two more still hung from their ropes.

Hurry!

A bark from above and Eroan's heart hammered faster. "Ready the ballista!"

Men and women burst into action, each knowing their places, and above, the dragon beat its wings, keeping itself aloft in a position far beyond the range of the arrow. Down the coast, three other winged beasts broke from their formation. Their dark marks grew larger against silvery clouds.

This was it.

This was the moment where it would all come together.

They could not fail.

He could not fail them.

CHAPTER 43

*L*ysander

LYSANDER DREW BACK Dokul's heavy curtains and entered the bronze chief's private chambers. Scattered wreckage glimmered in the corners of the room, a hollowed-out rock with holes above for ventilation. Torches illuminated alcoves, and as if their heat wasn't enough, a fireplace throbbed in one corner, throwing out wave after wave of sweltering air.

"Strip," Dokul ordered.

The bronze was sitting in a large, ornate chair, built from rusted and twisted metals. It resembled something Lysander's mother would have used to torture her prisoners in. He quickly pushed thoughts of his mother away and reached behind his neck to unlatch the lamé shirt.

"The elf?" he enquired, slowly making his way across the room.

Dokul didn't take his eyes from him. "She stays." Dilated pupils swallowed the sight Lysander presented.

Inwardly, Lysander winced. He had some pride left—a tiny kernel his mother hadn't beaten out of him—and had hoped the elf would be spared witnessing this.

"Mirann?" he asked.

The bronze's glare flashed with annoyance. "My daughter is preoccupied with repairs. As I have been..." He leaned forward, setting his armor and bangles rattling, and rolled his great shoulders. "Elf, come here." Still, he kept his eyes on Lysander's slow approach.

Seraph moved by him, and Lysander plucked the shirt off, over his head, using the motion to distract from what the bronze might have planned for the elf. The chief wouldn't touch her. They'd made a deal and there was no way, with the lust so raw on Dokul's face, that he'd risk losing Lysander's cooperation.

"Remove my chestplate," the chief ordered.

Seraph obeyed without hesitation. *Good.* She unlatched the heavy plates from behind and pulled them off, revealing Dokul's bronze-skinned chest and large, powerful shoulders. When she set it down beside the throne-like chair, her eyes flicked to Lysander. He kept his glare firmly locked with Dokul's and pushed his rattling nerves down.

Lysander preferred his males slimmer, built for stamina, not force. In fact, he would have preferred not to be here at all, but as half a dragon and without a flight, he had only his allegiance and body left to bargain with. His mother had figuratively fucked him over enough times. What difference was this?

Dokul brushed a hand over his smooth head and down the back of his neck. As Lysander drew close, the bronze settled back in the chair, roaming his hungry gaze where soon his hands might follow. The heat in his eyes wasn't entirely unwelcome, and Lysander's own desires began to stir awake. He could help by summoning the memory of a powerful, stubborn elf tied beneath him.

"Stop." Dokul flicked his fingers, lending the command weight. The male drew out the seconds. Heat stole the air and dried Lysander's throat. But the intensity of the older male's gaze set loose a shiver of goosebumps and shortened Lysander's breaths. A long, long time ago, Dokul had been a storm of destruction in an unprepared world. That beast still lurked deep inside, hidden so far down, Lysander wondered if he imagined the weight of it in the room. His mother had warned him but said nothing more. Surely, nothing could be worse than her.

Dokul swallowed and lifted his chin. "Remove your trousers. I want to see all of you."

Lysander opened his belt, let it hang loose, and flicked open the buttons, one. By. One. A lifetime under Elisandra meant he'd learned to hide the swirl of thoughts trying to trip him up. Thoughts like where this was going and how it would end. Thoughts like the one trying to root in him now, the one telling him this was wrong, that he didn't want Dokul, didn't want to be here in this fucking heat, in this mausoleum of a warren or anywhere near the salted air making everything taste like blood and rust. And doubts— like the one whispering how he shouldn't have killed the queen because at least under her, he'd had a place among his own kind.

He'd stopped undressing. Dokul's narrowing gaze

speared into his. His heart missed a beat, and with it, he caught Seraph's pale, wide-eyed face and felt his gut plummet. No, no, no... he had to stay in control if this—

"Don't look at the pet." Dokul shot to his feet. "You look at me and only me." The male was all he could see, all he could smell. A wall of slick muscle and ancient power that had the primal part of Lysander caught between hunkering down or snapping back. "You are mine now. You understand?"

Lysander swallowed a bitter taste and breathed hard through his nose. His heart was a galloping thing trying to break free and his blood like fire, trying to spur him into a fight he couldn't win. The bronze wasn't some lower dragon he could bully into submission. This creature was as old as earth.

Panic squeezed his chest. Lysander did the only thing he could think of. He caught the male by the back of the neck and pulled him into a forced kiss. The bronze felt like stone in his hands, on his lips. Didn't matter. He'd agreed to this. It would help unseat Akiem and save the fucking elf. Who was watching all of this like a damned rabbit caught out after dark. She reeked of fear and rage. The kind of heady concoction that would get her killed if Dokul noticed. So Lysander shoved his tongue into the bronze's yielding mouth like he hated the bastard, and gripped the male's neck harder. There was no getting away from this.

Dokul clamped both his huge, hot hands loosely around Lysander's throat and growled into the kiss. The deep, luscious sound rumbled through his chest and sank into Lysander's bones, stoking the fires hotter, brighter, luring the beast in him out of its hiding place and spilling its needs and wants through his veins. The shift tried to stretch beneath his skin and remake him. Lysander tore from the kiss and shoved Dokul back, more on instinct than thought, but it was a mistake. Dokul stumbled into the chair, caught himself, and growled low in his throat.

By diamonds, Lysander had just made this so much worse.

Dokul grabbed his wrist and pulled, either to trap Lysander against him or throw him into the chair, but the raw beast in Lysander wasn't submitting. The right hook was a tight, precise blow and it landed across Dokul's jaw, exactly where Lysander had imagined it would go. Had the chair not caught him, Dokul would have hit the floor.

Pain flared up Lysander's arm. He let it, and grabbed Seraph, then shoved her toward the door. "You can't see this. Get out of here!"

Seraph whirled, eyes so wide. "Look out!" she screamed.

The arm flew around Lysander's throat like a thick, muscled noose. His balance fell out from under him. Dokul dragged him into his heaving chest. Lysander's lungs stretched, fighting to draw in air. He dug his fingers into the male's forearm, trying to pry it from constricting his throat. Stars exploded. Red spilled into his vision.

"Get off him!" the elf screeched.

The arm was gone, but hot hands were still on him, shoving. Lysander hit the bed chest first. He sunk his fingers into the sheets and breathed too-hot air deep into his lungs. Every breath refilled his sight and pushed out the thumping in his head.

The elf screamed.

No! The deal! Lysander twisted. The room spun, all

shining metals ticking in the heat. Dokul had Seraph lifted in the air. She clawed at his grip on her neck.

"Hey, we had a deal!" Lysander growled out, letting some of the dragon slip through, lending his threat weight. "Are you going to fuck me or fuck with that tiny little elf? She's not worth your time. But I am."

Dokul's grip twitched. Seraph's eyelids fluttered closed.

"You son of a breeding-bitch!" Lysander rumbled. "Drop her or I'll kill you. Don't think I won't..."

Dokul's grin grew. He tossed Seraph away. Her little body hit a pile of metal at an awkward angle and crumpled into a heap at its base, but Lysander saw how she moved, tried to stand. Relief poured through him. She was alive. Of course she was. Elves kept right on surviving...

Something Lysander knew well.

Dokul tore open his belt and wiped his free hand across his leering grin. "Oh, I don't doubt you'd try, you jeweled whelp."

Shit, this was happening. He hadn't planned it this way. Not like this. He would have been the one controlling Dokul's desires, and now the brute was going to fuck him, just like he'd wanted years ago.

Seraph was shifting, rising, clawing her way off the floor, using the metal sculpture to haul herself up. If she stayed there, stayed out of this, she'd be all right. He tried to will her to turn, to look at him, to read the warning on his face.

"Got a thing for elves, haven't you." Dokul grabbed at Lysander's ankle. "I'll fuck that right out of you, pretty one."

Lysander kicked out, cracking the brute under the chin for all the good it did him. Dokul caught his other ankle and yanked, dragging Lysander down the bed to its edge. The bronze's fingers sank into Lysander's loose belt and pulled, tearing his trousers down, below his knees, then off altogether.

Finally, Seraph looked. But it wasn't fear on her face. That little elf's eyes had narrowed to knife-like slits, and her lips were pulled back in a vicious sneer, revealing tiny sharp teeth. Fuck, no. She was going to get herself killed.

Lysander shook his head. *Please don't.*

She sank her hand into her pocket and pulled out two rectangular blocks joined together with a length of chain. What...? Eroan's firestarter. She'd taken it from his room. When or why? She probably didn't even know Eroan had given it to Lysander, but there it was, like a talisman in her hand.

The bronze shoved his own loose trousers over his hips and down his thighs, freeing his taut erection. He cupped it, presenting the engorged cock to Lysander like a damned trophy. Lysander couldn't damn well miss it. He'd heard Dokul was endowed, but the rumors had undersold him.

"Scream, if you want." Dokul stroked from base to tip and planted a knee on the bed. "I prefer it when they do."

"I'm not screaming for you. We had a deal. You touched the elf. The deal's off."

Dokul laughed his deep, rumbling laughter. "Foolish kit. You think I care about any deal you make. You have nothing. Everything you are, I own. You walked into my warren and gave yourself to me. You are in no position to dictate my actions or your own."

"Sire!" someone called.

Dokul tensed at the sound of the new voice.

Lysander couldn't see behind Dokul's mass to pinpoint the new bronze in the room.

"Get out." Dokul's top lip rippled.

"Sire, the humans have a fleet—"

"Get out!" he roared, still staring at Lysander.

Lysander bared his teeth and let his own growl bubble.

"That's it, pretty green eyes. Growl for me."

Whether the lower had left, or where Seraph was, Lysander didn't know. All he knew for sure was that fighting Dokul would make it worse. He'd weathered his mother's twisted affections since the first memory of having her force him into her bed, among her harem. He'd lived with the shame of knowing he was broken among his kind. Lived as an outcast while still within the tower walls. This could not be any worse than that.

Dokul stroked his own erection, placed his other knee on the bed, straddling Lysander's knees, tore his belt free from where it hung from its loops and snapped it taut.

It can always be worse.

The brute braced an arm against the bed and looped one end of the belt behind Lysander's neck, bringing him close enough for Lysander to wonder if he could bite that grin right off the bastard's face.

"With every generation, the jeweled get stronger. Did you know that?" Dokul spoke softer now as he drew the tail of the belt through its loop and tightened it.

Leather brushed Lysander's collarbone, along with the bronze's warm fingers. Down those fingers sank, down over Lysander's right pec, down where his lungs heaved and then rippled over his abs.

"It's why your mother bred relentlessly. And you're the

one who taught her that amethyst quirk." Dokul slowly tightened the belt, choking Lysander.

"Amethyst, opal, diamond... and you, a nothing emerald. A weakness from the outside. She tried to kill you. When that didn't work, Akiem tried. She mentioned you to me—a throwaway comment about her wretched weakling of a son, but even then, she knew it to be a lie. You were no weaker than she was."

The leather dug in, closing Lysander's throat. It would be all right. Dokul wouldn't kill him, just so long as he played this game. But in Lysander's glare, he made sure Dokul saw the fire within. The bronze got off on it, soaked in it, the brute panted his lust and need, his cock nudging Lysander's hip. It didn't matter. Lysander could no more quell his own fire than he could shut out the starlight or fly again.

"Every time she tried to kill you or had Akiem attempt it, you came back stronger. Every time you flew with your flights and battled the lost ones to the north, you came back stronger." Dokul straightened and pulled the belt tighter, making Lysander's heart stutter. "Every single time." Dokul spread his hand on Lysander's chest, admiring the shuddering rise and fall. "She pushed you, and the stronger you became. Hate made your fire burn hotter. You were ore, rough and unwieldy, until she forced you to survive. There, you forged yourself into a weapon with a heart of steel. When you killed her... Tell me," he yanked tight and gasped, "tell me she was afraid."

Dokul kissed away any answer Lysander could have given, then shuddered, hips thrusting at nothing. Lysander knew lust when it danced on his tongue and clamped his hand against the back of Dokul's head, holding the bronze down, drowning him in a kiss drenched with that same hate he'd used to kill his mother.

None of this mattered because despite the belt, Lysander had control and the thrill of it spilled need into his veins. A need to take and own. He reached between them and dragged his fingertips from below Dokul's balls, up the male's hard shaft, making the ancient dragon gasp into his mouth.

Maybe he was like his mother, he realized, as he stroked the bronze into a panting, writhing, mindless creature. Hadn't she done the same to him over and over again?

Dokul pulled from the kiss and let out a wrought, agonized moan. "Stop," the male breathed. But Lysander had no intention of stopping. Only one of them had the power here. He circled his fingers, making the pulls shorter, faster and when his gaze captured Dokul's, the ancient beast inside peered back, lost to his primitive urges.

He should have known the elf would screw it up.

She sprang onto Dokul's back, looped her skinny arm around his neck and drew the steel portion of the firestarter across Dokul's throat, opening a second bloody smile.

Lysander blinked, trying to clear the sudden splash of red blurring his left eye. Dokul's hot seed spurted into his hand, but that seemed far less important now that the bastard had a shiny new smile in his neck where smiles should not be.

Dokul reared up, reached behind him, and tore Seraph from his back. He flung her across her room. She struck the chair. This time when she fell, she lay motionless, but the bronze wasn't done. He staggered off the bed, apparently oblivious to the stream of blood soaking his chest, made it two steps after her, then dropped to a knee.

If the son of a bitch died, Lysander was screwed whatever way he looked at it. "Fucking elves!" He wiped his hand clean on the sheet, clambered off the bed, pulled on his trousers, rounded on Dokul—still on his knees, gaping like a fish at the fallen elf. Between Seraph and the bronze chief lay the bloody firestarter. Lysander scooped it up and wiped blood from its edges. All right, so he hadn't planned for this.

Think!

He had to get the elf away before the bronze recovered —if the bronze chief recovered—and somehow make it so he wasn't implicated in trying to kill another leader.

"Father!"

Lysander whirled. Mirann stormed into the room, done up in her battle armor with an expression to match. She took one look at Lysander, at her father bleeding out on his knees, and barely even glanced at the elf.

He held his hands palm-out. "This is not what it looks like."

CHAPTER 44

 roan

FLAMES STRAFED the side of the ship, blasted over the deck and extinguished again in less than a second, leaving soot and embers dallying in the air. Steam momentarily blinded the crew and Eroan with them. Then a swift wind swept it off-deck, revealing the dragons circling for another blast.

"Fire!" Eroan yelled.

The ballista let loose its enormous arrow. It sailed high, whistling into the air. Other arrows whistled in a chorus of strikes. Eroan's heart thudded, his thoughts fell into silence, and the moment stretched on. He watched those arrows fly, willing them to strike home. *Alumn, make this be the moment, guide those arrows home. Guide me home...*

They missed. Some sailed on, some clanked off scales and tumbled out of the sky.

No!

Something cracked inside Eroan. Hopes, maybe. Dreams, certainly.

Arrows plunged into the sea, and the dragons spiraled higher, building height for their fatal swooping blows.

The skiffs. They had to make it now...

Eroan saw some riding the surf, oars stuck out at awkward angles. Yes, they still had a chance.

A dragon screamed. He'd heard the sound before, the first time he'd killed one. It sounded like ice breaking or the earth splitting. They screamed that way when they died.

Above, one of them was clawing at the air like it could try to climb it, but its wings were failing, its body falling. The beast twitched and tumbled, and at just the right moment, Eroan saw it clutch at an arrow protruding from its neck. The beast couldn't breathe.

An arrow had found its target. It was dying. Eroan knew it. "Reload!"

The men gawked at the twitching, falling beast.

"*Reload!*" he bellowed. They were too slow! He dashed in, scooped up a second enormous arrow and rammed it home. Then, taking the ballista's frame in both hands, it heaved its wheels into position, lifting its sights among the swirling beasts. He could taste blood, like he'd been able to taste the blood of those he'd killed fleeing the tower. Forcing his heart to slow, he pushed out the noise, the shouts, the swell of the ocean, and the screams until all that existed was the ballista in his hands and the dragon in his sights. The ship dropped, the dragon soared, wings spread, beginning its descent. *Yes, stay on that line.* The ocean lifted the ship once more and Eroan fired. The ballista jolted, the arrow flew, and the crew saw—Eroan saw—as the arrow punched into the beast's right eye. Whoops and cheers filled the air. The dragon didn't reach for the arrow like he'd expected, but simply stopped. Its right wing drooped, and the beast flipped over and down it went. Down, down, down until it crashed into the waves, sending up a blast of water.

Other arrows flew, and this time, they found their targets.

Dragons rained from above. One, two, five, eight... yes, yes! Every arrow was finding its mark now, and they screamed... they screamed so loudly Eroan was sure blessed Alumn herself would hear them.

He heard the warning shout too late and turned toward it in time to see the wings spread like they could encompass the whole ship, and the jaws open. The beast came down on the ship, planting its clawed-feet in the deck. It snapped the main mast with a single bite, sending ropes and rigging flying and sails tumbling. The ship listed suddenly toward its heavy side, tilting the deck at an impossible angle and sending anything not tied down crashing into the guardrails. Eroan fell hard and tumbled. He clutched at a rail only to find it rolling with him. He clawed at the deck, dug his nails in, cutting open his fingers, and snagged some kind of notch in the wood, jolting to a halt. Noise and fire and pain, cracking wood, cracking bones.

The dragon beat its wings to keep from falling backward into the sea then it let out a deafening screech.

Eroan freed his sword. In the chaos of motion and noise and screams and water, he heard the shouts of men and women dying. No, he had not led them here to die! He'd kill all the dragons himself if he had to. *For Alumn!*

The beast snapped at something slipping and sliding toward it. Its jaws clamped closed on a man. It tossed back its head and threw the still-screaming human into his mouth then smiled its reptilian smile. With its head up, Eroan saw the firepit low in its throat glow. He tightened his grip on the sword and let go of the deck. The tilt of the ship sent him skidding almost vertically down. *Stay there... Don't move, dragon.* The dragon's foreleg lifted. Then it saw Eroan, and its large, slitted eye widened, fixing him beneath its glare.

I am Eroan Ilanea, I was forged in the fires of Ifreann, quenched in Alumn's maelstrom, for one purpose... to kill.

He slammed his heel into the rail, sprang, and plunged the sword deep into the beast's fiery gullet. The sword sank in clean and true. The beast choked out its screams. Liquid fire spewed, splashing Eroan's face and neck. Then a blast of icy-cold water slammed over him, tore him free, and pulled him down, down, down into its cold embrace. He still clutched the sword like it might somehow save him, even as above him, the ship rolled into the pool of light and the dragon rolled with it, plunging into the water, throwing Eroan into a complete, churning darkness.

CHAPTER 45

ysander

MIRANN CAME AT LYSANDER, teeth and blades flashing. "The humans are attacking our lines," she exclaimed. "We're scattered and disorganized and our chief has his knees in a pool of his own blood with his cock hanging out? And you..." She stopped, tilted her head at her father, then eyed Lysander again from the corner of her eye. "I'm not sure about you yet."

He tensed for the attack, but as the seconds passed and she continued to regard him as though trying to place the pieces of a puzzle, he reassembled her words in his mind. "Humans are what?"

She snorted. "The parasites saw a weak spot and took advantage. It's being dealt with, but this..." She flung a hand at her gasping father. "His timing is terrible." Her gaze turned back toward Lysander, morphing into something slippery and sly. "Did he at least fuck you?"

"No."

"Pity. He'll only want you more now you've cut him."

Lysander wasn't about to correct her on who had been the one to cut her father. Seraph still lay out cold. Avoiding the growing pool of blood, he moved to the elf's side. Her pulse beat strong against his fingers, but there was no knowing what damage had been done internally. She would die here. Maybe not now, from this, but eventually. He had to get her away from the bronze for good.

Mirann's gaze sat heavy on his back. Apparently, she was impressed with the fuck-up she'd walked in on. And Lysander had thought amethyst were wired wrong. The bronze took fucked-up to a whole new level. Maybe all dragons were wired wrong. Now wasn't the time to think on it.

Seraph's face held a soft, peaceful expression. Did she dream of her home, now destroyed by Akiem? Lysander sighed. None of this felt right. The only time anything had felt right, he'd been watching an elf sleep through campfire flames.

"The humans are attacking... now?" He brushed Seraph's choppy black hair back from her face and let his fingers softly dally on her cheek.

"By boat. It's not unusual. They keep trying and dying. Why?"

Were they the humans Eroan had gone to? If they were, they'd be armed with new weapons, and this little routine attack wasn't routine at all.

The bronze were about to be very distracted.

If he could get Seraph to the beach, the humans might

take her in. And maybe he could help them in other ways too...

Dokul clutched at his neck and slumped to the side. Seraph's cut wouldn't kill him. It hadn't been deep enough. But he'd be weak and vulnerable for the next few hours.

"Dokul's no good to anyone like this." He tucked his arms under Seraph and scooped her body against his chest, then stood and headed for the door. "Someone needs to organize your flights. I'm assuming that someone is you?"

"Yes," Mirann agreed. "I should return..."

"Then go do that." On, he walked, heading back to his chamber. "I'll be right behind you."

"Where are you taking the elf?"

A barked alarm sounded somewhere far off but loud enough to shudder through the warren walls. A warning call for reinforcements. Mirann swore behind him, and his raggedy heart warmed at the sounds of chaos beginning to unfold around him. "Go."

She caught his arm and pulled him up short. Suspicion narrowed her eyes. She always had been smarter than her father. If they fought here over an elf, it would further weaken the line. Her place was elsewhere and she knew it.

"You're needed on the line," he said, a subtle reminder of her duty.

"So are you, Lysander Bronze."

He nodded. "I'll be there." He couldn't fly, but he'd be expected to hold the line from the battlements.

Another bark shook the walls. Mirann turned back toward the outer tunnels and marched away. The next time he saw her, Seraph would be safe, and that was all that mattered. He veered down a side-tunnel, toward the sound of waves thundering against rock and screaming dragons.

343

～

THE CAVE AIR GREW DAMP, and the heat gave way to a brisk, salted breeze. Torches flickered, their flames barely clinging on. In all the rumbling noise, Lysander didn't see the gang of humans until they were more almost upon him.

He stopped, positioned partially above them on a slippery rock as one by one they saw him in the gloom. Warriors, all of them, armed with short swords, compact crossbows, and grizzled expressions. Eight men and women, and all looked at him like the second he put the elf down they'd take great pleasure in killing him.

How had they even known about the tunnel?

Didn't matter now.

They were here, and Seraph in his arms was likely the only reason they hadn't attacked.

The leader, an older male at the front of the gang, rested his crossbow at his hip. "Put the elf down," he said, voice heavily accented as though from a foreign land.

If he did that, this would no longer be a civilized conversation. "I have no intention of hurting anyone."

"Put her down."

Eight dragon-killers. As dragon, he could crush them—maybe. Their weapons glinted with familiar tips. Eroan had been busy.

"I'm bringing her to you. I can help you."

"You can set her down right by your feet there, and we'll take good care of her." The man in charge had eyes like flint, like he'd seen so much death in his life it had crawled inside him and turned his soul to rock. He'd pull that trigger, and he wouldn't miss.

How could Lysander explain who he was, that he wouldn't hurt them? Seraph might have been able to speak up for him, but she wasn't waking anytime soon.

"I'm going to set her down nice and slow. You don't need to attack. I'm not going to hurt you. I can help you get inside... There's a forge deep inside the warren. If you get inside and disrupt the flow of molten iron, you can bring this whole operation to a stop. But you'll need me to find it."

They glared back, each one as cold and hard as the weapons they carried. Maybe they didn't all speak his language? His heart hammered faster. He'd come here to save Seraph, but dying for her hadn't been a part of that plan. If he set her down and went for his sword, they'd fire. If he moved, said the wrong thing, they'd fire. They'd likely fire the second they had a clear shot. And all for an elf he barely knew. He looked down at her face nestled against his shoulder. Her village was gone. Her whole world, her family, wrecked by Akiem.

Lysander sighed.

Very little had felt right in his life, but this did. Out of the two of them, she deserved to live.

He adjusted her weight and stepped down off the raised rock. The gang bristled and rattled their weapons. "Easy... I'm just putting her down, like you asked." Inch by inch he lowered her and set her gently down by his boots. She'd be all right. She was a fighter, like another elf he knew. He gritted his teeth, breathed in, and straightened.

They fired.

CHAPTER 46

roan

EROAN TOOK the hand offered to him and let the man yank him to his feet out of the shoving surf. He coughed and spat a mouthful of sand and salt water. His throat burned. His lungs heaved. But he was alive. For a while there, he'd felt and seen nothing but darkness...

"You all right?" The man... Jeremy, Eroan recalled from their training sessions, gripped Eroan's shoulder and looked him in the eyes. "You got a nasty cut... maybe you should sit this out. We'll come back for you."

Sit it out? Eroan's mouth found a smile even if the rest of him didn't feel much like grinning. His head throbbed, his arm too, where the sword he'd been holding had snagged in the rocks and nearly twisted it out of its socket. But he still had the sword and had used it to claw his way over the rocks.

Firelight blasted from behind. An explosion rocked the air. Eroan flinched, knowing men like Jeremy were dying on the ships. The skies above swarmed with wings, but they were falling too.

"I'm going in with you," he croaked.

"All right... but keep up." Jeremy patted him fondly on the shoulder. "I hear they caught one alive." The man's eyes gleamed with pride. "Got an elf too. They're bringing her out now."

An elf? Why would there be an elf at the bronze line? "Wait..." Eroan tried to draw Jeremy back, but the man was already stomping toward the gang readying their weapons.

There was no reason for an elf to be here unless they'd been caught. Perhaps they would have news of the elves' efforts to secure more dragons teeth. They could have launched an assault from their side!

With renewed fire in his blood, he followed Jeremy's boot prints in the shingle. Someone handed him a rag. He wiped at the wetness on his face and winced as it came away soaked in blood. He shouldn't go inside, he knew that, but nothing short of death would stop him now.

"There she is..."

Three men clambered toward them. One carried the elf in his arms. An elf missing the tip of her ear.

Eroan's heart stuttered. His blood turned to ice. "No..." It couldn't be Seraph. He'd told her not to follow him. She was supposed to stay behind... He took a few staggering steps forward and almost fell. Someone caught him, held him up. He should thank them, but he couldn't take his eyes from Seraph. Her pale face was thinner than he remembered. Her eyes were closed. He'd left her, and she'd followed. "Is she... dead?" he whispered.

"No, she's breathing. But she's been out a while. I'll see if I can signal one of the landing skiffs. It's going to be tough getting her off this beach, but we..."

The man's words vanished behind the *thump-thump* of Eroan's heart. The second man threw a sword in the sand. A sword identical to the one on Eroan's back. Of course, he'd given it to Seraph. But seeing it here drove another nail into his heart.

"Do you know her?" someone asked him.

"Y-yes... I..."

A third man frog-marched a prisoner in front of him. A bag covered his head. A bag like the one Eroan remembered. Pain knotted like a fist in his chest.

The dragonkin's wrists were bound. Blood dripped from his fingers. Eroan's insides knotted tighter at the sight of those restraints. He tasted bitterness on his tongue and swallowed the bile back down. The prisoner's boots left bloody prints in the sand. He was wounded, badly by the steady stream of red soaking his legs. The bag over his head hid his expression, but his bronze clothing marked his brood easily enough.

The warrior stopped with his quarry in front of Eroan. "What should we do with him?"

They were asking him? He looked at Seraph motionless in the man's arms. The dragons would have beaten her, mutilated her, used her in every way. Everything he'd narrowly avoided, they would have inflicted upon her. Rape, torture, starved of light. And the bronze were the worst of them. Perhaps it was better she had died than to live as a used, damaged thing. But she was here now, and she would live. He'd make sure she was safe.

"Kill him," Eroan growled. The dragonkin bucked against his bindings and mumbled into the hood. Whatever he had to say, a gag silenced him. Good. Delicious, vicious vengeance sizzled on Eroan's tongue. "Make him suffer."

The man jerked his prisoner by his wrists. "My pleasure."

Still, the dragon stumbled and twisted, bucking like panicked prey as he was led away. Dragons didn't often experience the fear of facing their own deaths. That one would, and Eroan was glad for it. It was just a shame they couldn't draw out his agony on this beach for days and weeks like the dragons would have with a captured elf.

A screech bore down on them from above.

"Go! Get inside! Do what we came to do!" Eroan barked. Eroan took Seraph from the man's arms. "I'll see to it she's safe." Seraph fell against him, so small and warm. His heart turned over, briefly choking him, and the strength that had kept him moving stuttered. He hadn't expected this, hadn't expected to see her again, and not here.

"It will be done, Eroan," the warrior said. "There's a forge inside, a weakness. If we can get there, we can break its channels and ruin this nest forever."

"Do it. Kill any and all you come across." He hugged Seraph close, vowing to keep her safe until this was done. "The bronze line falls this night."

CHAPTER 47

$\mathcal{L}$ysander

THE BASTARDS HAD SHOT him at near point-blank range, gagged him, and dumped a bag over his head. The bolts had gone in and straight through, although one was lodged somewhere below Lysander's right rib. His body burned and twitched and bled. But that wasn't the worst of it. He'd heard the voice over the sound of the waves and the panting of his own breaths muffled inside the hood. He would have heard the voice a million miles away.

Kill him, Eroan had said.

He'd screamed through the gag for Eroan to listen, for them to take off the hood and just let the elf see him, but all it had gotten was a walk down the beach and a knee in the back.

Make him suffer.

Eroan hadn't known it was Lysander they marched to his death. But even if he had, would it have mattered? What had Lysander hoped for really? That Eroan would be pleased to see him, that the elf would just cast aside thousands of years of racial slaughter because Lysander had concocted some ridiculous romance in his head?

But to be so close and have him not know? He would have liked to tell that elf what he thought of him. That he admired him, loved him, even, for everything he was. For everything he could be.

That hurt more than all the wounds, more than his broken wing, more than his mother's cruel words. It hurt so much he didn't even care when the hood was torn off and the man saw the tears.

"Huh, dragons can cry..." He tore the gag free. "Anything to say?"

Lysander let some of the dragon rumble up his throat. "Fuck you, human. You think you can take me just because I'm—"

The man grabbed the bolt, the one sticking out from between Lysander's ribs and twisted. Pain exploded like a fiery ball eating him from the inside. A scream tore from him. He couldn't have stopped it, and among the towering rocks and crashing waves, nobody would hear. The pain didn't end though. It changed, morphing into a thick, drowning agony that tried to drag him into unconsciousness. If it went dark, he'd never wake again.

"I know Eroan! I know him! Tell him, just... tell him it's Ly—!"

The fist almost tore his jaw off, and Lysander hit the sand. His consciousness swam and the pain rumbled, or perhaps that was his own growl. The shift wouldn't save him, it'd just rearrange all the wounds, and it wasn't like he could fly off the beach. They'd kill him, as surely as this one was killing him now.

"I saved that elf!" Lysander groaned. "Tell him!"

The fist found his gut this time and mingled with the fire from the shifting bolt rubbing against bone. He tasted blood and spat somewhere toward the asshole beating on him. "He doesn't know..." Lysander saw stars. Real stars. He wanted to be among them again, soaring free. "He doesn't know it's me," he tried to shout it, but his voice was breaking, coming undone. "Tell him..." Words cracked, a sob breaking through. "Just tell him my name."

The man sank his fingers into Lysander's hair and grinned into his face. "He doesn't give a shit who you are, dragon. He wants you dead. Didn't you hear him? And he wants it slow."

Oh by the great gods, it couldn't end like this. He had tried to do the right thing, tried to be better, to just live and survive in a world that had tried to chew him up and spit him out. Didn't that count for something? Didn't any of it matter? What was the fucking point if he was just going to die here on this wretched beach having done nothing, leaving no legacy besides Lysander... the broken one. His mother was a bitch, but she was right.

The man freed a dragon's tooth knife and pointed the tip an inch from Lysander's right eye. He'd taken his mother's right eye too. Oh, how she would laugh now if she saw him.

"Do it!" he snarled. "You piece of human filth. You'll never bring us down. You can't because you're all the same. You hesitate, just like you're doing now, and when you hesitate, you die!" Lysander smacked his forehead into his, sending him sprawling against the rocks, and managed to fight his way to his feet when the son of a bitch rammed him, driving Lysander against a sheer rock wall lined with skin-tearing barnacles. Each one like tiny teeth ripping into his flesh. But pain, it was an old friend, one that wouldn't fuck off after the party was over.

The blade touched Lysander's neck, right below his ear. Only the person holding it wasn't the gnarled asshole but some woman with short hair and a snarl to rival any dragon's.

Lysander spotted the original human over her shoulder, dabbing at a bloody mess over his left eye. "Eroan said to kill him slow," the man said.

"Eroan doesn't command this crew," she replied, clearly in charge. "I do."

Lysander panted, pinned between her and the rocks. It was a good thing she was holding him up because he figured his legs wouldn't. The stars were back, only they weren't in the skies anymore, they were dancing around his vision, dragging the darkness behind them.

"There, you're not going to fight me, are you..."

Maybe she sensed the weakness in him. He'd heard humans didn't sense much of anything until their fate was almost upon them, but this one seemed to realize he was beaten. Maybe it was all the blood, or the shivering, or the fact he was having a hard time holding his head up, and her blade wasn't helping.

"What's your name, huh?" she asked, peering down her nose at him.

She smelled like the sea, although everything smelled salty, her scent was lighter, freer and so very human it made his mouth water, and the dragon in him wanted to burst free and tear strips off her.

If she wanted his name, she was going to have to keep him alive for it.

"*Putain, merde,*" she muttered. "You're not to kill him. I have a new home for this one." She eased off, and Lysander breathed in, setting his wounds on fire again, but at least he'd live. She smacked his head against the rocks, and the stars were back, only this time, they swallowed him whole.

CHAPTER 48

roan

THE TIDE of battle turned in the darkness. Eroan could taste it—more than that, he could *feel* it. And then the screeching caws sounded barks and whoops of the withdrawal. And screams. So many dragons screams from deep inside the warren. He listened as the night swallowed the sounds of the bronze abandoning their line. It shouldn't have been possible, the line had stood for a thousand years, but here they were, a handful of human prides with the right weapons and knowledge had done what none had been able to do in living memory.

"Victory..." he whispered, clutching Seraph closer. He'd tried to carry her back toward the shoreline, but after almost falling, he realized he was in no condition to try to clamber over the rocks alone, and so he'd sat and waited

357

and listened and watched as the fruits of his work, as his dreams, had been made real.

Humans truly were remarkable. He *had* done the right thing bringing knowledge to them. He could return to Xena and Curan, Nye and Janna, look them in the eyes again knowing he was finally worthy of their admiration. The tide had definitely turned this night.

Debris had begun to wash up on the shoreline, and in the cresting morning light, the true cost of their assault began to wash up too.

Seraph stirred in his arms. He blinked down at her fluttering lashes and smiled into her sleepy gaze. "Hello."

It took her a moment to focus on him and then the jagged rocks lit by a blaze of morning sunlight. "Sassa? Where..." she croaked.

"You slept through a battle. Don't worry, I won't tell anyone."

Her eyes widened. She reached up a hand. "Your head. Your hair! You look like you washed up here."

"I did."

She twisted, looking around with fresher eyes. "You... Er... you can put me down..."

He'd held her for so long he wasn't sure he could move his arms, but as a trail of humans snaked over the rocks toward them, he finally relented and set her down.

She swayed a little and took his hand. "Whoa. It's all right... I'm all right. I just..." She bowed over and gripped her thighs. "Maybe I do need a minute."

"I think you might have all the time you need." Eroan straightened as the returning gangs approached. He could smell hot iron on them and saw some were splashed with globules of what had once been molten but had cooled to a solid and singed their clothes. They'd found this forge one had mentioned.

"They're gone!" Jeremy was back, his eyes crinkled in glee. "They're truly gone!"

It seemed almost impossible. "How?"

"Part of their defenses had already been exposed and their response was sporadic like I've never seen from the bronze before. The big one, the brute, we didn't even see him. Once we found the forge rooms, most of the lowers had fled. We upset their molten tanks, flooded the place in molten rock. If they ever come back to it, they'll have to dig a whole new warren. For now, the entire line is undefended."

The elves could finally pass through the lines. Or the humans could come in force. Some of both. They could combine forces, build an army. This was everything he'd hoped for. Almost everything. His smile faded.

"How many did we lose?" he asked.

"Three ships went down, including yours. One is barely afloat. We should be able to limp it back. As for the people... we don't know yet. But... they took dozens of dragons to their graves. Their sacrifice is not in vain. This is a new morning on a new era."

More men and women spilled from inside the cave-mouth. Some wounded, and some carried the dead. Eroan's thoughts sped up. He would return to the village, take Seraph, and rally more assassins. It had to be quick, the bronze would not abandon their warren for long if they thought it could be reclaimed. Bolstered by this success, the Order could take the fight inland to the tower.

He returned to Seraph and relayed the news. She lightly smiled, but it didn't reach her eyes. Perhaps news of returning home would rally her. He opened his mouth to explain his next plans, when Chloe called, "Eroan..."

She appeared with the same man who'd marched the dragonkin off hours ago.

"Wait here," he told Seraph and met them far enough away that she wouldn't hear how he'd sanctioned an execution. "Was it done?" Eroan asked.

"It was done," she replied, face grim. "He won't be hurting anyone ever again."

Eroan nodded. He would tell Seraph later, when they were on the trek back home. "I must return to my village. With the line down, we can send messengers again, rally more to our fight. We must maintain the momentum."

"*Merci beaucoup*, Eroan." Chloe dipped her chin in thanks. "None of this would have been possible without you. I'll be sorry to see you leave us." She looked past him, out at the crashing breaks and two remaining ship masts. "I do not know if Gabe..." Her voice caught. "His ship went down. We're scouring the shore, but there's a lot of debris..."

Eroan's duty to his people warred with wanting to help the humans. It seemed wrong abandoning them now. "I can stay, a little while—"

"Take the poor girl home and send a messenger when you can," she smiled fondly and offered her hand. "It was an honor to fight alongside you, Eroan Ilanea. May this be the first step toward a human and elven alliance against the dragon blight."

He took her hand, pride swelling in his chest. "May Alumn shine her light on you and yours."

"Now, go take your friend home." She sniffed and tucked her hands into her pockets. "Swift travels, elf."

~

Dancing flames licked at the campfire kindling. The wood was damp, but the fire had eventually taken hold, and they'd needed it. Winter was setting in, misting their breath, its bite sharp.

Seraph's silence was a concern. He watched her stare into the campfire flames now as though she were searching for something in their hypnotic motion. She would need time to recover from the bronze, time he'd denied he'd needed. He hadn't listened to the advice from Xena, from Curan, and knew she wouldn't either.

Not for the first time, he considered telling her how he'd had the bronze she was found with killed. Revenge like that might have given her closure or at least alleviate all those rotten and knotted feelings inside. He'd gotten his revenge on the bronze who'd threatened to rape him, but not the one from the dungeons, the one who'd left his mark all over Eroan's chest and back. And the one who had given that order. Akiem. He would taste vengeance again, one day.

He circled the camp, made from a small depression where a huge oak had fallen, pulling up its roots and breaking the canopy so stars sparkled above. Their small fire wasn't likely to attract any unwanted attention this far from any strongholds, but there was always a risk a wandering dragon might stumble upon them. "We should rest in shifts."

Seraph picked up a twig and tossed it into the flames. She hadn't heard. Eroan crouched beside her. He unclipped his sword and laid it next to hers. The two dragonblades looked right together, and it seemed fitting they should lie side by side now, as a pair, where they belonged. Seraph merely blinked at them.

"Do you want to talk?"

She looked up, tears shining in her eyes. Oh Alumn, he had to stop himself from pulling her close. He picked up a stick, tossed it into the fire, and watched the flames twist and warp it until nothing was left.

"After what they did to me, I tried to forget it, to deny anything had happened..." he swallowed. Then, feeling the cold, blew into his cupped hands before spreading them against the fire's glow. "It tore me apart until I had to tell someone, anyone... Those things I said to Curan—things you heard."

She looked up.

"As terrible as they were, they were true, and to speak them..." He winced and sighed, "It was painful to admit, but I'd been carrying all of that around and needed it out there. It lost me the Order, but I couldn't have continued there as I was. I would have gotten people killed."

"I need to tell you something," she blurted.

"You don't have to tell me anything, not until you're ready. I understand, better than most."

"No, I do, Eroan..." She twisted toward him. "I..."

The fire crackled. Wet wood hissed and popped.

Whatever she had to say, her glassy eyes shined in the dark. She seemed so small a thing to him now. He hadn't protected her and he should have. He should have been there for her.

"It's all right," he said.

"No," she sniffed. "You don't... I don't know how to say this." She pulled her knees up and hugged them close.

"There's nothing you can tell me that I don't already

know." He met her gaze. One tear fell. "You survived, and there was a time that hadn't been enough for me, but surviving what they do, it is heroic. Being a survivor, living with the pain, healing from it, it makes you strong. It takes time, but it will come. Trust yourself to heal and know I'll be here for you. Always. We'll get through this. Together."

She brushed her cheek dry. "They didn't hurt me. Not like... not like they did you. I mean, they would have..." She flicked her gaze down. "It's not that anyway."

She shook her head and threw her gaze up, toward the stars. More tears slipped from the corner of her lashes. Her bottom lip quivered, and Eroan's heart ached for her. "After you left," she said. "Curan did as you suggested. The assassins went out and harvested the teeth. We even got word to Cheen, but..." Her throat moved. She rested her chin on her knee and stared back into the fire. "The dragons saw a pride. They must have realized we were organizing. They followed and... and..." She hiccupped in and more tears fell. "Oh *Alumn*... there's nothing left, Eroan. Nothing left at all. It's all gone."

His thoughts stalled, and he figured he must have heard wrong. "What did you say?"

"I wanted to tell you," the words came in a rush now. "I wanted to, as soon as I saw you, but I couldn't believe you were there, and then the humans won their battle and I... I didn't want to take that away from you. You were happy like I haven't seen you happy in forever and I couldn't tell you, Eroan. I couldn't. And then... " The tears fell freely. "Today, all day, every step I wanted to tell you, but I couldn't get the words out—"

There was that darkness again, getting bigger inside, creeping through his veins like a poison. He listened, letting her words sink into his veins like the cold did, but sink deeper, into some part of his spirit—the part he'd always carefully guarded.

"We fought them, but there were too many. Nye... Nye got Xena out, and I was supposed to keep her safe. Just her. That was my job. I was supposed to protect her, and I failed." She sobbed, shoulders heaving. "The black dragon killed her and I couldn't do anything! If it wasn't for Lysander, I'd be dead too."

Ice. It was ice now, filling him up, cracking, turning him to ice inside. "Slow down. I... Seraph, look at me." She snuffled and gasped her short breaths, breaking apart in front of him. "Seraph." She jolted and stared wide-eyed. From all those words, from their terrible meaning, he gleaned one thing above all others. "Xena's dead?"

"They're all dead," she whispered.

No. That wasn't possible. He scrambled to his feet and paced to where the wall of oak roots reached outward like claws. "You're wrong. You weren't there? You said you weren't there. Nye had you leave..."

He'd left them, all of them, and the dragons had come. "Nye sent you away?" He asked, voice sounding distant like someone else was asking. "Then you don't know, you can't know what happened."

He'd left the village to save them and condemned them all instead.

Seraph's gaze tracked his pacing. "It was all on fire, Eroan," she whispered, words stammering from her shivering that had nothing to do with the cold. "I'm sorry. I'm so sorry."

The ice broke and fell away, and Eroan felt every shard, every jagged tip cut deeply, scoring his spirit open. Why would Alumn do this to him? Why would he go through all of this for nothing? "Please, Seraph... you're mistaken. You left. Some survived, surely?" He swallowed, and whispered, "Please... tell me some survived." If his home was gone, his people, then why was he even here, why had he survived?

"I... I suppose." She looked down and tucked her chin behind her knees, folding herself into a small ball.

There was a chance. A small chance. Curan could have gotten them out. The children... The assassin leader would have saved them. Just like Eroan should have.

He thrust his hands into his hair and laced them behind his head. Everything he had done, every sword he'd put in human hands, it had been for his people. So they might survive. And now...

He kicked at the root wall, thoughts coming undone.

They were dead. He knew it, knew it in his spirit. Dragons didn't leave elves alive. Ever.

Except one.

He turned his head. Firelight licked over Seraph's small frame. "You said... " His voice cracked. He tried again. "You said Lysander saved you?"

She nodded tightly.

"How?" How had the prince gotten involved in all of this when the last time Eroan had seen him, he'd been fighting Akiem? That was months ago. He tried to think, tried to recall their hierarchy, their plans... bronze lines, human attacks... Something about a bonding? "He was at the bronze line?"

"He..." she breathed in and puffed that breath out again to steady her voice. "He bargained with the bronze leader for me. He *saved* me. I mean, they... they tried to hurt me, but he was there and... I thought he just wanted

me for himself but... he was nice, actually. For a dragon."
Her lips hinted at a smile. "He talked about you." She
smiled. "A lot. Like... *a lot.*"

Eroan let his hands drop and fell back against the root
wall. Dirt rained over him. He didn't care. Didn't feel. It
was all too much. His village, Xena, and now... Lysander
had been at the bronze line and the humans had attacked.
Had he escaped? The prince was a survivor, like him, like
Seraph. He would have escaped. "He saved you?" Why?
Why did that prince keep saving elves? Was it something
to do with the old dragon's words, how Lysander was a
diamond in the rough? Why wasn't he like the others? And
why, when Eroan thought of him, did all the emptiness and
heartache thaw some?

"In the end, I... I couldn't take watching him suffer for
me. The bronze leader, Dokul—he's horrible—he was
going to... do things to Lysander. Bad things. At first, I
thought maybe he wanted it, he seemed to want it, and
then it all went wrong. Lysander had a firestarter tool.
Kinda strange, for a dragon. I stole it, and I was going to
ask him why he had it—"

Her words faded beneath the thudding in his ears,
beneath the memory of him throwing the firestarter at
Lysander's feet.

"You do realize, I'm a dragon."

"I'm done with being cold and wet, so if you don't mind..."

He remembered it so clearly. The campfire, like this
one. The dragon prince, all cocky smiles like those smiles
could paint over the hurt, but it always showed in his
green eyes. "He asked about me?" Eroan heard himself ask.

"I wasn't going to tell him anything about you, but he
wouldn't stop asking. When I overheard you and Curan,

you said his name, said some... things about him. So, I thought maybe it would be okay to tell him, to make him a friend. I needed one in that place."

Eroan dropped a hand over his eyes. It was too much. Lysander had befriended her, kept her safe, but an ugly, gnawing, barbed thought had begun to dig at all the others. To dig and dig until he couldn't ignore it.

"I shouldn't have. I'm so sorry!" She thought his pain was her doing. "But he seemed so sincere—"

"It's not that." He bit into his lip and swallowed the rising knot in his throat, but he couldn't swallow the yawning dread consuming him from the inside. "How..." His voice came out raw, as raw as the feeling inside. The world was tipping beneath him, breaking, coming apart. "How did you get to the beach?"

He knew.

He knew what her answer would be. And he knew. He had done something terrible. Something unforgivable.

She answered, but her words were lost inside the storm inside him.

Kill him.

Make him suffer.

The dragonkin bronze found with Seraph. Not bronze at all, just a dragon out of place, in the wrong place, at the wrong time.

Eroan had condemned Lysander, the only dragon who had dared think differently, the only dragon who looked to heal instead of hurt, the only dragon Eroan had ever cared for.

Kill him.

Make him suffer.

And Lysander had heard those words. He would have

known it was Eroan who had spoken them. The elf he'd saved time and time again had ordered his execution. The prince had been so close. Just a reach away.

If Eroan could have seen his face, if he could have heard him speak, he would have known... He never would have let it happen, never would have said those things.

Why, Alumn?! Why have you done this to me?!

His legs buckled. His knees hit the ground. He fell onto his hands and sank his fingers into the earth as though he could dig his fingers into the hurt and rip it out. And it hurt, it hurt so much he couldn't breathe, couldn't speak, like his heart was a rancid, barbed thing and it was pumping more guilt, more rage through his veins. His village, his friends and now... Lysander.

Seraph threw her arms around him. She held him, rocked him, and said sorry until her voice failed, until she could only whisper the words. But she had nothing to apologize for.

"It's not your fault, Eroan..." she whispered. "It's not." She crushed him close. "Please don't blame yourself. Please... stay with me. I can't be alone. I need you."

Oh, but he did blame himself. How could he not? She didn't know what he'd done. But she would ask what had become of the dragon who carried her out of that hell, the one who saved her, and he would have no choice but to tell her: *I killed him. I made him suffer.*

"Our people died, but we won," she said. "*A new dawn rises and the age of the dragons will soon be over.* Xena said those words, Eroan. They were her last. We won, and we'll keep on winning, but we need you." She took his wet face in her hands and stroked the tears away. "Eroan, I need you... Please... please be strong. Nye and Curan, they could be alive. We'll find them. And others too. This war needs you. We'll bring them down. All of them. Together."

Bring them all down... but one. The dragon with the green eyes and broken wing. The one who had dared think differently.

Eroan's heart broke into pieces, ripping shards of his spirit with them. Alumn had forsaken him. His village was gone. He'd failed. And he'd saved nobody but himself. He wished he could have saved one. Just one. The impossible dragon who had guided Eroan out of the dark.

CHAPTER 49

$\mathcal{L}$ysander

LYSANDER PACED HIS CRAMPED CAGE. Whatever it had been before, the narrow bars and low top weren't built for a dragon his size. With every turn, his scales scraped the sides. But he did turn and pace because if he hadn't, he might have lost his mind while staring at the warehouse walls. As for stretching his one good wing... Impossible. Like these fucking humans were impossible. After the one known as Chloe had knocked him out on the beach, he'd woken up as human, bandaged, and shut in here. They'd rattled off question after question about amethyst mostly, about the tower, its defenses. On and on the questions had come and he'd ignored them all. He'd grown so bored of their twittering he'd shifted to dragon in front of them just to see them lose their tiny little human minds.

Half had fled and hadn't returned, but Chloe had stayed, and she had stared back at him. And that was all she did now. Stared. And he stared right back. He liked to click his claws at her and bare his teeth—teeth like those daggers she had clipped on her belt. He'd tried to light the place on fire, but the metal beams and walls hadn't burned. Figures. They were smart enough for that if nothing else.

Then the questions stopped. And the people stopped coming too and all Lysander could do was pace and turn, pace and turn. And dream of a faraway freedom, one he'd never fully grasped, but vowed one day, he would.

On that day, he would soar again. And on that day, when it came, he would change the world forever, because if he'd learned anything from a stubborn elf, it was that he couldn't surrender:

Until it was done.

~

To be continued in
Iron & Fire, Silk & Steel, #2

If you enjoyed Silk & Steel, please leave a review. Your support and more reviews means the series will continue. Just a few words will do.

For a free short-story, sign up to Ariana's mailing list at www.ariananashbooks.com and get all the news first.

ALSO BY ARIANA NASH

Sealed with a Kiss, Silk & Steel, #0.5

A short and spicy encounter between a Cheen messenger
and Eroan.

Join Ariana's mailing list at www.ariananashbooks.com and get it
for free.

∼

Coming soon:

Iron & Fire, Silk & Steel, #2

∼

Ariana also writes sci-fi and fantasy as Pippa DaCosta. Visit her
website at www.pippadacosta.com for more thrilling action,
romance and adventure books.

Lightning Source UK Ltd.
Milton Keynes UK
UKHW010739060223
416537UK00003B/1037

9 780995 711372